"Did you bring gloves?"

Cody eyed Dustin's baggy jeans. A person could hide a small child and two dogs in the pockets of those things.

"Don't need 'em."

Cody bit back a sigh, "Yeah, you do." He leaned forward and took the small pair of leather gloves he'd picked up at the feed store out of the glove compartment and tossed them in Dustin's lap. The boy glared at him, but Cody ignored him.

"I'm not a hick." Dustin spoke the word in such a way that it let Cody know exactly what he thought of him.

"I believe the politically correct term is cowboy," Cody shot back. Then he softened. He was supposed to be setting a good example, not arguing with the boy. "Look, the gloves are for your safety, like I told you before. I'm not trying to make you into a hick."

"Don't you mean *cowboy*?" Dustin looked out the passenger window as though bored out of his mind. "How can you stand living out here in the middle of nowhere?"

Cody resisted his initial impulse to throttle the kid. The ranch meant almost as much to him as his marriage. It might be the only one of the two he had left at the moment.

Hell, if he lost Nikki, nothing else would matter.

Dear Reader,

Sometimes the old saying "Blood is thicker than water" doesn't hold true. I have friends who are closer to me and who know me better than many of my blood relatives. There's another old saying—"You can pick your friends, but not your family." Again, not always true. Many children are chosen to be part of a family through adoption.

When the hero and heroine of this book, Nikki and Cody Somers, discover they cannot have a child of their own by traditional means, they turn to in vitro fertilization and surrogacy. But a tragic accident changes their plans.

As so often happens, Nikki and Cody find themselves journeying down an unexpected path. And when a special boy enters the picture, they must take a step back and explore the true meaning of family.

I invite you to take the journey with Nikki and Cody, and see that in today's world, where there is often so much darkness, there is a ray of light, as well. We just have to be willing to look for it.

I love hearing from my readers. You can e-mail me at BrendaMott@hotmail.com. Please reference the book title in the subject line. Or stop by my author's page at the Smoky Mountain Romance Writer Web site at smrw.org. Happy reading!

Brenda Mott

The Chosen Child

Brenda Mott

HARLEQUIN®

TORONTO • NEW YORK • LONDON
AMSTERDAM • PARIS • SYDNEY • HAMBURG
STOCKHOLM • ATHENS • TOKYO • MILAN • MADRID
PRAGUE • WARSAW • BUDAPEST • AUCKLAND

ISBN 0-373-71257-X

THE CHOSEN CHILD

Copyright © 2005 by Brenda Mott.

All rights reserved. Except for use in any review, the reproduction or utilization of this work in whole or in part in any form by any electronic, mechanical or other means, now known or hereafter invented, including xerography, photocopying and recording, or in any information storage or retrieval system, is forbidden without the written permission of the publisher, Harlequin Enterprises Limited, 225 Duncan Mill Road, Don Mills, Ontario, Canada M3B 3K9.

All characters in this book have no existence outside the imagination of the author and have no relation whatsoever to anyone bearing the same name or names. They are not even distantly inspired by any individual known or unknown to the author, and all incidents are pure invention.

This edition published by arrangement with Harlequin Books S.A.

® and TM are trademarks of the publisher. Trademarks indicated with ® are registered in the United States Patent and Trademark Office, the Canadian Trade Marks Office and in other countries.

www.eHarlequin.com

Printed in U.S.A.

This book is dedicated to Sam and her lost boys.
And also to the women who are my sisters, if not by blood,
then of the heart: Wanda Barnes, D'Ann Linscott-Dunham,
Judy Meister, Jennifer Niles, Kayla Perrin, Janet Swanson,
Joanne Ward ("Sissy") and Brenda Williams. I love you all.

With special acknowledgment to retired 911 operator
Barb Dimich, The Silt, Colorado and Rifle, Colorado Police
Departments, and MADD—Mothers Against Drunk Driving.
Any errors in this work of fiction are my own.

PROLOGUE

THE GLASS DOORS of the hospital emergency room slid open with a mechanical hiss, throwing Nikki Somers into a world tipped off its axis. Bright light and the sterile odors of medicine and cleaning solutions enveloped her, pitching her stomach into a nervous roll.

Faces, voices, blurred around her as she bypassed the busy front desk receptionist to find someone with answers. "Excuse me!" Hands shaking, Nikki waved down a woman in a nurse's uniform. "You contacted me. My sister—Amanda Kelly—was brought in by Flight For Life. She was in an accident. I need to find her—now. Please." The words poured out, nearly choking her. She felt as if she'd been dropped into some strange netherworld, and her real life was back there, somewhere outside the hospital doors.

Eyes filled with sympathy, the nurse met Nikki's gaze. "Your sister is in surgery."

Nikki's heart nearly leapt from her chest. "Surgery! My God, how bad is she? What about the baby?"

"I'm afraid I don't have the details, ma'am. The

doctor will talk to you after Ms. Kelly is taken to recovery. There's a waiting room upstairs, third floor.
Take the elevator—" she pointed "—and follow the
yellow line."

"Isn't there anything you can tell me?" Nikki per-
sisted. "Anything I can do?"

The nurse shook her head. "I'm sorry. You'll need
to wait for Doctor Smith."

"Thank you." Nikki could barely bring herself to
utter the words. She didn't want to wait. She rushed
to the elevator and pressed the Up arrow.

Please, God, no. Not my sister…and not the baby.

The elevator bell dinged and the doors slid open.
Nikki stepped inside. In what felt like slow motion,
the car ascended to the third floor, where a lemon-
colored line painted on the polished linoleum pointed
the way to the waiting room. Nikki followed it, feeling as though she were on an alternate yellow brick
road—one that led to nightmares.

The waiting room seemed small and close. She
avoided eye contact with the four people who sat
around the perimeter of the room. She had no interest in speaking to them, trading horror stories about
why a group of strangers had been brought together
in this room. Yet she couldn't help but steal a glance
in their direction.

In the far corner, a middle-aged woman sat with
her coat unbuttoned, her dark hair pulled into a flawless bun. Beside her, a young man stared unseeingly

at the television centered on one wall. The woman's pantsuit looked designer, her nails professionally manicured, her makeup perfect. Nikki saw that she'd been crying and looked away as she sat, perched on the edge of one of the mustard chairs.

But she couldn't block the whispers of the man and woman who commiserated with the elegantly dressed lady. She caught the words *drunk driver* and *hit-and-run*. And the fact that someone named Caitlin now hovered at death's door. The dark-haired woman's next words brought Nikki's head up with a snap.

"The other woman was pregnant."

And the man. "Dear Lord."

My God. They were here because of the same accident Amanda had been in. She didn't want to share this common bond with them, though she prayed their loved one—Caitlin—would live. Instead, she willed this all to go away and not be real, and for Amanda and the baby to be safe…alive.

The woman had said *was pregnant.* Surely she'd meant *is.* Nikki felt faint, but before she could address the woman, the door to the waiting area opened.

"Mrs. Somers?" Nikki turned toward the doctor as he entered the room.

"Yes." Quickly, she rose to her feet and hurried to him.

"I'm Doctor Smith." He held out his hand, and Nikki shook it reflexively. "Your sister is in recovery. You can see her in a little while, once she's been taken to her room." He pressed his lips together, looking grim. "I'm afraid the news isn't good. Ms. Kelly suffered a placental abruption as a result of the impact from the accident. I understand her Blazer rolled into the ravine."

Nikki's throat constricted. "And the baby?"

"She lost the baby. I'm so very sorry." He gently squeezed her shoulder, then went on to describe the extent of Amanda's injuries—a concussion, cracked ribs...she'd required blood transfusions. She had yet to learn that the baby had died.

Nikki could only stare at the man, one hand over her mouth. This wasn't happening. It couldn't be real. She bit her lip, trying to hold back the tears, wishing Cody were here instead of on duty some seventy miles away. When the hospital had phoned to say Amanda had been in an accident, she hadn't even taken time to call the Deer Creek police station. The Colorado State Highway Patrol had responded to the accident, which meant Cody didn't know. She needed to call him.

"Are you all right, Mrs. Somers?" Doctor Smith's words barely penetrated the fog shrouding her mind.

She managed a nod. "I just want to see my sister."

"Well, like I said, it'll be a little while yet." He gestured toward the phone on the wall. "That's an in-house line. A nurse will call you with your sister's room number once she's been transferred from recovery. I'll be dropping in later to talk to her as well." He looked as if he didn't know what else to say, as if he'd like to move on to his next duty, his next patient. The smartly dressed woman had risen to her feet as soon as Doctor Smith entered the room, and she now moved forward, questions of her own at the ready. He started to turn toward her.

"Doctor." Nikki laid her hand on his arm. "Was the baby a girl?" The ultrasound had indicated it was.

His eyes softened with genuine sympathy. "Yes. Again, I'm so very sorry for your sister's loss."

Nikki mumbled a thank-you, but for what, she wasn't sure. She amended the thought, thanking God that Amanda was alive.

An eternity later, the wall phone rang and Nikki hurried to pick it up. She listened as the nurse gave directions to Amanda's room. Once more, she followed the yellow line to where her sister lay on sterile white sheets, her blond hair spread across the pillow, eyes closed. Fighting back tears, Nikki moved up beside the bed. Amanda's eyelids fluttered open.

"Amanda." Nikki reached for her hand.

"Nikki?" The fear in Amanda's voice devastated her, and it was all she could do to stand. She couldn't speak to answer the question in Amanda's eyes. All she could do was shake her head.

Amanda's wail tore her apart, and Nikki's emotions whirled in confusion. Relief at knowing Amanda would live mixed with sorrow at seeing her sister in pain. At the same time, the sickening loss in knowing the baby had not made it continued to grip her.

Not Amanda's baby, as the doctor had assumed. Amanda had been a surrogate mother.

Nikki squeezed her eyes shut and wished she could melt into nothing.

Wished with all her heart that she could slip into a dark, quiet place where there was no pain.

Where her little girl was not dead.

CHAPTER ONE

NIKKI STRUGGLED to control her anger as she looked at her husband. "Vengeance won't bring Anna back." In the four months since the accident, they'd made little progress in working through their grief, moving past the loss of their baby girl. And Cody's attitude wasn't helping.

His dark blue eyes held hers. "Maybe not. But I still intend to find the son of a bitch who killed our daughter." He rose from his chair and walked out of the room.

Embarrassed, Nikki sighed, leaned back in her chair and faced Regina Jeffries. "I'm sorry."

"Don't apologize. Cody needs to work out his feelings in his own way." She studied Nikki with her expressive eyes. "Obviously, revenge against the hit-and-run driver responsible for your sister's accident is not your first concern."

"No, that's just it." Nikki shook her head, the heated words she and Cody had exchanged ringing in her mind, giving her a headache.

Why are you so hell-bent on finding the guy,

Cody? Let the State Highway Patrol and the sheriff's office do their jobs.

It's not that simple, Nikki. I wish you'd try to understand.

"Let's talk about what you think is more important." Regina glanced at her watch. "We've still got fifteen minutes left."

Nikki shook her head. "I think I'd better go after Cody." She stood and gave Regina a small smile. "Thanks. Hopefully we'll see you next week."

"I'll be here."

Outside the three-story brick building of Colorado Family Counseling Services, Nikki paused. Cody wasn't in their truck, parked at the curb. He wasn't anywhere in sight. Where had he gone? Her patience wearing thin, Nikki craned her neck, looking up and down the few blocks that made up Main Street in their little mountain town of Deer Creek. Through the plateglass window of Pearl's Diner she caught sight of him, sulking over a cup of coffee. Head bent so that his black cowboy hat partially hid his face, he reminded her more of a pouting teenager than a thirty-one-year-old man. Half tempted to get in the pickup and drive away without him, Nikki instead took a deep breath and strode across the street. The bell on the door tinkled as she entered.

Cody didn't look up when she slid into the booth across from him, and she waited until the waitress left with her order for coffee and a doughnut before she spoke, keeping her voice low. "Care to tell me what that was all about?"

He stared into his coffee. "I'm tired, Nikki. That's all."

"Maybe you should try coming to bed at night then, instead of falling asleep in front of the television." She knew he purposely did that to avoid sleeping with her.

He looked up. "I'm tired of fighting with you."

"I thought that was the purpose of counseling. To sort things out instead of arguing." She hated what Anna's death had done to their already shaky marriage. Their relationship had been tested by the injustice of three miscarriages in two years, and now they'd lost Anna. "How can we do that if you walk out in the middle of our session?"

"Do we have to do this here?" He indicated the room full of patrons enjoying Pearl's down-home cooking and conversation with friends and neighbors.

"No, we don't." Nikki stood. "You know what, Cody? I'm just as tired as you are. I'll see you at home."

She turned and nearly collided with the waitress who'd brought the coffee and doughnut she'd ordered. Nikki eyed the huge, chocolate-glazed pastry, anticipating the comfort she knew she'd find in curling up with the treat in a quiet corner of her bedroom. "Can I get that to go, Sherry? Sorry to trouble you."

"It's no trouble." Sherry smiled and darted back around the counter.

Cody was at Nikki's elbow before she reached the cash register.

"We drove here together," he reminded her.

"I thought I'd go see Jana." Nikki's longtime friend owned the bookstore down the street. "She can give me a ride home on her noon break. It's my turn to buy her lunch anyway."

"Fine." He pressed his mouth into a thin line and slapped money down on the counter to pay for their order. "See you later." He shot out the door and drove away in the Chevy.

Take-out bag in hand, Nikki headed down the block.

An hour and a half later, Jana drove her home, pulling up the long driveway of the sixty-acre ranch. Not even the welcome sight of the horses grazing in the sun was enough to lift Nikki's spirits. She climbed from Jana's car, palms sweating at the thought of picking up where she and Cody had left off. Both the truck and Cody's squad car were parked in front of the garage, today being his day off.

"You'll call if you need me?" Jana's voice drew her from her thoughts.

"Of course." Nikki lifted her hand in a wave. "Thanks again."

"You bet."

Inside, she found Cody in the kitchen. He'd made a sandwich, but had left it half-eaten. She sat at the table near his elbow. "What's happening to us?"

"I don't know," he said quietly.

Silence gripped the room. "We need to find a way to get past this," Nikki said. "How can we do that if you're not willing to try?"

There were sorrow and hurt in the look he gave her. "I am trying, Nikki. But you don't seem to understand that. You think going to town once a week to spill our guts to some stranger is going to make everything right. But it won't."

"And neither will your obsession with finding the drunk driver." Nikki struggled to contain her temper. "Cody, I want to see justice for Anna, too. I want the jerk who ruined our lives to pay." She leaned toward him, and laid her hand on his wrist. "But if you let revenge consume you, we'll never be able to move on with our lives."

He pulled away from her and stood. Raking his hands through his dark hair, he began to pace. "I'm a cop. It's my duty to uphold the law."

"You're too close. Let the Highway Patrol and the sheriff handle this."

Cody stopped pacing. "You do what you need to do to cope with Anna's death. Why can't you leave me to do what I need to?"

She leaned back in her chair. "What's that supposed to mean?"

"Your hair. Your clothes." He shook his head. "I've known you since high school, and this—" he indicated her bright pink jeans, lacy blouse and pink cowboy boots "—is not you."

Stung, Nikki's jaw dropped. "I thought you liked my new look." She fiddled with a strand of her recently dyed-blond, shoulder-length cut. "And what's wrong with my clothes?"

"Nothing is wrong with the clothes, Nikki." Heaving a sigh, Cody sat down again and stared at her. "They're just not you. The colors, your makeup, none of it is you. Even Regina noticed the changes."

"Yes, but she said they were good changes." Defensively, Nikki folded her arms, suddenly conscious of her extra weight. She'd eaten her way through her depression, until she'd gone from the severe weight-loss she'd suffered since Anna's death, to being ten pounds past her normal body size. But food gave her comfort. Something she hadn't found anyplace else lately.

"Exactly my point." Cody looked at her as if she were dense. "You cope your way, now let me cope in mine."

"So, what you're saying is that once you've tracked down the hit-and-run driver and put him away, things will be A-OK again? Everything will just go back to normal?"

"You know that's not what I mean." He pursed his lips and shook his head. "And women say men don't listen."

"I'm listening, Cody. You're the one who's not." Tears burned her eyes, and her throat tightened as she struggled not to cry. "I've found a *healthy* outlet for my feelings. Revenge isn't healthy. You've got to find a better way than that to move past our little girl's death. Regina can help us get back on track and work through this together."

"I'm not so sure that's the answer." The look in his eyes chilled her.

"What are you saying?"

He was silent a moment before he answered. "I've been thinking about moving in with Jordan for a while. I need some time and space."

Fear gripped her. "You don't mean that."

"Yes," he said. "I do."

Nikki fought to control her panic. She'd never been one to let emotions overrule good judgment. "Please don't."

"I'm not giving up, I just…" He let the sentence trail away. A fly landed on his discarded sandwich and he flicked it away, scowling. "I'm just taking a step back, Nikki. I think it's best."

Best. Not the word she'd use to describe what he proposed. "Please, Cody, just…wait." *God*, if he moved out there might be no turning back.

"Wait for what?"

For us. For whatever it took to stop this hell they'd lived in for the past four months. She took a deep breath. "When I talked to Amanda on the phone last week, she asked me to come to Tennessee for a visit." The accident had left Amanda unable to cope with her job as an RN in the maternity ward of the local hospital, or with anything else for that matter, including the tension between the three of them. She'd fled Colorado and now lived in the hills of Tennessee, in the cabin where their granny had taken care of them for the better part of their childhood. "I've been thinking I might take her up on her offer. I had planned to talk to you about it today, after our session with Regina."

Now it was Cody's turn to look apprehensive. "You're going to fly out there?"

She shook her head. "Drive."

His eyes widened. "Nikki, it's fifteen hundred miles to Boone's Crossing."

"I know. That's why I want to drive. It'll give me some time to think." She stared at the tabletop. "If I leave in the morning, I can be there by Saturday. I don't want Amanda to face Sunday by herself." She felt his gaze on her, and out of the corner of her eye, recognized the set of his jaw.

Sunday, June twentieth, would've been Amanda's due date.

Cody would talk about little else besides his need for revenge. He had yet to open up and talk to her about their baby girl.

"Amanda's been through hell," he said quietly. "And *you* need to be with her, too."

It hurt Nikki to admit that she couldn't let herself lean on him. She nodded. "And when I come back, you and I can decide what our next step should be."

"How long will you be gone?"

Her job as a kindergarten teacher left her with the summer months off, school having let out last month, the end of May. "I don't know. Two weeks, maybe three?"

Cody's jaw muscles tightened and she knew he wasn't happy with the idea. "I really hate for you to be out on the highway alone like that. Especially after…" His words trailed away, but she knew what he'd been about to say.

After what had happened to Amanda.

"I'll be fine, Cody. I'll take my cell phone and check in with you."

"Sounds like your mind's made up."

"It is." She hadn't fully realized it until now. But maybe this was best. Time apart might give them both a chance to cool down. Maybe when she got back home, Cody would be more willing to talk.

And less willing to simply give up and move out.

"All right." Cody turned his hands palm up in a gesture of resignation.

"Will you wait until I get back to discuss moving in with Jordan?" Her heart raced, and she held her breath.

He nodded. "Yeah, I'll wait."

"Okay then." She got up from the table. "Guess I'd better start packing."

Nikki headed for the bedroom, half hoping Cody would call out for her not to go. To instead stay with him.

But he said nothing as she left the room.

THE DRONE of the dispatcher's radio faded into the background as Cody tried to focus on the paperwork at hand, a task he normally hated. But he didn't want to go home.

Nikki had been gone only two days, and already it felt like forever. He hated the emptiness of their house without her. It felt as if his life had suddenly veered south to hell the minute she'd driven away. One minute he'd had it all, right down to the proverbial white picket fence and family dog—if you could call a retired police dog with an attitude proverbial. And now he sat looking for excuses not to go home.

He scooted his chair closer to his desk and bent over it a little more intently. But his thoughts circled back to Nikki.

He'd called her on her cell phone so many times he'd lost count and had been relieved to know she'd made it to Boone's Crossing safely. But when he'd hung up after their last conversation, he'd felt alone and empty, as though a lifeline to her had been broken.

He hoped her visit to Amanda would help Nikki. She felt so much guilt for having asked her sister to act as a surrogate in the first place.

And he knew he needed to call Amanda himself

to apologize for the horrible things he'd said to her before she'd left Colorado, running from demons of her own.

How could you be so stupid, Amanda? So irresponsible. Stopping on a dark highway like that, for God's sake!

He hadn't meant it. In the pain of losing his baby girl, he'd lashed out at everyone. The fact that Amanda had pulled over to offer her cell phone to Caitlin Kramer—stranded on the side of a mountain highway with a flat tire—was typical of Amanda's generous and caring nature. She couldn't have known what would happen. Dear Lord, it had taken him longer than it should have to realize the depth of Amanda's suffering. Baby Anna had been hers as much as she'd been his and Nikki's.

The thought instantly caused Cody's self-imposed safety mechanism to kick in, the one that kicked in every time his thoughts veered too close to little Anna. The hurt was still too great, too fresh. Instead, he tunneled all his energy, his grief, into revenge. He'd find the scumbag responsible for tearing apart his family if it was the last thing he did, and see to it that the guy went to prison.

"Man, now I know you're desperate."

Cody looked up at the sound of his partner's voice. Jordan Blake had been with the Deer Creek PD a year longer than Cody, his tenth anniversary around the corner. A beefy man with a deep voice, Jordan had a way of putting the fear of God into a suspect with nothing more than a sharp word or two. He'd cover your back with his life, and Cody couldn't think of anyone he considered a better friend.

"Yeah, well, it beats going home to my remote control and a cranky police dog that only understands German." The dog had been trained in non-English commands so that a perp couldn't distract him.

Jordan perched on the corner of Cody's desk, his dark eyes sober. "You know the invitation to stay at my place is still open. You can even bring Max. I think I've finally figured out what kind of dog biscuits he really likes."

Cody laughed, then shook his head. "That I doubt, but thanks."

Jordan sat there a minute, as though fishing for something more to say. Apparently, he came up empty. "I'm out of here," he said, standing. He gave Cody's shoulder an affectionate cuff. "Don't stay too long, cowboy. Go home and take a ride. You know what they say…nothing better for the inside of a man than the outside of a horse."

Cody nodded. "I might just do that." The horses could always use a workout, and riding usually helped clear his head and bring things into perspective. Only this time, he was afraid there were no answers.

A short time later, he made his way to the parking lot. The sun beat down on the blacktop, the evening temperature still hovering high enough to make him glad his squad car had air-conditioning. He strode toward where it was parked off to one side of the building. And did a double take.

A boy who looked to be perhaps ten or eleven crouched in front of the car, a can of spray paint clutched in his hand, and as Cody watched, he reached up to finish the job he'd already started. Red initials—*DH*—big enough to read even from this distance, spread across the hood of Cody's squad car as the kid's finger depressed the button on the paint can.

"Hey!" Cody sprang forward. "What the hell are you doing!"

The boy's eyes widened as he cast a hurried look over his shoulder. Then he ran. Thin as a whip, he wasn't very tall, but the kid could move. He sprinted from the parking lot and into a field of unmowed grass behind the police station. The mountainous, rural area that surrounded Deer Creek offered plenty of places for a boy to hide. If Cody didn't catch the kid quickly, he'd be out of sight and long gone.

The boy sped on like a downhill train. He ditched the paint can in a clump of bushes and vaulted over a six-foot chain-link fence at the end of the field as if it were nothing. Berating himself for spending a lot less time at the gym lately than he should have, Cody kept after him. He clambered over the fence but, as he hit the ground, the toe of his shoe caught in a tangle of deep grass, and down he went.

His knee slammed into a rock hard enough to

bring a string of creative curses to his lips. With a grunt, Cody scrambled to his feet, feeling like an idiot, hoping the kid hadn't seen him fall. Even madder than he'd been moments before, he took off again, trying to ignore the fresh shot of pain through his knee. *Great.* He gave chase as the boy zigzagged through the quiet neighborhood, down a side street.

"I'm warning you, halt!" Cody shouted. *Or what?* He couldn't exactly draw his gun on a kid who'd been armed with nothing more than an aerosol can. The boy cast a glance back at him, but made no move to slow down. He wore baggy jeans that exposed colorful boxer shorts, and Cody couldn't see how he could possibly run without his pants falling around his ankles. Shaggy hair stuck out from under a black ballcap, bill tilted at an angle, and a yellow basketball jersey with the number twelve bunched above his skinny hips.

Cody swerved, taking a shortcut across the front lawn of Old Man Parker's place—a retired Navy admiral well-known for his dislike of children. The kid was already headed toward the backyard, ready to rocket over the fence, where he could cut across the alley and likely lose Cody by ducking through the next yard, then on into the sagebrush of the surrounding countryside. Cody's heart flew to his throat, knowing what was on the other side of Parker's fence.

Luckily, the enormous Doberman pinscher hit the chain-link before the boy did. Teeth bared, the dog barked in a way that said he meant business. The boy skidded to a halt and turned to run the other way, too late. Cody caught him by the arm and spun him around. "Hold it right there!" Fuming, out of breath, he glared at the child.

For a moment, Cody saw fear flicker behind the boy's brown eyes, but then it was gone, replaced by defiance. The kid squirmed in his grasp. "Let go of me, man."

"What the hell were you doing—spray-painting my squad car?"

"I don't know what you're talking about." Breathing rapidly, the boy shrugged from Cody's grasp and tried to bolt again.

Cody caught hold of him, simultaneously reaching for his handcuffs. "Oh, really? I suppose that red paint on your hands got there by itself." He snapped the cuffs on the kid's scrawny wrists.

"Hey! What the hell are you doing, dude?" The kid squirmed and twisted, tossing a fiery look of resentment over his shoulder.

"That's Officer Somers to you, and I'm placing you under arrest."

Panic snaked across the boy's features before hiding behind a defiant mask once more. "You can't arrest me. I didn't *do* nothin'."

"Tell it to the judge." With a not-so-gentle push, Cody set the boy walking, back toward the station.

The kid cursed loudly and vehemently.

From the yard, Parker's Dobie barked with renewed fervor, and the old man jerked his door open to see what the commotion was about. "Everything's under control, Admiral Parker," Cody said. He hurried the kid away before Parker could utter a word. Given the choice between facing the dog or facing the old man, Cody would've chosen the Doberman.

Limping along, he sighed, still holding on to the boy, whose face looked vaguely familiar. "What's your name, son?"

"I ain't your son," the kid spat, "and I don't have to tell you a damned thing."

"Thank God for small favors," Cody quipped. "If I had a kid like you…" If he had a kid like this boy, he'd be so grateful for a child of his own, it wouldn't matter what sort of discipline problems arose.

The boy, looking younger and more frightened by the minute, set his jaw and scowled. "Damned dog."

"Yeah—a damned *good* dog. Thor lets Parker know when somebody's up to no good—like when someone spray-painted the side of his garage last week. You wouldn't happen to know anything about that, would you?"

"No." The boy smirked. "I could've outrun you, if it weren't for that stupid dog."

"Yeah, yeah." He hated to admit the kid was probably right. His knee felt as though someone had wedged a grapefruit beneath his skin.

"Maybe you oughta lay off the doughnuts."

Cody's already stretched temper snapped. "And maybe you ought to lay off with the smart mouth."

The kid glared at him, and suddenly Cody remembered where he'd seen him before. He'd been in Nikki's kindergarten class a few years ago. Dustin Holbrook. Child of an alcoholic mother and a father who'd left shortly after the boy was born, Dustin had been in the foster care system for the better part of his life. Cody hadn't seen him in a year or two, but if memory served him right, Dustin was eleven. Naturally, he'd grown and changed as he neared puberty. But when Cody looked for it, he could still see the face of the little boy Nikki had taught and cared so much about.

Dustin's slight build made Cody feel like a big bully, shoving him along down the street. But the kid refused to walk under his own steam. "You know," Cody continued, shooting Dustin a smirk of his own, "you might want to be thinking about what your foster parents are going to say when I call them."

"How do you know—" Dustin began, then clamped his mouth shut.

"That you're in foster care?" Cody gave him a piercing stare. "I know a lot of things, including your name, Dustin."

Dustin scuffed his toe against the ground as they walked. "Big deal. My foster parents will ground me for a couple of days, maybe take away my video games. Who cares?"

"You've got a lot more to worry about than having your video game privileges revoked."

"What do you mean?" Dustin tried to hide behind his air of bravado, but he looked worried.

"You're going to juvie."

CHAPTER TWO

NIKKI TURNED INTO the driveway, with mixed emotions at being home. The three weeks she'd been gone had felt like an eternity. Her pulse picked up speed as she parked in front of the garage. Cody's squad car was in the driveway. She hadn't talked to him for a couple of days. The fact that he had kept in touch with her on the drive to and from Tennessee showed he still cared. Yet her stomach churned at the thought of walking through the front door to face him. She wondered if he'd made up his mind about moving in with Jordan.

"One way to find out," Nikki mumbled. She climbed from behind the wheel of her Saturn and retrieved her luggage from the trunk. Suitcases in hand, she strode up the front walk, frowning. She'd thought Cody would at least come outside when he heard her pull in. It wasn't like him not to help her with her luggage. The house was quiet and empty when she unlocked the door and pushed it open. Not even Max came to greet her. Which meant one thing. Cody was out on a ride. He often took off for hours on one of the horses when something was on his mind.

Nikki carried her suitcases upstairs to their room. Ignoring how empty it seemed without him, she began to unpack. She couldn't stand to leave things in a mess when she traveled. Had to unpack right away, before she could allow herself to relax.

As she sorted through her clothes, hanging the clean, tossing the dirty into a pile to be toted to the bathroom hamper, Nikki glanced out the second-story window of the ranch house. It offered a view of the mountains, which encircled the one-hundred-year-old house like a lover's embrace. For as far as the eye could see, the lush, gold-green pasture stretched out behind the ranch, rising to meet public BLM land beyond. There the grass gave way to sage-brush, and the ground grew rocky as flat became hills and hills became mountains. Aspen and blue spruce dotted the distance with color, and somewhere out there Nikki imagined her husband rode, lost in thoughts of his own.

On an impulse, she abandoned her unpacking. No matter what their differences, she'd missed Cody, and she didn't want to wait one more minute to see him. She'd stalled, putting off the return home for far too long. Whatever their marriage had come to, she needed to stop running from it. She traded her shorts and blouse for jeans and a T-shirt, her sandals for socks and cowboy boots.

Minutes later, she made her way to the eight-stall barn, white with blue trim, that stood behind the house. Armed with a halter, lead rope and a handful of treats, she exited a stall through one of the connecting paddocks and walked out into the pasture. A shrill whistle snagged the attention of the four horses in the distance. Always game for a treat, they raised their heads and cast a hopeful look in her direction. "Come on!" Nikki called. "I've got cookies. Come on Cheyenne! Dancer!" She took a step toward them, noting that Cody's gelding, Raven, was not in the group. Her movement was all the encouragement the horses needed. They trotted briskly toward her, then broke into a lope. She smiled, loving the way their muscles rippled beneath their well-groomed coats. There was nothing more beautiful than a quarter horse in motion.

She cooed to them as they gathered around, nudging and nuzzling her for their treats. She handed out the oversized alfalfa pellets, then slipped the nylon halter on her favorite mare, Cheyenne. The palomino lowered her head willingly into the noseband, and Nikki buckled the blue halter into place, then led her back toward the barn. The other horses tagged along, hopeful for more treats, and she laughingly commanded them back so she could open the paddock gate and slip through with Cheyenne.

A short time later, she had the mare saddled. After leading her from the barn, Nikki rechecked the cinch, then swung aboard. She sighed in pleasure at the familiar creak and scent of the leather beneath her, and

relished the movement of the powerful golden horse
as Cheyenne moved out at a smart walk. Nikki
guided her to the trail that led away from the ranch
through the hills, glancing at the ground. The pattern
of shod hoof marks in the dirt told her Cody had been
doing a lot of riding lately.

Clucking to the palomino, Nikki set off at a lope
and was soon rewarded with the sight of a black
horse in the distance, trailed by a large German shepherd. Her pulse quickened at the sight of Cody in his
cowboy gear. She loved the way he looked when he
dressed in his Wranglers, western shirt, boots and
cowboy hat. The getup did even more for her than his
police uniform, though he looked sexy in that, too.

A little tug of sadness pulled at her. It would take
far more than physical attraction to save their marriage. No matter how strong. She let Cheyenne
stretch into a gallop, closing the distance between her
and Raven, not slowing to a lope again until Cody
turned in the saddle and spotted them.

The look on his face as she drew close was enough
to melt Nikki's resolve to take things slow and easy.
Clearly, he'd missed her every bit as much as she'd
missed him.

Max gave a welcoming bark, and Raven whinnied
a greeting to Cheyenne. Cody swung the gelding
around to face Nikki, and her mouth went dry.

"You're back." His eyes feasted on her. "I didn't
expect you until tomorrow."

"I left Nashville a little sooner than I'd expected." On the way home from Amanda's, Nikki had stopped off in the Music City to see the sights. Or so she'd told herself. Truthfully, she'd been afraid. Afraid to go home and find out things were really over between her and Cody. So she'd stalled, which had turned out to be a good thing, since Amanda had joined her in Nashville with good news. News she would share with Cody later, though she wasn't sure how he'd take it. That's why she had cut her sightseeing side trip short.

"I'm glad you did." He urged Raven up beside her, and she could tell he was about to do what he'd so often done, what came so naturally when the two of them rode together. Lean from his saddle and kiss her.

She braced herself. It had been a while since they'd shared more than a casual parting kiss. As a matter of fact, the farewell kiss Cody had given her when she'd left for Tennessee had been a long time coming. But as she was anticipating his lips on hers, Cody stopped, pulling the black horse up short.

His expression sobered. "I'm also glad you rode out here." The tone of his voice, the look in his eyes, put her on edge. "I have something to show you."

With that, he swung Raven around, and Nikki urged Cheyenne into a trot, following along after him. She felt disappointed and irritated. He hadn't even asked her how her trip had been or how Amanda was. Hadn't welcomed her home. But then, what had she expected? That three weeks apart would automatically solve their problems? That he would welcome her with open arms and everything would be the same as it used to be before the accident?

Cody glanced over at her as the horses settled into a brisk walk side by side. "How was your trip?"

"It was good." Nikki's heart pounded. Should she tell him now?

He pursed his lips in a thin line, focusing on the trail ahead. "I meant to call so I could talk to Amanda. I owe her an apology."

"I'm glad to hear that. But I guess I'd better tell you her good news first."

"Yeah?" He watched her expectantly.

"Amanda's seeing a really wonderful man. His name's Ian Bonner. They're engaged."

"That's great. I'm happy for her."

"That's not all, Cody." She took a deep breath. "She's pregnant."

His head turned so fast, Nikki heard his neck pop. His expression shifted from shocked surprise to something she couldn't quite read before he adopted the neutral mask he'd worn so often lately. A mask she hated worse than his anger and hurt.

"That is good news," he said. "Good for her, anyway."

Nikki scowled at him. "Well, I'm happy for her."

For a moment, she didn't think he was going to answer. He reached down and absently flicked a wayward strand of Raven's mane onto the right side of the gelding's neck where it belonged. "I can't say that I'm not," he said, his voice low and husky. "But you're going to have to give me some time to let it sink in."

The fact that Amanda could have what they couldn't obviously bothered him.

"How can you possibly begrudge her a child of her own after what she sacrificed, what she went through for us?"

"I don't. I just wish…forget it."

"No, what were you going to say?"

The sorrow she saw in his eyes immediately washed away the resentment she'd felt moments before. "I just wish Anna hadn't died."

Familiar pain laced through her. "Me, too. But we've got to get past this somehow. We've got to get on with our lives." She guided Cheyenne around a dip in the trail, her movements automatic. "Cody, we've got to start with us."

"I know. I've done nothing but think about us while you've been gone. And I believe I've come up with a compromise."

Her hands felt like ice. "Are you moving in with Jordan?"

"No." He shook his head. At that moment they rounded a bend in the trail, and Nikki knew exactly what he had in mind.

A three-room, white frame house stood butted up

against the rock face in front of them. In days past, when their place had been a larger working ranch, it had served as a bunkhouse and later as a home for the many live-in hired hands that came and went. But over time, they had left it abandoned and empty, except for some ancient pieces of furniture and the cobwebs the spiders had taken to spinning in the undisturbed corners.

Only from the look of things, there were no longer cobwebs in the house.

The cozy building bore a new coat of paint, and the broken-down steps of the porch had been recently repaired. Two chairs sat side by side near the front door, facing the panoramic view beyond. And through the curtainless front windows, Nikki could see the inside of the little house had been cleaned and painted as well.

She sat frozen in the saddle, her hands and legs numb. Her mind raced. "What have you done?" she asked, feeling betrayed. That he would fix up the bunkhouse—and so quickly—meant only one thing. "How on earth did you manage all this…?"

"I've had some help," Cody said, "which I'll tell you about later. What do you think?"

"It looks great." Maybe she was wrong. Maybe he had something else in mind. "Why did you do it?"

"I'm going to move in here," he said quietly.

She sat her horse in silence, not sure what to say. A temporary stay in the bunkhouse would've required cleaning the place up, even repairing the broken steps. But the new paint, the yard cleared of brush and rock…it all looked too permanent. Too much as though Cody meant to stay here, on the ranch that had been in his family for three generations. But away from the home they'd known together—away from their bed—for good.

"Do you want to go inside and see it?"

Nikki blinked and tried to focus on Cody's question. Tried not to let her emotions show. She gave a casual lift of her shoulders. "Sure."

Telling herself to stay calm, that she could handle this, she swung down off Cheyenne's back. The old hitching rail in front of the house had also been replaced, and she looped her reins around it before preceding Cody up the steps.

His boot heels clipped against the porch's wooden surface as he moved past her to hold open the door. The scent of fresh paint greeted her as she stepped inside and looked around. Arms crossed, Nikki turned to face him. "It looks great. You got a lot accomplished in a short time."

If he noticed the apprehension in her voice, he gave no indication. "Like I said, I had some help."

"Jordan?"

"Some. But mostly I had a kid helping me. One of the boys I'm supervising during his community service."

She raised a brow. "The judge assigned him community service on our ranch?"

"No, but his foster parents did."

"Who is he?"

"Dustin Holbrook. He was in your class—what— five years ago?"

Her jaw dropped. "Dusty?" She remembered a bright, shy, little boy with brown eyes and chestnut hair. A boy whose mother and stepfather had gone through a divorce the year he was in her kindergarten class. She'd heard whispered rumors around the school of the parents' alcohol and drug addiction. "My God, I haven't seen him in ages. What did he do?"

Cody's mouth quirked. "Painted his initials on the hood of my squad car."

"What? I didn't see…" She gestured over her shoulder in the direction of the house, where his squad car was parked. "How did I miss that?"

"It just came back from the body shop."

"I can't believe he had the nerve to do that. What on earth possessed him?"

"Gang initiation."

"In Deer Creek?" She wasn't naive, and their little town was by no means immune to crime, but it usually came in the form of domestic disputes…and drunk driving.

Nikki cringed inwardly and refocused on her conversation with Cody.

"Apparently Dustin and two of his pals decided to form a 'gang.' They thought spray-painting their initials on a cop car would be a good way to get 'jumped in.'" He shook his head. "They have no idea what the term even means."

Nikki shuddered, thinking of the things cops in bigger cities had to deal with. Things like kids as young as Dustin being jumped in to gangs through initiation beatings and worse.

"So, his friends painted a squad car, too?"

"Nope." He chuckled, and the sound sent a pleasant shiver up her spine. It had been a while since she and Cody had laughed together. "The trouble Dustin got into with me and his foster parents was enough to make his pals change their minds. He cooled his heels in juvie for a couple of days, then the judge assigned him forty hours of community service. I've had him pulling weeds and mowing the grass around the station, the senior housing units and the park. But his foster parents—Frank and Sylvia Thompson—have been harder on him than I've been.

"Dustin's been getting into quite a bit of mischief lately, though he hasn't broken any laws, until now. Or at least, none that we know of. They're fed up with his nonsense. Asked me to keep him busy here on the ranch, too. So I have." He gestured at the walls around them, bringing Nikki's focus back to the reality of her and Cody's circumstances.

She looked through the doorway that divided the living area and kitchen from the bedroom and bath. Cody's clothes hung from pegs on the walls, and she saw several personal belongings on top of a small chest of drawers squeezed into one corner between the window and the foot of the bed. Her throat constricted, and she fought back the hurt. "So, are you already sleeping here?"

"Not yet," he said. "I figured I'd wait until you got back."

Nikki plastered a humorless smile on her face and lifted her hands. "Well, I'm home. So I guess that means you'll be sleeping here tonight." She spun on her heel and left the room.

"Nikki." Cody followed her, but she was already halfway across the room, halfway to her horse before he could close the door and catch up to her. She gathered Cheyenne's reins, swung into the saddle and faced him. "What did you expect?" he asked.

"I don't know." She tried to sit up straighter in the saddle. To cowboy up. "I guess I knew this was coming…well, not *this* specifically, but that you might move out."

"I thought it would be better this way." Cody shrugged and leaned against a newel post, shoving his hands into the pockets of his jeans. Damn but he looked tempting standing there, hip cocked, black cowboy hat shadowing his face. He looked like a man who belonged here.

Nikki felt like the outcast, a stranger. Maybe she should be the one leaving.

It was going to be a long, hard summer.

"Sure." She gave Cody a tight smile. "It'll be better this way." She lifted the reins and backed Cheyenne away from the hitching post. "I've got to finish unpacking. I'll see you later."

She spun the mare around and galloped down the trail toward the barn.

CHAPTER THREE

CODY WATCHED NIKKI ride away, his heart heavy. He wanted to go after her, sit her down and make things right between them. But he didn't exactly know how to go about doing that.

He shook off the thought. Nikki needed a little time to let it sink in. Lord knew, it hadn't yet sunk in for him—that they would actually be living apart. Sure, he was still on the ranch, but the acreage separating him from Nikki felt like the Grand Canyon. Still, he needed to focus on work and his search for Anna's killer.

Not expecting Nikki to be home until tomorrow, he'd made arrangements for Dustin's foster parents to bring him to the ranch this morning. Cody had a long row of fencing that needed to be repaired and replaced, and he figured it would keep Dustin out of trouble. It was also a good way to get to know him better. The more time he'd spent around the kid, the more curious he was about Dustin Holbrook.

In spite of his penchant for mischief, the only previous trouble Sylvia could recall was Dustin's shoplifting a candy bar when he was eight. According to her and Frank, Dustin did things to get attention, even if that attention was negative. Like joining a gang and spray-painting a squad car. But his attitude made it difficult to find him a permanent home.

Cody rode back to the barn, but not until he'd given Nikki ample time to put her mare up and return to the house. He unsaddled Raven and rubbed him down before turning the gelding back out with the other horses. Forcing himself not to so much as glance at the ranch house, Cody made his way to his pickup truck, Max at his heels, and checked to make sure he had the tools and supplies he and Dustin would need for the fence.

Minutes later, the sound of a vehicle drew his attention, and Max barked a warning as the Thompsons' minivan pulled into the drive. Sylvia parked beside Cody's Chevy and leaned through the open window, her long, gray-streaked ponytail hanging over one shoulder. She gave him the same warm smile she always wore whenever he went through her checkout line at Wal-Mart. "Hi, Cody. How's it going?"

"Not bad, Sylvia." The lie rolled easily off his tongue. He nodded toward Sylvia's husband. "Good to see you again, Frank." He didn't know Frank well, but he seemed like a pretty good guy. Walked with a limp as the result of some shrapnel he'd taken in his hip in Nam.

"Likewise." Frank nodded. "I sure appreciate you finding some more chores for Dustin." The older man shot the kid a look.

"No problem." Cody craned his neck to peer into the van where Dustin sat in the middle seat beside one of his foster siblings, brooding as usual. He hadn't taken kindly to the community service he'd been assigned, much less to the extra work Frank and Sylvia had sentenced him to. "Ready to string some fence, Dustin?"

"I guess."

Progress. Not much, but some.

"I wanna help, too." Five-year-old Michael spoke from the back seat. Beside him, the two-year-old, Jessica, began to fuss in her car seat.

"So do I." Michelle, seven, smiled widely at Cody.

He smiled back. "You keep eating your vegetables, kids, so you'll grow big and strong, and then we'll talk."

"I am big and strong," Michelle insisted.

"I think I'm going to puke." Dustin rolled his eyes and climbed from the van, his body language letting everyone know there were a thousand places he'd rather be than here.

"Dustin," Frank warned, "mind your manners."

But Dustin only scowled, ignoring Frank. With both hands he ruffled Max's fur, avoiding further conversation. Cody had been surprised by the way the big German shepherd had taken to the boy—and vice versa—the first time the two had met.

Max's normal attitude ran the gamut from aloof to forbearance. He'd been Cody's dog for two years now, after a gunshot wound had put him out of commission as a K-9 officer with the neighboring Ferguson Police Department. Though he tolerated and respected Cody, Max had never shown much interest in bonding or being overly friendly toward anyone after losing contact with his partner. Until Dustin came along. Even now, despite his normal pickiness, he took the bone-shaped treat the boy withdrew from his pocket and chomped it down with enthusiasm.

Turning his attention from dog to boy, Cody noticed Dustin's previously long and shaggy, chestnut-brown hair trimmed to a reasonable length. Yet he still wore baggy jeans and running shoes with his ball cap at a cocked angle to match his attitude. Instead of his usual oversized T-shirt, he'd put on a long-sleeved shirt, untucked. Stringing fence, even if it was barbless wire, wasn't something a person wanted to do without the protection of sleeves and leather gloves.

"Let's get to it." Cody gave the van's door a friendly tap. "'Bye, kids." He waved at Jessica, who paused in the throes of fussing to stare at Cody, wide-eyed. Cody tried not to think about how the little girl's big, blue eyes reminded him of the child he'd lost. "Frank, Sylvia, see you later."

"Keep him busy," Frank said. "Dustin, you remember what I said about minding your manners."

"Yeah, whatever." Dustin sulked away from the minivan, hands shoved into deep front pockets.

A long chain hung from the wallet in his back pocket down to his knees, then disappeared back up beneath his shirttail, attached to his belt, the end of which also dangled down the leg of his pants. He postured a gangsta walk as he made his way to the Chevy and climbed inside. Cody shook his head and followed as the sound of the Thompsons' van faded down the driveway. He opened the driver's door of the pickup and let Max jump up onto the seat before sliding in after him.

Dustin remained silent as Cody started the truck and headed out a ranch road that led to the back half of the property.

"Did you bring gloves?" Cody eyed Dustin's baggy jeans. A person could hide a small child and two dogs in the pockets of those things.

"Don't need 'em."

Cody bit back a sigh. "Yeah, you do need 'em." He leaned forward and retrieved the kid-sized pair of leather gloves he'd picked up at the feed store yesterday, and tossed them in Dustin's lap. Dustin glared at him, but Cody ignored him.

"I'm not a *hick*." Dustin spoke the word in such a way that let Cody know exactly what he thought of him.

"I believe the politically correct term is cowboy," Cody shot back. Then he softened. He was supposed to be setting a good example, not arguing with the kid. "Look, the gloves are for your safety, like I told you before. I'm not trying to make you be a hick."

"Don't you mean 'cowboy'?" Dustin looked out the passenger side window as though bored out of his mind. "How can you stand living out here in the middle of nowhere?"

Cody resisted his initial impulse to throttle the kid. The ranch meant almost as much to him as his marriage. It might be the only one of the two he had left at the moment.

Hell, if he lost Nikki, nothing else would matter.

"This ranch has been in my family for almost seventy years."

"That's probably because nobody else would want it."

This time, Cody was unable to hold his emotions in check. "Look, Dustin, you put yourself in this situation," he snapped. "You might as well make the best of it."

Dustin faced him, his dark brown eyes narrowed and his freckled cheeks red. "I didn't ask to do stupid cowboy chores on some stupid ranch."

"No, but you chose to spray-paint my squad car. Negative actions have consequences."

"Oh, *excuse* me. I'll remember to write that down in my journal."

"You do that."

Dustin rolled his eyes, then postured his shoulders,

hands, and arms gangsta-like. "So me and my homies decided to spray-paint a few buckets. Big deal."

"I'd hardly call a Crown Vic with a souped-up 460 a bucket. And while you're busy taking notes, remember that your homies decided extracurricular art wasn't such a good idea after all." Cody steered the pickup around a pothole in the dirt road. "They obviously learned something from what happened to you."

"Yeah, right." Dustin slumped against the seat and stared out the window at the rolling grassland and the groves of trees beyond.

Frustrated, Cody was nonetheless determined. He'd overseen juvenile community service on more than one occasion and had managed to see those kids through their assigned hours with a fair amount of success. He'd find a way to work things out with Dustin, too.

Minutes later, Cody veered off the dirt road. He drove across the pasture to the corner of a section of fence that sagged between posts, some of it broken, where the horses had leaned on the wire to reach grass that was always greener on the other side. With the Chevy parked, he got out and closed the door behind him, Max tagging at his heels.

Dustin did likewise and stood staring at the five strands of barbless wire that stretched out of sight from both points of the corner post. "We have to fix *all* of that?"

"Most of it." Cody moved to the back of the truck and dropped the tailgate. He reached for the heavy roll of wire and dropped it onto the ground, rolling it along with his booted foot. Leaving it by the corner fence post, he returned to the truck for the tools they would need. He handed the fence stretcher to Dustin.

"What's this thing?" The boy looked at the metal, saw-toothed and jointed contraption as though it might bite.

Cody grinned. "Don't worry. I'll show you."

Two hours later, Dustin had the operation of the fence stretcher down pretty well, and Cody thought the boy even seemed to be enjoying the pleasure of working with tools. "Let's take a break." He lifted his cowboy hat and ran his sleeve across his damp forehead. The July sun burned down on them without mercy. Max had long ago retreated to the shade beneath the pickup truck, where he lay on his side, snoring loudly.

"Canteen's empty," Dustin said, tipping it upside down and giving it a shake.

"So, go fill it." Cody put his hat back on. This wasn't the best time of day to be out here stringing fence in the heat. Had he purposely picked late morning to early afternoon to make things harder on Dustin—or was he punishing himself? He'd done a lot of that, ever since Anna's death.

"Where?" Dustin crinkled his features in a mask

of adolescent sarcasm. "I don't exactly see a convenience store anywhere nearby."

"Try the water pump." Cody gestured to the west.
"It's over that knoll, by the stock tank. You can't
miss it."

"You want me to drink horse water?"

Cody gave him a look of exasperation. "The pump
is fed by an underground spring. It's better than any
bottled water you'll ever taste. Just lift up on the
handle, but watch out. It'll come out hard and fast."

"O-kay." Dustin spun on his heel and ambled off.

DUSTIN TOPPED the knoll and eyed the neighboring
ranch house that sat a short distance from the fence bor-
dering the Somers' pasture. Great. He knew who lived
there. Mr. Super Jock himself—Eric Vanderhurst.

Running back on the seventh grade football team
last year, as well as a wrestling champ and basketball center, Eric thought he was all that. He had blond
hair and blue eyes, and practically every girl at school
hanging on his every word. He made Dustin want to
puke. But worse, Eric was a bully who enjoyed picking on boys younger and smaller than him. He'd long
ago singled out Dustin as one of his targets.

It was no secret that a lot of kids resented Dustin
for having been bumped up a year. He was the youn-
gest kid in Deer Creek Middle School's seventh
grade class. In the first grade, he'd been skipped to
second because of his ability to learn quickly and eas-

ily. With a photographic memory, it took him little effort to retain whatever the teachers threw his way, and acing tests was so simple, Dustin found them boring.

But then, that had been before his mom had given herself completely to the drugs and alcohol. Before the foster care system had swallowed him up and spit him out again and again.

Frank and Sylvia were okay. He'd lived with them for about a year now. But he didn't give a rat's ass about school anymore, and he'd recently let his grades slip to the point where he'd barely passed seventh grade. Everyone was on his case—Frank, Sylvia, his teachers and school counselor. But Eric Vanderhurst made his life all the more miserable.

Dustin had been relieved when summer vacation finally arrived so he could hang with his friends. But Eric wouldn't leave him alone, even now that school was out. He made it his mission in life to make Dustin's life hell, which was part of the reason Dustin and his homies had decided to form Tech-9. As a gang, they would show jocks like Eric that they weren't to be messed with, and spray-painting their initials on cop cars had seemed a good way to start. It was something Dustin was sure Eric would be too chickenshit to do.

But now all that had been blown to hell, thanks to Officer Do-Good, and even Frank and Sylvia had turned on him, making him do these lame chores on this stupid ranch. Like he'd told Cody, he wasn't a hick. And the last thing he wanted was for Eric Vanderhurst to see him filling up some Roy Rogers canteen at a horse trough.

Seeing no one in the Vanderhursts' yard, Dustin heaved a sigh of relief and headed down the other side of the knoll, toward the stock tank and the shiny red pump. And came to an abrupt stop when he saw Eric standing beside the tank. It was as though his fears had conjured up the worst-case scenario.

What was he doing on this side of the fence, on the Somers' land? Too late to run, and with nowhere to hide, Dustin swaggered toward the big, round stock tank. "I didn't expect to see your ugly face today, Vanderhurst." The words of false bravado nearly choked him, but he refused to let Eric know he was afraid. He willed his heart to stop pounding. Glancing back, he saw that the knoll effectively blocked Cody from seeing them. The Vanderhursts didn't have a clear view from their house, either. *No witnesses.* No one to see if Eric acted on the threats he so often dished out in the hallways at school, and at the mall.

But to his surprise, it was Eric who fidgeted and looked as though he'd been cornered. "What the hell are *you* doing here?" A good three inches taller than Dustin, Eric scowled down at him as Dustin halted near the tank.

"I could ask you the same thing." Belatedly, he noticed Eric had something hidden behind his back. His pulse gave another jump. What if it was a gun? Or a knife? But as Eric shifted, he saw it was merely a pillowcase. "What are you doing with that?" He nodded toward it.

"None of your damned business."

Dustin raised his eyebrows in another show of bravado. "Ew-w. Testy, aren't we? What are you hiding, Vanderhurst?"

Eric looked as though he wanted to bolt. As though he were seriously thinking about doing just that. Dustin's fear gave way to puzzlement. And then he saw movement in the pillowcase. Saw that it had been knotted shut, and from inside he heard a soft mewling.

Adrenaline surged through him. He dropped the canteen. "I said what is it?" he demanded. "Let me see." He darted a glance from the pillowcase to the water tank and back again, suddenly putting two and two together. No longer thinking about Eric's size or the fact that they were out here alone, Dustin moved forward and, lightning quick, snatched the sack from Eric's grasp.

"Give it back," Eric demanded. His arm shot out in a hard shove that sent Dustin stumbling, nearly tripping over his own feet. He managed to dodge Eric's next maneuver, knowing the boy was capable of taking him down. But anger fueled his reflexes, lending him agility. He loosened the knot in the pillowcase and spread it open to peer inside.

Kittens. Four tiny, helpless kittens, their eyes barely open, mewed and clambered inside the blue sack.

Dustin felt sick and fought the urge to gag.

"You bastard!" Without hesitation, Dustin lowered the sack to the ground and dived at Eric.

The look of surprise on Eric's face barely registered.

Rage filled Dustin. With everything he had, he plowed his fist into the older boy's gut, and took deep satisfaction in his pain-filled grunt.

Drawing back his arm, he hit him again.

CHAPTER FOUR

MAX SCRAMBLED FROM beneath the pickup truck as if he'd been goosed. Cody watched as the German shepherd paused and tensed. "What's wrong, boy?" Max's response was an excited yip of warning. Seconds later, Cody heard the sound of muffled shouts, coming from over the knoll. He threw the fencing pliers on the ground and raced in that direction. As soon as he topped the rise his heart sank. Dustin. Fighting. With Eric Vanderhurst.

And Max straining, eager to help Cody stop the fight. *"Nein! Bleib!"* Cody called out the command in German for the dog to stay, then rushed forward, shouting at the boys.

"Hey! That's enough." He seized them by the backs of their shirts and hauled them apart. They writhed like two fish on hooks, arms flailing, trying to get at one another. "I said that's enough. I mean it!" He twisted the material of their shirts, pulling them farther apart.

Dustin was the last to stop struggling, to finally stand still, chest heaving—anger making him shake, darkening his eyes. "You should've let Max have him."

Cody let go of both boys and faced Dustin. "What is wrong with you?" He fixed him with a firm gaze, unable to believe what he'd just seen, yet realizing he shouldn't be surprised. The cynic in him—the cop who saw the worst side of people on a regular basis—told him Dustin was trouble and likely always would be. "You're out here working with me," he gestured toward the distant fence, "because you're in trouble, Dustin. And now you're fighting?" He shook his head. "What were you thinking? What in God's name possessed you?"

The expression in Dustin's eyes changed so quickly, Cody almost didn't notice. Hurt, disappointment and resignation before jolting back to anger. Still trembling, Dustin said nothing for a moment. Instead, he walked around the huge water tank and bent to retrieve something from the ground. Cody frowned. *What the hell?*

Dustin returned and stood with a pillowcase, of all things, in his hands. Cody's heart leapt. Had Dustin stolen something? Had shoplifting accelerated to petty theft without the Thompsons' knowledge? Had Eric caught him with the loot?

As quickly as the thought came, he pushed it away. Where and when would Dustin have gotten the chance? Beyond curious, Cody watched Dustin set the pillowcase at his feet, and suddenly the sharp little cries coming from inside reached his ears.

Jaw set, Dustin bent to spread the sack's opening

wide. "This," he said, his voice tight, hard, "this is why I was fighting." Disappointment filled his eyes again before his gaze darted from Cody to Eric, the hate and resentment darkening his expression.

"I want him arrested!" Eric pointed an accusing finger. "You saw it yourself, Officer Somers. He attacked me. I didn't do nothin' to him."

"He was going to drown the kittens." Dustin's quiet anger was frightening, and Cody could relate.

That anyone would hurt an animal made him furious. Along with that fury, he felt guilt. He'd been quick to judge Dustin and, apparently, this hadn't escaped Dustin's notice. The boy shot Cody a look that said it all.

"Go ahead and arrest me. I don't care." He narrowed his gaze on Eric. "It was well worth it."

Biting his tongue to keep his own temper in check, Cody examined the kittens to see that they were okay. They appeared unharmed, though they mewed pitifully. He needed to get them out of the pillowcase right away. "Take them," he said to Dustin. "Go back to the house and find Nikki. I'll be there in a minute."

Dustin held the opening wide, to allow air to flow to the kittens. With a final black look at Eric, he turned and hustled off toward the ranch house.

Cody waited until he was out of earshot before speaking. "Why did you do that, Eric? Where did you get the kittens?"

Eric's face reddened, and he scuffed one running

shoe against the ground. "There was a feral cat hanging out under our porch. She got hit by a car. My dad didn't mind her there catching mice, but now that she's gone he doesn't want to mess with the kittens, so I'm getting rid of them."

Cody made a mental note to have a serious talk with Mr. Vanderhurst.

Before he could respond, Eric struck another defensive posture.

"So, are you going to arrest Dustin?"

"I can do that," Cody said. He didn't bother to explain that they were in Garfield County, outside the town limits, and this wasn't his jurisdiction. He wanted to put a scare into Eric, one that would make him think twice before mistreating an animal again. "But then I'll also have to arrest you."

Eric's eyes bulged. "For what? He hit me first."

"Ever hear of animal cruelty?" Cody folded his arms, planting his feet in an official-looking stance. "It's a class one misdemeanor in this state, Eric, with a mandatory minimum fine of five hundred dollars, plus sentencing to anger management classes…" He shrugged. "A second conviction is a class six felony."

"Second?" Eric's jaw dropped. "I've never hurt an animal before." But the way his gaze darted to the side made Cody wonder.

"Good. Let's make sure you never do it again." He leaned closer. "What you did to those kittens, even putting them in that pillowcase, was cruel in itself.

And what you were about to do was a million times worse. I wonder what your father would say about this…." He rubbed his chin as though pondering. "Or maybe he already knows about it. You said he didn't really want the kittens around. If that's the case, he might be charged as an accessory to the crime."

Now Eric's face went pale. "He didn't know what I was going to do. I swear."

"Okay. We'll see. Should I call the sheriff's office or would you like to?"

Eric swallowed visibly. "The sheriff?"

"Sure. I'll want to make sure everything is done by the book when you and Dustin are arrested on your separate charges." He frowned. "Did your mother know anything about this?"

"Leave my mom out of this," Eric said. "She likes cats. She's the one who started feeding the stupid mother cat in the first place. If she hadn't, it never would've had those dumb kittens under our porch."

"If I were you," Cody spoke each word quietly, distinctly, "I'd go home and tell your parents to call me. We'll talk about what happened here, and see what you can do to make amends. Maybe you can volunteer at the animal shelter."

"Man, don't tell my parents." Eric slumped in defeat, raking one hand through his short-cropped hair. "They'll kill me."

"You mean like you were going to kill those kittens? I doubt it. However, it's up to you. I can talk to your folks or I can call the sheriff. What's it gonna be?"

Eric scowled at him. "That isn't fair." He shot a glare in the direction in which Dustin had disappeared. "Dustin's a little troublemaker. Everyone at school knows that."

"Uh-huh. You're probably right. I guess the best thing to do, then, is have you both arrested." Cody patted his pockets. "I don't have my handcuffs on me. But you'll come along peacefully, won't you?"

"Wait." Eric held up his hands defensively. "I don't see any reason to press charges against Dustin. He didn't hurt me that bad."

Cody noted the beginnings of a shiner puffing beneath the kid's eye. He refused to feel petty for the amount of satisfaction he felt. Eric deserved what Dustin had dished out.

"I'm glad to hear it. Actually, never mind the phone call. Just tell your parents I'll come over and talk to them later." He gave Eric a final piercing stare. "I hope they'll be home."

Cody called out to Max to heel, with the German word that rhymed with moose. *"Fuss."* The big dog rushed forward, and Eric took a step back, eyes wide.

But Max was well-trained and, though retired, kept sharp by the practice search-and-find exercises Cody and Jordan performed with him on a regular basis. The dog fell into place at Cody's side without so much as another glance in Eric's direction.

Cody headed back toward the pickup truck, still feeling bad about having misjudged Dustin.

NIKKI ROSE from the couch at the knock on the screen door. She'd seen a minivan pull in earlier and, when she'd looked out the window, realized it must have been Dustin's foster parents, dropping him off. She wondered why Cody hadn't mentioned that the boy was coming out today and felt annoyed that he'd already fallen into a pattern of doing things without her.

She made her way to the door and smiled at the sight of the boy standing on the porch. "Dusty? Is that really you?" She held the screen open and he stepped inside. He'd grown and changed so much. It never ceased to amaze and delight her, watching each year's group of kindergartners mature into bigger children, preteens and finally teenagers.

He squirmed. "It's Dustin. Hey, Mrs. Somers. How're you?"

"I'm okay." Her gaze fell on the pillowcase he held out in front of him like a trick-or-treat bag. "What have you got there?"

"Kittens."

"What?" She listened, horrified, as he explained the incident with Eric Vanderhurst. Belatedly, she noticed that Dustin's lower lip had a small cut on it. Otherwise, she saw no marks on him. Apparently Cody had stopped the fight before it got out of hand.

A small part of her was sorry. The part that wanted

to throttle Eric Vanderhurst herself. "I can't believe people can be so cruel." She reached inside the pillowcase and pulled a tiny silver-gray tabby kitten from inside. It hissed and spat at her, making her chuckle in spite of the sad situation. "Look how cute they are. Already full of spit and vinegar." Cradling the kitten against her chest, she reached for another, this one orange.

Dustin gently extracted the third and fourth kittens—a calico and a black one. "I wanted to throw Eric in that horse tank."

"I'll bet you did. I don't normally condone violence, but when it comes to animal cruelty...well, hold me back."

He frowned. "I wonder where their mother is."

"Did Eric say?"

Dustin lifted a shoulder in a careless shrug. "I didn't give him much of a chance."

"I see. Where's Cody?"

"Talking to Vanderhurst." He smirked. "I bet he's giving him he—" He broke off. "Giving him what for."

"I'm sure he is." Her heart gave a little jump. More than likely, Cody would come back to the house when he was finished with Eric. "Well, maybe he'll know more about the situation. In the meantime, we need to get these poor little kittens someplace safe and secure." She knelt on the living room carpet near the couch and gently placed the kittens on the rug be-

fore reaching for some throw pillows to make a little wall around the tiny cats. "I'll be right back."

Moments later, she returned with a laundry basket lined with towels and a heating pad, an extra
towel draped over her arm. In a corner of the room,
she placed the heating pad on the rug and plugged it
in, then put the towel over it, followed by the laundry basket, positioning half of it over the electric pad.
Then she put the kittens in the basket. "This way they
can move off the heated area if they get too warm."

Dustin reached to stroke the kittens with one index
finger. "How will they eat if we don't find their
mother?"

"They do look hungry." Nikki pondered. "I'll go
to the feed store and see if they have some pet nursing bottles and a milk substitute. Can you keep an eye
on the kittens while I'm gone?"

He shrugged. "I guess so."

Telling herself she wasn't avoiding Cody, that the
kittens needed immediate care, Nikki gathered her
purse and headed for the door. "I'll be right back.
When Cody comes to the house, tell him where I
went, will you?"

"Yeah, okay."

Nikki paused briefly in the doorway, studying
Dustin's face. He focused intently on the kittens, his
jaw set in determination. It was easy to see he wanted
them to live as much as she did. His gaze softened
as he watched the babies moving around, and he

smiled and began to talk in a low voice to them. Reassuring. So different from the boy Cody had described, who had wanted to join a gang and who seemed to look for trouble. This time, trouble had found him, and he'd been right to stop it.

Nikki turned and headed out the door. She felt partial to Dustin because he'd been one of her kindergarten kids.

The only kids she had now. The only kids she'd ever have.

She could and would learn to live with that.

CODY WATCHED as Nikki and Dustin took turns feeding the kittens in pairs. The little buggers had taken surprisingly well to the two doll-sized, pet nursing bottles Nikki had bought and soon fell asleep in a multi-colored pile of cotton-soft fur, curled into the towel above the heating pad, their tiny eyes closed, their paws tucked into various positions of comfort.

And he saw that Nikki used the kittens so she wouldn't have to look at him as he sat on the edge of the couch near the basket. Every time she avoided his gaze, it wrenched his heart.

He damned sure wasn't about to sit here and take the old cold shoulder routine.

Cody stood. "Come on, Dustin. We'd better get back out and finish up that section of fence before Frank and Sylvia get here."

Dustin protested at having to leave the kittens,

but followed him back to the truck. Inside, he gave Cody the same silent treatment Nikki had, obviously still ticked off at the way Cody had jumped all over him earlier.

They reached the section of fence where they'd left off, and the two worked in stubborn silence. After some time in the hot sun, Cody realized they hadn't refilled the canteen. As a matter of fact, he hadn't even remembered to pick it up back at the pump by the horse tank. Unable to stand the silence another minute, he looked at Dustin. "Guess we never did get our canteen filled, huh?"

"Nope." Dustin stared straight ahead, mechanically hammering a fence staple into place.

"I suppose it's still by the water tank?"

"I'll get it." Huffily, Dustin dropped the hammer to the ground and spun to go.

"Hold up a minute."

"What?" Dustin slumped his shoulders in a show of impatience and gave Cody a look that said he had his attention under duress.

Cody stood with one hand on his hip. "I'm sorry I came down on you for fighting with Eric. I didn't realize what was happening."

"It doesn't matter." Dustin turned away.

"Dustin." Cody spoke firmly, and Dustin sighed and scowled at him. "It does matter. I had no right to jump to conclusions that way." His lips turned upward. "You did good, partner."

"I told you," Dustin said gruffly, blushing. "I'm not a *cowboy*, partner."

Cody watched him walk away. The little brat.

No wonder no one wanted to adopt him.

WHEN THE THOMPSONS came to pick Dustin up, Nikki went out to meet them. Now that she'd gotten reacquainted with Dustin, she was curious about Frank and Sylvia. They were delighted to meet Dustin's former teacher, and she liked them right away. Sylvia was friendly and easy to talk to, and Frank was chatty and had a great laugh.

When the couple went in search of Dustin, Nikki returned to the house. She sat in the corner, watching the kittens sleep, knowing Cody would likely not come back to the house with Dustin gone, unless it was to get the rest of his clothes. Maybe he would simply wait to get them another time, when Nikki wasn't home. Should she leave for a while? Maybe go to Jana's house, or to the mall to kill a little time.

She and Jana had been good friends since high school, even before she and Cody had started dating in Nikki's junior year, Cody's senior. Jana had been extremely supportive during Nikki's attempts to have a baby, but still, she missed Amanda, who wasn't just her sister. She was her best friend. Devastated when Amanda moved to Tennessee, it had been hard to say goodbye to her all over again after their three-week visit.

Nikki was startled by the sound of Cody's footsteps on the porch. The screen creaked open and he stepped inside, his gaze immediately finding hers. "So, what do you think of Dustin?"

Relieved he wasn't going to pick up where their earlier conversation had ended, Nikki managed a smile. "He's a kid with potential."

"I hope you're right. With his attitude, I'm beginning to wonder."

"Attitude? He was gentle with the kittens."

"That's not exactly typical of his behavior." Cody shook his head. "Dustin's not easy to get close to."

"Can you blame him? He's been through a lot, from what little I've heard."

"I've been hoping that working on the ranch will give him the chance to open up. Sometimes it's easier to talk to a stranger."

Nikki's chest constricted as she studied Cody's face. It was easy to see how caring a person he was. He'd always had a deep-seated desire to help others. It was a large part of why he'd become a police officer in the first place. So why couldn't he reach out and help her—help himself—through this trying time in their marriage?

"Speaking of heart-to-heart talks," Cody said, "I've put off calling Amanda long enough. Do you think she might be home now?"

Nikki glanced over her shoulder at the clock on the wall. It was almost four-thirty, two hours later in eastern Tennessee. "She should be. Unless she's gone out somewhere with Ian." She moved toward the door. "I'll give you a little privacy."

Their eyes met before she stepped outside.

"Thanks," he said quietly.

"Sure. I'll be right out here if…if Amanda wants to talk to me." *If you need me.*

Without another word, she closed the door behind her.

"HELLO?" Amanda's voice came across the line, and Cody's mouth went dry. How much did she know about their failing marriage? Probably everything. Nikki had always confided in her sister.

"Amanda, it's Cody." He took a deep breath. "Nikki told me you got engaged. Congratulations." He knew he should congratulate her on her pregnancy as well, but couldn't bring himself to do it. The words clogged in his throat like backed-up sewage. He tried to swallow as Amanda spoke.

"Thank you." Her tone seemed hesitant, as though she wasn't sure whether to trust his sincerity.

He felt ashamed of himself. "I mean that, Amanda. And I want you to know how sorry I am for the way I acted toward you after the accident. I said some horrible things, and that was wrong. I didn't mean them."

"I know you didn't." The familiar warmth was back in her voice, just like that. Cody admired his sister-in-law so much for her ability to forgive and forget. He wished he could forgive Anna's killer so easily. But black thoughts overwhelmed him at the thought, and he had to force himself to focus on what Amanda was saying. "It's all right, Cody. I don't want you to give it another thought. Just be good to yourself. Be happy." She hesitated. "Nikki seems to be doing better."

"Yeah." He didn't want to get into his marriage. Didn't want to listen to any lectures on why he should save it. "Speaking of which, she'd like to say hello. Hang on and I'll get her."

He bid Amanda a quick goodbye and laid down the phone. Going out to the porch to get Nikki, he was stopped by her beauty as she stood in profile, leaning against the rail, looking out at the distant mountains.

She turned to face him, saying nothing, and he knew she was waiting. Waiting to see how things had turned out between him and Amanda.

"We're okay," he said. "We made peace with one another."

"So, do you feel better?"

She was really asking if talking to Amanda had helped him put the accident behind him. He struggled not to be irritated.

"I feel better about the way things are between me and your sister, yes." He looked her in the eye. "But I still want to catch the bastard who murdered our daughter." He gestured over his shoulder. "Amanda's still on the phone. She wants to talk to you."

The hurt and anger in Nikki's expression nearly undid him. He saw something else there—bitterness and frustration. All the same things he was feeling.

"I'm going over to the Vanderhursts to talk to them about Eric. I'll be back later to get my stuff." He turned on his heel and walked away, leaving Nikki staring after him. He could feel her gaze on his back, and wished for the millionth time he could somehow make things right between them.

The sound of the screen door, creaking open, then closing again as she went inside the house reached him as he neared his pickup truck. Then the sharp click of the door as she shut it firmly behind her. Not exactly slamming it, but still sending a message to Cody.

He climbed into his pickup truck and slammed the door shut. He hated this. Hated what his life had become.

And he used that hatred to fuel his anger and his need for justice. He would find Anna's killer, whether or not Nikki understood.

CHAPTER FIVE

NIKKI STOOD in the hallway outside the door of what was to have been Anna's room, knowing she'd put off the inevitable long enough. In the five days since her last conversation with Cody, after he'd spoken with Amanda, she had looked for anything and everything to keep her mind off Cody's harsh words and the fact that they now lived in separate houses. Restoring the nursery to a guest room would help keep her busy.

Turning the knob of the closed door, she took a deep breath before shoving it open. Stepping inside, she braced herself for the emotional blow that landed every time she walked into this room.

It was empty, except for the crib and changing table. But in Nikki's mind, she saw it the way it had been five months ago after she, Cody and Amanda had spent days preparing for the arrival of the baby. She had been so excited, so certain that nothing would go wrong this time.

Cody, too.

Amanda had come over the weekend before the baby shower to help decorate the room with stuffed animals and wall hangings. On the night of the baby shower, she had stayed after the guests all left, and the two of them put the shower gifts away in the dresser drawers and closet. Laughing, talking, planning.

Then Amanda left to drive home, and within moments, she was lying in the hospital emergency room, her life in jeopardy, the baby dead.

Nikki shook away the overwhelming thoughts. Morning sunlight filtered in through the bedroom window, accenting the cheeriness of the soft, yellow walls. Such an anomaly.

She crossed the room and rested her hand on the crib rail. The bare mattress said it all. The baby bed was as empty as her heart. Jana had come and helped her pack away the bedding, the clothes, the toys. And the gifts from the shower.

It had all been boxed up and put in the attic— Nikki wasn't ready to part with Anna's things.

Swallowing against the tightness in her throat, Nikki reached out to touch the mobile that hung from the crib's headboard. The colorful zoo animals dangled on the end of their strings. It was the one item she'd been reluctant to pack. With a turn of her wrist she wound it, sending the elephants, giraffes and monkeys in a circular dance to the melody of a soft lullaby.

A tear squeezed from the corner of her eye and slid down her cheek; impatiently, she wiped it away. *Get over it,* she reprimanded herself. *There is no baby, and there never will be.* Right now, she'd settle for having her marriage back.

Nikki removed the mobile, then focused on the crib itself, irritated that Cody had yet to take it apart and pack it away in the attic as promised.

Taking a deep breath, Nikki reached for the screwdrivers to dismantle the crib. She barely noticed the gathering storm clouds outside the window as she set to work.

"I told you I'd do that."

She spun around to face Cody. He strode through the doorway and took the Phillips screwdriver from her hand.

She glared at him. "You startled me. And I can do this just fine by myself, thank you very much." She tried to snatch the screwdriver back, but Cody avoided her grasp.

"I said I'll do it."

Nikki rolled her eyes in frustration. "Yeah, now that you see me doing it."

"What's that supposed to mean?"

She struggled for patience. "You procrastinate over *everything,* this included." She gestured at the crib.

"I do not."

"Oh, that's right. You just thought about procrastinating, but then you decided to put it off until later."

"Very funny." He turned away from her, lifted the mattress out and leaned it against the wall, then began removing screws that fastened the headboard to the frame.

"What are you doing here anyway?" The realization that Cody had come to the house, even though he'd moved the majority of his things to the bunkhouse days ago, finally registered.

He didn't look up. "I forgot my rain slicker, and it looks like I'm gonna need it before feeding time."

She'd planned to feed the horses herself when evening chores rolled around, since he'd fed them that morning. "I thought we'd split the chores.... Maybe you should knock from now on."

He stopped what he was doing and finally looked up at her. "Knock? You want me to *knock* on my own damned door?"

"Well, you did move out."

"This is still my house," he said, scowling at her before resuming his task of taking the crib apart.

"Our house," she said. Now she was really annoyed. "Actually, I guess you had it right the first time. Your family has lived on this ranch for three generations. It is your house more than mine, so maybe I should move out."

"No!"

His sudden protest took her by surprise. Nikki raised her brows as Cody spun to face her. Panic etched his features, then quickly disappeared as he mastered it.

"I don't want you to move out," he said. He laid

down the screwdriver and took hold of her arms. "Nikki, I moved into the bunkhouse because I thought it would be better than moving off the ranch. Rooming with Jordan felt too permanent, and I'm not sure we're ready to take that step yet, are we?" His gaze flickered across her face, and for a moment she thought she saw longing in his eyes. She knew he felt the same way she did, wished things between them hadn't changed. But they had changed, and she could no longer deny that.

She backed away, shrugging from Cody's grasp. "You've got a point. There's no reason to act in haste." Her words disguised her true emotions, betrayed only by her rapid pulse. The urge to slip into Cody's arms and invite him to move back into the house, back to their room and their bed, was strong.

She held that urge in check. They'd tried working things out, and had managed only to do more damage. Like it or not, living in separate houses was the only answer for the moment. Whether that would change, Nikki didn't know and didn't even want to think about it.

"So for once you agree that putting something off can be a good thing?" Cody's lips twitched in a half smile that tugged at her heart.

"Funny ha-ha." She gestured toward the changing table. "I'll take that out of here while you work on the crib." Again, emotion overwhelmed her. That they should have to dismantle the last of Anna's belongings seemed so unfair, so wrong. "I never pictured things this way," she whispered. She had dreamed of the two of them together in this room singing their baby girl to sleep.

Cody's eyes met hers, and he swallowed. "The changing table's too heavy for you. Leave it and I'll get it."

"Fine." Nikki let her arms flop against her thighs in resignation. "I'll open the attic door. I've got to get the painting supplies anyway." She went down the hall to the kitchen, where a flight of stairs in one corner led to the attic.

She only meant to hold the door for Cody, since, being unlevel, it tended to swing shut. It also had a loose knob and squeaky hinges…. Mentally, Nikki rattled off the items that she would now learn to take care of herself instead of adding to Cody's *Honey-do* list.

She hadn't intended to linger in the room. But when she pulled the door open, her gaze fell on the wooden rocking horse in the corner.

Cody had spent hours making the horse for Anna, and Nikki had teased him, telling him it would be a few years before their baby girl grew up enough to ride it.

Nikki walked across the room and knelt in front of the wooden horse. Her eyes burned, and she fought back tears. She supposed she should donate Anna's things to the local women's shelter or whatever charity needed them most. Even though Amanda was now expecting a baby of her own, there was no way she would want the items meant for Baby Anna. Nikki wouldn't want that either.

Yet she couldn't bear the thought of giving up the rocking horse. Cody had put so much time and effort, so much love, into making the horse with its carved flaring nostrils and lifelike eyes. Like the handcarved cherrywood cradle her grandfather had once made, which would now be used for Amanda's baby, the rocking horse had been crafted to pass down through the generations.

Nikki ran her hand over the arched neck, tracing the carved lines of the flowing mane. The rocking horse looked as though it might, like Pinocchio, come to life at any moment and turn from cold, hard wood to warm silkiness.

Hearing Cody coming up the stairs, she moved away from the rocking horse and hurriedly ran her index fingers beneath her eyes, determined to hide her tears, before heading to the door.

Without a word, Cody came in and set the headboard and footboard of the crib against the wall, then went back down the steps to retrieve the rest of it. Nikki knew there was no good reason why she shouldn't find something in the attic to prop the door open for Cody and leave. No reason other than she wasn't ready to put distance between them. She liked watching Cody work, loved the way his jeans cupped his backside as he bent over.

As if on cue, Cody returned, carrying the mattress. This time, Nikki did prop the door open, yet she still stayed in the attic. A few trips later, the baby furniture was tucked neatly into the corner opposite the rocking horse.

Cody faced her, one hand cocked on his hip, and she found herself staring at his snug-fitting Wranglers.

"Is that it?"

Quickly she looked up, as though she'd been caught doing something wrong. Truthfully, she *shouldn't* be looking at Cody that way. The idea that eyeing her husband was now taboo put her on the defensive. "How can you say it like that?"

"What?" He gave her a puzzled frown.

"Is that it—as though moving Anna's things up here is just another chore to scratch off your list."

Cody's chest heaved in an audible sigh, but the expression on his face softened. "I didn't mean it that way, Nikki, and you know it. I just wondered if there was anything else you needed me to do before I go. Since I tend to procrastinate so much."

She folded her arms. "No. There's nothing." *Except to fix the leaky faucet you said you'd get to last winter and to finish the outdoor barbecue pit you started building this spring.* She moved to brush past him, determined to get out of the attic before he could leave her standing there alone, and she promptly stubbed her toe on the rocking horse. "Ouch." Cross, she balanced on one leg and rubbed her injured foot.

"You okay?"

Cody reached out to steady her. There'd been a time when he would have jokingly offered to kiss her hurt and make it better. Which would've led to him kissing the arch of her foot and her ankle, running his hand up her bare leg to the cuff of her shorts....

Nikki swallowed hard, unable to tear her gaze away from him. "I'm fine. I just wasn't paying attention to where I was walking. I should have worn tennis shoes or boots instead of these stupid sandals."

Cody grinned. "They're not very practical for moving furniture, that's for sure. Or ranch work." He eyed the red leather sandals, and she could practically read his mind.

He'd loved the way she used to dress in plain western clothes. Faded jeans, cowboy boots and T-shirts with her hair tucked into a carefree ponytail beneath a beat-up cowboy hat. But that was the old Nikki, the one who had died along with their baby girl. The new Nikki wore bold colors and fashions. She'd traded her dusty-brown Tony Lamas for hot-pink Justin ropers, her faded Levi's for dress jeans in aqua, red and violet.

She straightened her shoulders. "Maybe not, but I happen to like my shoes."

Cody shrugged, then leaned toward her, invading her space. Breaching the line she'd drawn between them. A line that could be seen, not with the eye, but with the heart. Closing his eyes, he inhaled deeply, then opened them and looked at her. "That's one thing that hasn't changed," he said, his voice low and husky.

"What's that?" She did her best not to stammer.

"Your perfume. You always smell so sweet, like a juicy tangerine." His tongue flicked briefly over his bottom lip, and Nikki forced herself to tear her gaze from his mouth before she did something stupid.

She took a step backward and immediately his hand shot out to grasp her arm, his touch warm and strong as he steadied her on her feet. "Careful there. You almost tripped over the rocking horse again."

"Yeah." She glanced around, taking in the sight of the wooden horse, the dismantled crib, the empty changing table, and suddenly it hit her. Here she stood with the man she'd loved unconditionally for the better part of her life, in the house they'd shared for a decade, surrounded by the very items that were symbols of what had ultimately torn them apart.

Anna wasn't coming back. And neither was the relationship she and Cody once shared.

"Be sure to shut the door tight on your way out," Nikki said, without looking back. "It'll keep this hot, stale air from wafting downstairs."

She descended the steps and went to the bedroom to change into tennis shoes and old clothes she could paint in. It was time to finish it. Time to lay the past to rest.

So why did her aching heart say otherwise?

CODY FOUGHT THE URGE to slam the attic door behind him. He wasn't sure if he was more annoyed with Nikki for the way she'd treated him, like some damned intruder in his own home, or with himself for nearly kissing her. But a tumble between the sheets— or on the attic floor—wouldn't solve their problems.

It was a given that the two of them got along just fine in bed. The only time that had been an area of contention had been during the strained months of trying to make a baby over and over again each time Nikki suffered another loss. Sex definitely was not the trouble. It was their marriage they needed to straighten out. *But damn, Nikki smelled so sweet, so good.* And even though he missed the way she looked in her cowgirl clothes, he had to admit he liked looking at her bare legs. There was a curvy fullness to her breasts and hips she'd never had before, and he liked it. She also had a suntan, and the white shorts she wore showed it off enough to put his libido on the rise, especially when they rode up high enough to reveal her tan line.

Sexy. Hot. Words he associated with Nikki on a regular basis. He'd loved touching her body, kissing and caressing her into wanting him as badly as he wanted her. The act of burying himself deep within her had been pure ecstasy.

Being without her was pure hell.

Shaking his head, he reminded himself that he'd

just taken Anna's furniture to the attic and closed yet another chapter in their lives. Cody tromped down the stairs to the hall closet for his rain slicker. It had nearly killed him to have to take that crib apart, but watching Nikki do it had been worse.

It was a punishment. For not being able to do a damned thing to stop what had happened to Anna, to Amanda. To all of them. His job was to serve and protect, and yet when the chips had been down, there was nothing he could do to stop the fatal crash.

Nobody could've stopped it except the drunken bastard behind the wheel of the SUV.

In a routine that had become familiar, Cody used his anger to drive thoughts of making love to Nikki from his mind. He shrugged into the rain slicker and walked out onto the porch. His supervisor had made him take the last four days off, said he was working too hard. Looking for the hit-and-run driver.

He'd been expecting Dustin today, but with the gathering storm clouds he supposed he should call the Thompsons and tell them not to come out.

Retracing his steps, he went back inside to use the phone since there wasn't one in the bunkhouse and the mountains were blocking his cell phone. Half expecting Nikki to pop around the corner and ask what he was doing using *her* telephone, Cody dialed. When no one answered on the other end, he hung up. Too late. They must already be on their way. Would they turn around and go back once they realized a storm threatened? He called back and left them a message.

Back out onto the porch, in spite of his resolve, his thoughts strayed to Nikki once more. Five days in the bunkhouse and already he missed her.

Sitting on the porch to wait for Dustin, Cody clung stubbornly to the hope of reconciliation, even as the voice inside his head told him it was too late.

That his marriage was hell-bound on a downhill slide to nowhere.

CHAPTER SIX

THE THOMPSONS' MINIVAN pulled up the driveway, and Sylvia rolled the window down and leaned out to speak to Cody, her hair covered by a hooded raincoat. "Hey, Cody. How are you?" Dustin sat in the passenger seat beside her and shot a dark, surly look at Cody as Cody stepped off the porch and walked over to the van. Raindrops began to spatter the ground, the sweet scent of the storm filling the air.

"A little wet," Cody said as the rain began to hammer down in earnest. "I left you a message. I wasn't sure you'd bring Dustin over, what with this weather." '

"I wasn't sure I should either. But Frank had planned to take Michael and Michelle to see the new Disney movie, and I had to drop them off since his truck's leaking transmission fluid, so I thought we might as well stop by." She rolled her eyes. "It's always something."

"Yeah, that's for sure."

"Besides, Dustin and I wanted to see how the kittens are doing."

"They're doing great, far as I know." Cody looked across the seat at Dustin. "Nikki's going to paint one of the bedrooms today. Wanna help?"

Dustin shrugged. But Cody noticed a spark of anticipation in his eyes. A lot of kids liked painting, which, for the life of him, Cody didn't know why. He had no desire to repaint the nursery, though he would gladly help Nikki if she wanted him to. He doubted she did.

"Okay, then. If that's all right with you, Sylvia, we'll put him to work and see that he gets a ride home later."

"Great. Thank you, Cody." She gave him a smile.

"No problem." Cody made a funny face at little Jessica, who sat in her car seat, and the toddler rewarded him with a giggle that turned his heart in his chest. The kid was so cute. Cody forced himself to turn away from the minivan. With a wave to Sylvia, he hurried to the house with Dustin.

On the porch, Cody shook the rain from his slicker and slipping out of it, placed it on a chair to avoid tracking water into the house. Dustin wore his usual ball cap, jeans and a windbreaker. "You can hang that in the kitchen." Cody gestured. "Just drape it over a chair."

"'Kay." Dustin headed through the living room and disappeared into the kitchen.

Nikki appeared in the doorway that led from the hall, a paintbrush poised in her hand. She'd changed from shorts to faded jeans and a T-shirt, and Cody's pulse jumped at the sight of her.

"Dustin's here?" She glanced toward the other room.

"Uh-huh." Cody hoped she wouldn't mind the fact that he'd taken it upon himself to recruit help for her, but he really did hate leaving Nikki to face the task alone. "I'd intended to have him work on the fence, but with the rain...well, I thought you might want some help painting the, uh, guest room." He hated that he could no longer call it a nursery.

"Sure," Nikki said. "I could use his help." For a moment Cody thought she was about to ask him to join them, but instead, she headed for the kitchen as Dustin appeared in the doorway.

She looked at his clothes. "You know, we'd better cover up your jersey with something so you don't ruin it with paint." She frowned. "I'm sure I can come up with an old shirt for you to wear, but what about your jeans?"

Dustin quirked his mouth. "It doesn't matter. They're old."

Nikki laughed. "I wasn't sure if they were old or in style."

"I've got an old shirt you can borrow, Dustin," Cody said. "I'll get it." Avoiding Nikki's gaze, he moved down the hall to the bedroom. He glanced at the neatly made bed, and all he could think of was lying there with Nikki in his arms, watching her sleep while he held her.

It was no wonder he'd taken to sleeping on the couch.

When he returned with the shirt, he found her and Dustin in the living room, looking at the kittens, debating their progress and chance of survival.

"I think they'll make it." Dustin spoke with force and determination, and Cody wondered why the boy wouldn't apply that same ardor to his own life.

"Are you two all right then?" Cody asked. "You don't need my help?"

"No." Nikki spoke without looking at him. "We can handle it."

"Okay. I've got to go run some errands. My truck's making a knocking sound, so I thought I'd let Lester look at it." He was the only decent mechanic in Deer Creek, and his time was usually booked well in advance. Cody doubted he'd be able to get him to look at the Chevy on such short notice, but the garage Lester worked for took care of all the squad cars, so maybe he'd squeeze Cody in. If not, the truck could probably wait. He had a pretty good idea himself of what was likely causing the sound. But shooting the breeze with Lester while he worked was better than sticking around here where he wasn't needed.

Still, Cody hesitated.

"Need anything while I'm in town?"

"No, thanks."

"Hey, look at the orange one." Dustin chatted excitedly about something the kitten did, and Nikki continued to focus on the little cats.

Cody turned away, the sound of Nikki's soft laughter washing over him as he headed outside through the rain to his pickup.

"YOU MIGHT WANT to use a paint roller," Nikki said. A few feet from her, Dustin stood, stroking pale green paint over the wall. "It'll go faster that way on the bigger areas."

"Okay. Where's it at?"

"There's a couple in the attic."

"The attic?" Dustin's voice bore a funny hitch. Was he afraid of heights? Ladders?

"Uh-huh. Ours has stairs instead of a ladder. If you go up those steps in the kitchen, you'll find a little shelf off to one side of the door with painting supplies on it. There should be two rollers. I meant to grab one." She frowned as she studied Dustin's face. He looked a little pale. "Are you all right? Do you want me to go get it?"

"No." He waved her words away. "I'll do it." He walked off, and Nikki went back to painting the trim on the window. A sudden clap of thunder made her jump and smear paint on the window pane. "Dang it. Dustin!" She turned to call again, but he was already out of earshot. There was a pile of rags on the attic shelf which she'd also meant to gather, but her mind had been on Cody.

Laying down the paintbrush, she was heading for the kitchen when she heard the sound of pounding on the attic door. And Dustin's frantic voice. Immediately her stomach pitched.

"Let me out! Mrs. Somers, help!" From the other side of the door, his fists thudded against the wood.

"I'm coming, Dustin. It's okay." Nikki hurried up the steps, surprised to find the door tightly closed, considering it wouldn't stay put unless it had been pulled shut.

"Open the door." Dustin's voice trembled.

What on earth? "I'm here." Nikki tugged on the old-fashioned brass doorknob, but the door wouldn't budge.

"Dustin, it's stuck. It never does shut right because it's old, and the wood sometimes swells in the damp."

"The doorknob came off!" He all but shouted the words.

Nikki sighed. Of course. She knew it was loose and had thought to tighten it while she had the screwdriver in hand to dismantle the crib. Then Cody had come to help, and she'd gotten sidetracked.

"Listen, Dustin. You need to thread the shaft back into the hole so it'll connect with the outside knob. Then just push on the door while you turn the knob and it will come unstuck."

She leaned close to the door, listening, and heard the sound of metal against metal as Dustin tried to insert the shaft into the square-shaped hole.

"It won't fit." His voice tight with panic, Dustin sounded as if he were about to start crying. Nikki jumped as he slammed his fist against the door. "I can't stay in here!"

"All right. Calm down." She automatically turned to call out to Cody. But he'd left for town. "Dustin, listen to me. The door will open once the knob is in place, but you have to thread the shaft into the hole just right so the shape of it matches up. See how it's square?"

Silence filled the air for a moment. "Yeah. I see."

"Okay, then. Try it again." She held her breath, listening to the scraping of metal. A moment later, the door nearly smacked Nikki in the face as Dustin turned the knob and pushed it open so hard that it banged against the stairwell wall.

He stepped across the threshold onto the landing and stood shaking, sweat beading his temples. The color had drained from his face. "Man. I didn't think I was gonna be able to get it open. I thought it swung in, so when I yanked it that way to try to open it, it got stuck." He continued to tremble.

Frowning, Nikki gently took ahold of his shoulders. "Are you all right?"

"Yeah." His cheeks flushed. "I—uh—sort of have this thing about closed spaces." He shrugged as if the incident hadn't been a big deal. "I'm okay." He turned to lean back into the room. "I found the roller."

"Good." Choosing not to push the issue, Nikki stepped inside and came back with a handful of rags. "We'll probably need these, too."

Dustin nodded, then gestured toward the open door. "How come you have all that baby stuff in there?"

Nikki took a deep breath and decided that a simple explanation was best. "Cody and I lost a baby a few months ago."

He looked stunned. "She died?"

She pursed her lips and nodded. "Yes."

He hesitated. "How?"

"In a car accident."

"Gosh." Dustin stood awkwardly holding the paint roller. "I'm really sorry, Mrs. Somers."

"Thank you, Dustin. It was hard." She gave his shoulder a squeeze. "You know if you're going to be my painting partner, you might as well call me Nikki."

"Okay." He blushed. "You always were my favorite teacher."

"Aw-w, flattery. That's good." She winked. "I'd say it's worth a couple of chocolate chip cookies and a big glass of milk."

He grinned. "In that case, you're my favorite painting partner, too."

NIKKI MADE SURE Dustin got home in plenty of time for supper. She walked him to the door, and when he disappeared down the hallway to wash up and change his clothes, she lowered her voice and spoke to Sylvia. "Have you got a few minutes? There's something I'd like to talk to you about."

"Sure. Coffee's always on in this house. Come on in."

Nikki joined her in the kitchen and by the time she left, she had a whole new insight on what Dustin had been through. She drove from the Thompsons' house to Jana's, her mind drifting back to her conversation with Sylvia. She'd thought it best to tell the woman about the attic incident, but to her surprise she didn't seem at all startled by what had happened. Instead, she'd been extremely concerned.

"Lordy, I thought he'd gotten past that."

"Past what?" Nikki had asked, stirring sugar into her coffee.

"I'm adamant about protecting the privacy of my kids." Sylvia laid down her spoon and stared solemnly at her. "But since Dustin is spending a lot of time with you and Cody…well, I think it's best you know." She sighed. "Dustin was abused by his stepfather when he was five. Not sexually," she hurried to add. "The guy used to lock him in the attic for punishment, poor little thing. Can you imagine?"

Nikki couldn't. She thought about the quiet little boy she'd known as Dusty, when he'd been in her kindergarten class. She knew his birth father had abandoned him early on, and that both his stepfather and mother had a drinking problem and were going through a divorce, but she hadn't heard anything about abuse. She was stunned by what Sylvia had told her.

It had taken over a year for Child Protective Services to finally intervene and pull him from his mother's home. By then, he'd been subjected to beatings at the hands of his mother and some of the men she'd called boyfriends. He'd gone hungry on more than one occasion. But what bothered Nikki most was the thought of a five-year-old boy being locked in an attic. All day. With nothing to eat or drink, and no place to go to the bathroom.

Dear God. No wonder the kid had an attitude.

Nikki turned onto Jana's street and pulled over to the curb. Glancing down the block, she caught sight of Cody's squad car, along with Jordan's, parked in front of Admiral Parker's house. *What in the world...?*

Today was supposed to be his day off, so that meant he had to have gotten called in on his cell phone while he was in town.

Curious, and somewhat disappointed that she wouldn't be able to talk to Cody right away about Dustin, Nikki knocked on Jana's door.

"THERE WERE TWO of 'em." Admiral Parker's deep voice boomed through the living room, echoing off the walls. Cody stood with Jordan, scribbling on his clipboard. "I looked out that side window over there," Parker went on, pointing, "and saw 'em. They were pokin' a stick at Thor. I tell you, I had half a mind to open the gate and set him on their sorry hides."

"Can you describe the boys for me?" Cody asked.

"Darn tootin' I can. Baggy pants and ball caps on crooked." Parker gestured. "'Bout junior high age. One had earrings in both ears. The other boy didn't have any as far as I could tell."

"Hair color?"

"Hard to say with the caps on. Maybe brown on the boy with the earrings. The other one looked lighter—dirty blond I think."

"Mind if we take a look outside?" Jordan asked. "Just to make sure nothing was tampered with?"

"Go right ahead. I'll call Thor in." He went to the kitchen, opened the back door and whistled, and the big black-and-rust Doberman trotted in, stubby tail wagging. He spotted Cody and Jordan and began to growl low in his throat.

"Fall in!" Parker commanded.

Cody raised a brow as the Dobie came to heel and dropped into a sitting position at Parker's left side. "Nicely trained dog," he said. But he kept a wary eye on Thor as he and Jordan passed to exit.

They checked the perimeter of the fenced yard, as well as the area between the house and garage. Cody went through the gate and circled the garage. The graffiti he'd found there over a month ago had since been painted over, but a faint shadow of it still showed through on closer inspection. *Tech-9*. He shook his head, wondering if Dustin had played a part in spray-painting the garage. Possibly. But Cody was certain he'd had nothing to do with teasing Thor. Not after the way he'd defended the kittens. Plus he would've barely had time to get home under Nikki's care, then turn right around and go back out again with his friends.

Of course, it wasn't altogether impossible. And kids were known to get into unexpected situations and trouble hanging out with the wrong crowd. Sometimes, two or more of them together would do things that, alone, would never cross their minds. Dustin and his buddies—Chad and Ryan—gave the appearance of boys trying to act bigger and badder than they actually were. Maybe Dustin carried a chip on his shoulder after what had happened when Parker's Dobie stopped him at the fence.

Making a mental note to ask Nikki exactly what time she'd taken Dustin home, Cody eased around the back of the building, alert for any signs of tampering or vandalism. A dirt and gravel alleyway passed between the garage and the neighbor's house. Parker's trash barrels stood lined against the wall; three of them, industrial-sized with snap-on lids. One lid was ajar, and Cody leaned over to secure it against animals.

His hand froze when he spied the contents. The

entire trash can, top to bottom, was piled high with empty gin bottles. Gingerly, he lifted one and peered at it before giving the can a nudge with his toe. Glass rattled. The container held no other trash, just gin bottles, their frosted glass showing the admiral's preference for one particular brand. Cody had thought he'd detected the faint scent of liquor on the old boy's breath. Of course, there was nothing wrong with drinking in your own home, if that's what you had a mind to do. Nothing illegal about it, either.

It was none of his business, not even as an officer of the law, unless Parker was doing something that *was* illegal, something more than drinking at home. A cold chill crept up his spine. Would a man who drank so heavily drink and drive? It was possible. Cody snapped the trash can lid in place and walked back around the garage.

"See anything?" Jordan asked, coming around the other side from the yard.

"Not really."

"What?" His partner knew him well, read him easily.

Cody told him about the gin bottles. "So he likes his booze." Jordan shrugged. "Doesn't mean anything."

"Yeah, I guess you're right."

Cody went back into the house long enough to tell Admiral Parker that they'd found nothing suspicious, and to call if he had any more trouble. But once outside again, he fought the urge to go back and ask Parker to open his garage. The man owned a mid-sized car, but if memory served Cody right, he'd once seen the admiral in an SUV at the grocery store.

"You coming?" Jordan halted on his way to his squad car to glance back at Cody.

"In a minute." Cody gave in and knocked on Parker's door.

"Find something after all?" the old man asked, peering through the screen.

"Actually, no," Cody said. "But I'd feel better if I looked in your garage. Just in case, you know."

"Good thinking," Parker said. "I never actually went in there. I was just upset over the dog, you see. Thor's my partner."

"I understand," Cody said. "If you wouldn't mind, then?"

"Certainly, certainly." Parker retrieved his garage door opener, stepped outside and popped the door open.

Cody's stomach lurched when he saw the SUV parked there. A dark blue Chevy Suburban. He entered the garage, pretending to survey the area for possible vandalism, and gave the SUV a quick visual check. He saw nothing out of the ordinary on the vehicle, outside of the normal wear and tear—dead bugs on the grill and bumper, pock marks from gravel. No sign of damage to any part of the Suburban, no indication that it had been recently painted or repaired.

To make things look right, Cody walked around

the admiral's car as well, then checked the windows on the garage and the rear entrance that led to the backyard. "Everything looks okay to me," he said. "You don't see anything out of place or missing, do you, sir?"

"No," Parker said. "I think Thor scared them off, riled by their teasing. They likely would've tried something more if I didn't have the dog."

"Probably. Guess that'll do it, then. As I said, call us if we can be of any more assistance."

"Will do."

Jordan had stood quietly by while Cody looked around the garage, and he now walked with Cody toward their squad cars. "You want to tell me what that was all about?"

Cody shrugged. "I had to be sure." Maybe Nikki was right, at least in part. Maybe he was becoming obsessed with the hit-and-run driver to the point of paranoia. After all, Parker had been a longtime resident of Deer Creek.

Jordan's eyes held sympathy. "Hey, buddy, hang tight. We're gonna get that creep. But I doubt you'll find him here."

Cody grunted. "Guess not." As he climbed into his squad car, he saw that Nikki's Saturn was parked at Jana's. He hesitated, wondering if he should drive over and tell her he and Jordan had been called in to work. Henderson and Schmidt, who normally covered the mid-shift, had been unable to come in because Schmidt was sick and Henderson had a family emergency.

You're separated, a cold voice inside his head reminded him.

He was no longer obligated to tell Nikki where he was or what his schedule might be. Not that he'd ever felt it was an obligation.

Feeling grumpy, Cody pulled onto Willow Street heading, not toward Jana's house, but away from it.

"SOUNDS LIKE the poor kid has some serious issues to deal with." Jana poured tea from an old-fashioned copper teapot into Nikki's cup. Her waist-length, strawberry-blond hair fell down her back in a French braid, her full figure nicely complemented by the black slacks and loose-fitting tunic she wore.

Pulling the dessert plate Jana had set in front of her closer, Nikki used the edge of her fork to slice off a bite of homemade peach cobbler. She wasn't really hungry, but the treat was too much to resist. "I'll say. I just hope Cody and I can convince him there are more constructive ways to spend his time and energy." She started to lift the bite of cobbler to her mouth, then paused and laughed without humor. "Listen to me. 'Cody and I.' As if we're still a team."

"Hey, no negative thoughts." Jana put the teapot down on the table before sitting in the chair next to Nikki.

Nikki toyed with the edge of the hunter-green

place mat in front of her. "I can't help it. It's hard to think positively when my marriage is falling apart, and I can't even get Cody to continue with our counseling."

"Have you talked about that since you got home from Tennessee?"

She shook her head. "No. I've been waiting for the right moment. Whenever that might be."

"Well, as the old cliché goes, there's no time like the present. I don't think you should put it off any longer, hon."

Nikki wrinkled her nose. "You're right. I'd planned to talk to Cody this evening about Dustin, and I was hoping we might also talk about us. But apparently Cody got called in to work. I saw his squad car down the block at Admiral Parker's."

"Really?" Jana raised her eyebrows. "Hmm. I wonder if Parker's had more trouble with those kids who spray-painted his garage. You don't think Dustin had something to do with that, do you?"

"I don't know. I hope not."

Jana leaned back in her chair, and her pretty hazel eyes studied Nikki. "You're awfully good at taking care of others, Dustin a case in point. But you know what I think you need? To do something for you. Something totally positive to focus your energy on."

"Like what?"

"Have you ever thought about joining MADD?"

"Mothers Against Drunk Driving?" Nikki sipped

her tea. "I'm aware of the group of course, but no, I never really thought about joining."

"You should. There's a local chapter that meets monthly in Deer Creek."

"Really? Cody never mentioned it."

Jana shrugged. "I suppose just because he's a cop doesn't mean he's involved with the chapter, though that's not a bad idea, either. But for now, I think you need to do this alone." She hesitated. "It beats the heck out of curling up with a pan full of brownies. Trust me, I've been there."

Nikki scowled. "Hey, don't mess with my chocolate."

Jana chuckled and raised one hand in surrender. "Okay! But seriously, why don't you give it some thought. I've got the information handy if you'd like to have it. The chapter coordinator is a regular at the bookstore."

"Yeah, I think I would." She took another bite of the cobbler, then pushed it away, realizing Jana was right. She'd taken enough comfort in food lately. Enough to move up a pant size, and the shorts she now wore were beginning to feel snug.

Jana got her phone book, copied down a name and number on a sticky note, and handed it to her. "Savannah Webster is the coordinator. Give her a call. I believe they meet on the second Wednesday of each month, which is tomorrow."

Nikki folded the note and tucked it in her pocket.

"Thanks, Jana." She smiled. The two of them had always been good friends, but they'd grown closer after Amanda moved away.

"You're welcome, but what do you think you're doing pushing away my homemade peach cobbler?" Jana put her hands on her hips in a stance of mock indignation.

Nikki laughed. "Turning over a new leaf. My pants are so tight I can barely breathe."

"Well, turn it over another day." Jana pushed the plate back Nikki's way, then shook one finger threateningly. "I made that from scratch, and you're not going to waste it."

"Yes, ma'am." She dug into the cobbler and swirled a bite on her tongue, savoring the tangy-sweet combination of juicy peaches and cinnamon. "I love it when you twist my arm."

CHAPTER SEVEN

THE RAIN had let up a couple of hours ago, but storm clouds continued to darken the sky, bringing dusk early. After leaving Admiral Parker's, Cody cruised the downtown area, his thoughts wandering. How much longer could he continue like this, with no new leads on the hit-and-run driver? With nothing to go on beyond the meager information provided by the victims to the Highway Patrol. His frustration grew daily. Merely hoping to stumble upon something that might provide a lead—like Parker's trash can full of gin bottles—wasn't good enough. He'd dug through every possibility and then some. He had to keep trying.

Hey, buddy, hang tight. We're gonna get that creep. Jordan's optimism.

But Cody was beginning to wonder if they ever would. He turned the squad car around and headed toward the hated two-lane highway. The one he could barely stand to drive. Except he had to keep returning to investigate the area, looking for clues, expanding his search. How many times had he parked near the crash site and combed the surrounding area, poking through the grass, climbing down the embankment? He'd searched the riverbank, the shoulder of the road...

Twenty times? Fifty? It didn't matter. He'd come back a hundred times, if that's what it took.

Cody pulled his car well off the road onto a spot where the shoulder widened, yards from where Amanda's Blazer had pitched into the ravine. He sat behind the wheel and took a couple of deep breaths. Tried not to picture torn and twisted metal...shattered glass...

He got out and began the familiar routine, using his flashlight to penetrate the dusky-gray light. Thunder rumbled in the distance, and a flash of lightning briefly draped the sky in a fluorescent sheet of white. He likely didn't have long before the storm inched its way back in.

Cody nudged the grass with the toe of his shoe, parting the knee-high clumps. He picked his way through litter—the careless laziness of people too ignorant to use a trash can made him sick, and he vowed to bring Dustin back here to clean up. That would chap his rotten little butt. He kicked at the grass again, and his toe struck something metal. A pop can? No, something bigger, heavier.

He bent and shone the flashlight into a clump of weeds. A license plate, bent and dusty. He picked it up, staring at the personalized lettering: *SIXPAC*. His heart raced, and his hands began to shake. What sort of person would engrave something like that on their car plates?

Maybe the kind who would run down two helpless women and an unborn baby and leave them to die.

Cody ran the plates on his Mobile Data Terminal then radioed the sheriff's department and the State Highway Patrol. Minutes later, Deputy Rick Stillwell and Trooper Phil Johnson arrived on the scene. Cody got out of his car and walked over to Johnson's black-and-silver patrol unit.

Johnson spoke through his open window. "What's up?"

"Got something here for you." He held up the license plate. "I found it down there in the ravine." Cody reached inside himself to retain his professionalism. "I ran the plate. It came back revoked—DUI. Interesting thing is, it belongs to a 1986 Ford Bronco. Black. I think we'd better look into it." He turned toward Stillwell, who'd parked his car near Cody's and walked over to join them. "The driver lives in your jurisdiction, Rick."

"Wanna tag along?" Stillwell asked.

"You bet." Cody climbed back into his squad car and laid the plate on the seat beside him. Making sure the road was clear, he made a U-turn and fell into place between Stillwell and Johnson as they headed to the address of the registered owner of the vehicle. Veronica Dover.

Cody had always pictured the driver of the hit-

and-run vehicle to be a man. Some creep he could have the satisfaction of busting, of putting away behind bars. He'd never imagined the monster who killed his baby girl to be a woman.

Chastising himself for not keeping a more open mind, for letting his personal feelings give him tunnel vision, Cody parked in front of the farmhouse where Veronica Dover lived. He headed for the house along with Johnson and Stillwell, noting the black Ford Bronco that sat, weeds growing around the tires and in front of the grill, in an overgrown area near the edge of the well-lit yard.

Cody stepped up onto the porch. The woman who answered the door looked ten years older than the DOB on her vehicle registration. Her straw-colored hair stuck out in helter-skelter tufts, dark roots showing. She squinted at him and his fellow officers through a cloud of cigarette smoke. "Yes?"

"Are you Veronica Dover?" Stillwell spoke.

"Yeah, what do you want?"

"We'd like to ask you a few questions. Will you please step outside?"

She complied, and Stillwell nodded in the direction of the SUV. "You the owner of that Bronco?"

"Yeah, what about it?"

"Is this your license plate?" Cody held up the personalized plate.

Veronica's face brightened. "Man, where did you find that? I didn't think I'd ever see it again."

"When was the last time you drove the vehicle?" Cody asked, ignoring her question.

"New Year's Eve," she said without hesitation. She inhaled on the cigarette, then tossed it down and ground the butt out. "Got a fine coming home after drinking at a party. Had my license revoked for a year." She nodded toward the Ford. "That's why my Bronco's gathering spider webs."

Cody moved toward the SUV for a closer look. There really were spider webs, woven into the grill. Cody lifted the hood for a closer look and saw the spiders had made themselves at home in the engine compartment as well. Obviously, it hadn't been driven in a while, but he inspected every inch of the Bronco anyway, inside and out, and found nothing to indicate it had been in any recent accidents. While rusty and a bit run-down, it bore no dents or scrapes, other than a small one near the rear bumper. And that was rusted enough to tell him it had been there a good long while. The right rear tire had obviously been flat for some time.

"So, you haven't driven the vehicle since January," Stillwell asked, inspecting the front end of it for himself.

"Like I said, I had my license taken away on New Year's Eve, and I'm not about to screw up anymore."

Cody moved to the rear of the Bronco and noted that the license plate was indeed missing, a rusty set of baling wire dangling from holes in the homemade rear bumper where the plate belonged. The scratch marks on the mounting holes of the plate he held were the same type of marks that would be made by wire, not to mention the fact that the front plate also read *SIXPAC*.

He stared at it, wanting desperately to make a connection to the crash, practically willing Veronica to be the one who'd hit Amanda back in February. Then he could haul her off to jail and put his demons to rest. But evidence didn't lie, and when Cody looked in Veronica's eyes, he saw no signs of deception. Only a person who'd made a mistake and seemed to regret it.

With a sigh, he handed her the bent and dirty license plate. "This must've fallen off of your Bronco." He nodded toward the Ford. "You might want to find a better way to attach it to your bumper than with baling wire."

"Yeah, thanks." Veronica nodded as she held the plate. "I sure appreciate you taking time to come all the way out here and bring it to me."

She actually thought that he, Johnson and Stillwell had come out here just to return a lost plate? Short of her previous DUI charges, the woman was apparently guilty of nothing more than being a little slow.

She lit up another cigarette and moved to sit on the porch steps. "Do I gotta sign a paper or something? For the plate?"

"No." Johnson shook his head. "Just keep yourself on track." He gave her a firm stare before bidding Cody and Stillwell goodbye and heading out in the black-and-silver Crown Vic.

"Oh, I will," Veronica called after him. "Don't you worry, officers."

"Have a nice day," Stillwell said. He followed Cody back to his squad car. "You okay, buddy?"

"Yeah." Cody sighed. "Just disappointed."

"We're still on the case. I'm not about to let it go cold either."

"Appreciate it. See ya later." He climbed behind the wheel of his squad car and drove away.

CODY HEADED HOME after his shift ended at eleven, tired and ready to crawl into bed. He ignored the pain in the pit of his stomach as his headlights lit the ranch house, silhouetted against the backdrop of the night. His hands automatically began to steer the squad car over to his usual parking spot in front of the house, before his head reminded him his destination was the bunkhouse.

But he did a double take at the sight of Nikki sitting on the porch. She wasn't much of a night owl. He hoped nothing was wrong. Max stood near her, tail wagging in greeting as he gave a welcoming bark. Cody let his hands have their way, guiding the patrol car beside Nikki's Saturn. A moment later, he stood at the foot of the porch steps, looking up at her.

"What are you doing up?" He tried to hide the

concern in his voice, which made the question sound accusatory, as if she had no right to sit in the dark without him.

Nikki raised one brow in a way that always set his libido on edge. Sexy, sassy. *What's it to you, cowboy?*

He half expected the words to come out of her mouth. Instead, she leaned back against the navy-blue cushion of the wooden chair. "I was waiting for you."

His heart leapt. With hope? Dread? He wasn't quite sure. "Oh?" He forced his voice to remain neutral.

"I wanted to talk to you about Dustin. Have you got time, or are you beat?"

"No, I'm okay." He climbed the steps and sat in the chair beside her. Her citrus perfume tickled his senses. "What's going on?"

"We had a bit of an incident after you left for town today." She explained what had happened in the attic.

Cody listened, appalled, as Nikki told him of the abuse Dustin had suffered at the hands of his stepfather and, later, his mother's boyfriends. He mumbled a curse under his breath.

Nikki pressed her lips together. "Apparently, he needs positive influences in his life more than we originally imagined."

And with those simple words, Cody's thoughts began to click and whirl. He pictured Dustin, working on the fence with him. It made him feel good whenever he'd managed to pull a smile or a laugh out of the sullen boy. He pictured Dustin and Nikki as they'd sat beside the basket of kittens, Dustin's tough facade softened by his obvious love of animals. *Wouldn't it be nice...to be a family....*

"Thank goodness he has Frank and Sylvia."

Cody blinked, jarred by Nikki's comment. The Thompsons were good people, yes, but he knew they'd been foster parents for a number of years now, preferring to help many children rather than adopting a few. It wasn't likely Dustin would find a permanent home with them.

"He needs more than that."

"What do you mean?"

Cody leaned forward, resting his clasped hands on his knees. "All he's ever known is a temporary home, instability. He needs parents of his own."

Nikki nodded. "I hope he finds that. But most people want to adopt a baby, not an older child, especially one with attitude."

Cody avoided looking directly at her. They had considered adoption prior to choosing surrogacy. And yes, they'd had a baby in mind.

He was through dreaming about babies.

But he still longed to be a father. "What about us?"

"What?"

Nikki's puzzled look faded as realization dawned, and she stared at him as though he'd lost his mind.

He supposed he had, but he plunged on. "We could give Dustin a home."

"What?" she repeated, gaping at him.

"Dustin needs a home with two responsible, loving parents," Cody continued, "and we could give him that. Come on, Nikki, you know Anna's death is what put this damned rift between us." He waved his hand, knowing even as he spoke that Anna's death was only part of what had gone wrong with their marriage. Still, he felt he was headed down the right track. "I realize we've got a lot of things to iron out, but this might be the place to start. With us and Dustin as a family."

"Are you crazy?" Nikki jerked away from his grasp and stood. "We can't bring a child into our home when we're not even living together. I can't believe you would suggest such a thing."

He stood as well. "Just think about it. That's all I ask. We could do this. We could be the mom and dad Dustin needs."

"How about being the husband and wife we need to be to each other?"

Cody refused to give up. "I understand what you're saying, but you told me yourself that we need to start somewhere."

"Yes. With *us*."

"Yes." He nodded. "Us. You, me, Dustin…a family." He shrugged. "I know it's not as simple as all that, but just give it some thought," he repeated, raising one hand to hold off whatever else she was about to say. "I could use some sleep, and you probably could, too." Turning his attention to Max he bid the dog good-night, ruffling the shepherd's fur before commanding him to stay put. He didn't like the idea of Nikki being in the house alone.

"Good night, Nikki." Quickly he moved down the steps toward his squad car, before she could protest more.

He paused, leaning on the car's open door. "Let me know when you want to talk."

She merely pursed her lips, arms still folded. Looking as cute as she had the first day he'd laid eyes on her.

He knew she was probably right. That he was just that—crazy. And maybe it was only his emotions over what had happened tonight…running into yet another dead end on tracking down the hit-and-run driver…that had him tied in knots. Had him thinking off-the-wall thoughts, and wishing for things that weren't likely to happen. But Dustin had begun to grow on him. Any kid who would stand up to a boy a head taller than him to save a sack of kittens was okay in his book.

NIKKI LET MAX back in the house midmorning, then curled up in the rocking chair near the living room window with a giant cinnamon roll and a glass of chocolate milk, the resolve she'd made at Jana's to watch what she ate already forgotten. What did it matter anyway? At the moment she couldn't care less if she ballooned up to five hundred pounds, not that her size would ever matter to Cody. She could look like a runway model, a movie star or a homeless woman, and it wouldn't make a darned bit of difference to him. Unlike a lot of men, he wasn't shallow. That was the problem. Cody *wasn't* like a lot of men. He was one in a million, and if her marriage dissolved, Nikki never wanted a man to look at her again. Because the only man she had ever loved and *would* ever love had driven away last night in his squad car.

He'd also driven it past the house this morning. She'd purposely stayed in bed until she heard the sound of his tires crunching on the narrow dirt-and-gravel road that led from the bunkhouse. She'd waited until she knew he was gone, reasoning that if he found her awake he might stop in and pick up their conversation where they'd left off the night before.

Adopting Dustin! Nikki shook her head and stuffed a chunk of cinnamon roll into her mouth. She liked Dustin. And she was more sorry than words could say for the things the poor kid had suffered. But Cody was out of his mind. She'd been through way too much lately to think about adopting a child. Especially one who could be trouble.

Nikki carried her empty plate and glass to the kitchen, wondering if she should call Regina's office and see if she had time open today. Just because Cody wouldn't go to counseling didn't mean she shouldn't.

Maybe Regina would have some advice on how to handle the fireball he'd thrown at her last night.

Nikki flipped open the phone book and reached for the cordless, then hesitated. Jana's words raced through her mind. *Have you ever thought about joining MADD?* She closed the phone book and got out her purse, where she'd tucked away Savannah Webster's phone number. She could talk to Regina at their next regular appointment. Right now, she needed to do something just for herself, and if taking a stand against drunk drivers—fighting the cause of what had killed Anna—would help others in the process, so much the better.

"Hello," Nikki said in response to the woman on the other end of the line. "Is this Savannah Webster? My name is Nikki Somers, and I'd love to come to your next meeting."

THE WARMTH she'd felt in talking with Savannah over the phone turned to nervous anticipation as Nikki parked in front of the Town Hall where the Deer Creek chapter of Mothers Against Drunk Driving held their meetings. She looked across the lot to the adjacent building of the police station where Cody's squad car was still parked. He'd pulled his regular shift even after filling in for mid-shift yesterday, and he should be leaving the building any time now. Would he see her Saturn and come over?

Nikki took a deep breath and entered the building.

Inside, a sign pointed the way, and she easily found the conference room where a group of people were gathered in a circle of chairs.

A woman with ash-blond hair cut short and practical greeted her warmly. "I'm Savannah Webster. You must be Nikki."

She nodded, taking the woman's proffered hand. "It's nice to meet you." All eyes turned toward her. Several people nodded or gave a polite smile, and Nikki began to relax.

"Sit anywhere you like," Savannah said. "We're not at all formal here." She took her own seat and waited while people continued to file in and sit down.

Nikki glanced around, studying the variety of people who filled the room. Men and women of various ages, teenagers and even a couple of kids about Dustin's age. Somehow she'd pictured a room full of angry mothers, demanding prohibition. She wondered what each person's story was. Had they lost a child? A sister? An uncle?

"Good afternoon." Savannah spoke, bringing the meeting to order.

Nikki listened, barely noticing the slight creak as the door opened, then closed, at the back of the room. From the corner of her eye, she saw the latecomer slip into the last empty chair. The woman looked familiar, and it took Nikki a moment to register who she was and where she'd previously seen her.

Her heart began to pound. The emergency room,

on the night of Amanda's accident. She was the well-dressed woman with the flawless makeup and dark hair, whose loved one, Caitlin, had been in the same wreck as Amanda. *Dear God. Had she died?*

Nikki recalled reading in the paper that Caitlin had been severely injured and lay in a coma. But she'd been so shaken over her own loss, she hadn't thought to follow up on Caitlin…Kroger? Krieger? She couldn't even remember the poor girl's last name.

The woman wore a lightweight summer blouse and slacks, her hair pulled into the same flawless bun she'd worn that night in the hospital waiting room. Was she Caitlin's mother? By her silky complexion and high cheekbones, she could've been in her mid-thirties to forties, but Nikki guessed she was older than she looked. The woman caught her eye and gave her a polite smile, showing no sign of recognition.

Nikki smiled back, then faced forward as Savannah spoke. "We've got a newcomer to welcome to the group today, so let's begin by introducing ourselves. Nikki, you can speak if you'd like when your turn comes, but you don't have to. Nobody here has to talk if they're uncomfortable about it. But if you'd like to share a little about yourself and why you're here, that's fine, too."

Nikki squirmed as all eyes turned back to her, but everyone seemed so full of warmth and compassion, she began to relax again. These were people who could relate to what she'd been through.

"Henry, we'll let you start tonight." Savannah indicated a man who sat to Nikki's far right.

"I'm here," Henry began, "because I lost my son, Jamie, to a drunk driver on the night of his twenty-first birthday." Everyone listened with rapt attention as he told how Jamie had gone with friends to dinner, then to a party. "They were on their way home when an eighteen-year-old girl with a blood alcohol level of .16, hit them. The irony is that Jamie and his buddies made sure they had a designated driver. For all the good it did them." Henry's voice cracked and he shook his head, looking down at his lap.

"Designated drivers *are* a good thing," Savannah said gently. "Jamie and his friends did the right thing, the responsible thing. And if the girl who hit him had done the same, you wouldn't be sitting with us right now. That's why we're here. MADD isn't an anti-alcohol group. We're about not driving drunk." She focused on Nikki, eyes questioning.

Nikki couldn't remain silent. She'd come here by choice, to be with this group. If they were willing to bare their hearts, she couldn't do less. "My name is Nikki Somers, and I don't know if it's accurate to say I'm glad to be here, because I wish none of us had a reason to be in this room right now. But it feels good to be with people who understand what I've been through." She took a deep breath. "I lost my baby daughter to a drunk driver." Her eyes flitted to the dark-haired woman, who pressed her fingers against her lips, her pretty brown eyes immediately filling with moisture.

Nikki forced herself to look away. She focused on Savannah. "My husband and I had some difficulties getting pregnant, so we opted for surrogacy. My sister Amanda was the surrogate mother of our child, and when she was well into her second trimester, our friends threw us a baby shower. We held it at my house…."

She tried not to cry. She'd come here for strength and to give back in whatever way she could. She did not look to see how others in the room were reacting, but she could feel them watching her. "After the baby shower was over, Amanda stayed to help me put the gifts away in the nursery." Her voice hitched and she forcefully swallowed back a sob.

"It was starting to snow, and I live a few miles outside of town, so Amanda had a bit of a drive ahead of her and wanted to leave before the roads got bad. She doesn't remember much of what happened, but we put the pieces together. Amanda saw a young woman on the side of the road with a flat tire, and she pulled over to offer her cell phone. That's when someone in a dark SUV, who'd been seen swerving on the road, and by all accounts appeared to be drunk, hit them both."

A joint gasp rippled through the group.

"That was my daughter Caitlin—on the roadside," the dark-haired woman said. Nikki looked over at her. "Forgive me for speaking out of turn, but I'm Evelyn Kramer, and I remember you from the hospital emergency room that night."

Nikki nodded as murmurs of sympathy filled the room.

"I remember reading about that crash in the paper," one woman said. "I was outraged." She spoke with the deep, raspy voice of a longtime smoker, and tears slid down her round face. "Honey, I lost my own little girl to a drunk driver fifteen years ago. She was three years old. The pain just never goes away."

Seeing her cry was Nikki's undoing. These people—these strangers who suddenly didn't feel like strangers at all—were mourning for her Anna. "No, it doesn't," she said, wiping at her cheeks. She addressed Evelyn. "So Caitlin…she…"

"No," Evelyn said quickly. "She didn't die, but she was in a coma for nine days and her physical therapy has been intense. I thank God she's alive, but she's been through hell."

"I'm so sorry," Nikki said. Savannah handed her a tissue, and she took it and thanked her.

After everyone had taken a turn speaking about the reasons why they were here, Savannah shared her own story of losing a cousin in an alcohol-related crash, and then talked about literature she'd brought back from a recent state board meeting. Nikki began to feel excited that there were ways she could help make a difference. Ways she could perhaps save someone else from going through the pain she'd suffered.

When the meeting ended, she was surprised at how the time had flown. As people shuffled out of the room or mingled in smaller groups to continue talking, Evelyn Kramer approached her.

"I didn't recognize you at first." She smiled, and her gaze took in Nikki's new hairstyle. "I'm so sorry for what you've been through. And I'm ashamed of myself, because I meant to follow up and see how your sister was doing. But I got so wrapped up in my own worries over Caitlin—well…I obviously never got around to it."

"Don't feel bad," Nikki said. "I meant to do the same thing after the accident…see how Caitlin was."

"Crash."

"Excuse me?"

"Forgive me." Evelyn laid a hand on Nikki's arm. "I didn't mean to sound as though I was correcting you. It's just that here at MADD we refer to them as crashes, not accidents. There's nothing accidental about what happens when a drunk chooses to get behind the wheel of a vehicle and endanger other people."

Nikki blinked. "You're right." She gave a small laugh. "I'm married to a cop. You'd think I'd know that, wouldn't you?" But somehow, she'd always thought of Anna's death as an accident, as something beyond her control. It was one of the ways she'd coped with what had happened. Thinking of it as a crash upset her stomach.

"It's no different than brandishing a weapon," Evelyn went on. "The man who hurt your sister and my daughter, the man who killed your precious little baby, is just as guilty as if he'd pointed a gun at them." Her hands began to shake, and she took a deep breath and pulled herself up straighter. "I'm sorry. Sometimes my fury gets the better of me. I'm probably making things worse for you."

"No." Nikki shook her head. "You're not. Sometimes it's better to be angry than sad." *Unless you went too far.* Cody's obsession with vengeance had seemed extreme to her, but maybe it wasn't. Maybe it was the only way he *did* know how to cope.

"How is your sister?" Evelyn asked.

"She's doing well." Nikki smiled. "She's going to have a baby of her own next spring."

"Oh." Evelyn's dark eyes lit up. "I'm so happy to hear that. It brings me some comfort to know she's moved on."

"Yes." Nikki sighed and glanced down at her feet. She didn't want to talk about moving on. Evelyn hadn't lost her child. She couldn't possibly know how deep the pain ran. Immediately, the uncharitable thought wrenched Nikki's conscience. "I'm very glad to hear that Caitlin survived the acci—the crash."

"She was going to ride with the U.S. equestrian

team in the Olympics, show jumping." The woman's exquisite face abruptly looked pinched and tired. "It's what she's wanted for as long as I can remember. All that is gone now."

"I'm so sorry," Nikki said. "But at least she's still with you." Every day she gave a prayer of thanks that God had spared Amanda's life.

Yet she couldn't stop wishing He'd spared Anna's as well.

"Yes, and for that I am eternally grateful," Evelyn said. Her lips curved in a smile of warmth and sympathy. "If you need anyone to talk to at any time," she said, "please don't hesitate to call me. We're listed in the phone book—Foxwood Farms."

"Ah." Olympic-level horses…Foxwood…the biggest, most well-to-do spread in the county. The place covered an enormous amount of acreage—probably at least five hundred acres—and boasted showy white rail fences, emerald-green pastures and barns with a quality of architecture superior to a lot of people's houses.

Proof that even money couldn't buy the way out of tragedy and sorrow.

On impulse, Nikki reached out and gave Evelyn a hug. "Thank you. And please give Caitlin my best."

Evelyn returned the hug, her perfume enveloping Nikki. "I hope we'll see you here again."

"You will," Nikki said as they parted.

Evelyn bid Savannah goodbye before leaving the

room. As the woman exited, Nikki heard her speak to someone coming in.

Cody.

He stepped through the doorway, looking sharp in his uniform. His eyes found Nikki's. Her pulse picked up like a steam engine burning coal, and she felt a surge of happiness at seeing him here. But just because he'd come into the building didn't mean anything. It didn't mean he'd decided to check out MADD himself, or that he'd come to check up on her.

"Hi," he said. "I saw your car outside. I didn't know you were coming here."

"It was rather on impulse," Nikki said.

Cody hesitated. "Have you got any plans for supper?"

His question threw her off balance, considering they weren't exactly socializing these days. "Not really. Why?"

"I was going to grab a burger with Jordan, but actually, I'd rather talk to you about Dustin."

Any hope she'd had, fled. "Cody, you said last night you'd wait until I was ready to talk."

He held up his hand. "I know, but just hear me out."

She glanced over her shoulder. Savannah was still in the room, along with a couple of other women. "Not here." Nikki took Cody by the arm, ignoring how good he felt, and pointed him toward the exit. He held the door for her, and together they went to her car.

Leaning against the Saturn, she faced him. "What's going on?"

"I talked to Frank and Sylvia this afternoon. You'll be interested in what they had to say."

CHAPTER EIGHT

DUSTIN SLOUCHED along the sidewalk, head down, sipping from the oversized soda he'd bought with money he'd earned working for Cody. He couldn't believe Cody had actually *paid* him. Here he'd thought he'd be working his ass off doing chores for free at the Somers' ranch for the rest of his natural life. But the last time he'd worked on the fence with Cody, Cody'd slipped him a twenty.

Dustin had taken the money hesitantly. "What's that for?"

"A man works hard, he ought to get paid for it." Cody had given him a smile that lifted his spirits higher than they'd been in quite a while. "You did a good job."

Dustin slipped the money into his pocket. "Thanks."

"Don't thank me too soon," Cody had shot back. "You'll be out here mucking stalls next time."

Hell. He wasn't looking forward to that, but Cody was all right. Dustin didn't mind working on the ranch as much as he'd first thought he would. And Mrs. Somers—Nikki—was pretty cool. She'd even

trusted him enough to feed the kittens by himself the
other day. They were growing fast, and pride swelled
his chest, knowing that was in large part because of
him. That Cody had praised him for standing up to
that jerk Vanderhurst made it all the sweeter.

"Hey, Holbrook. What're you drinking there?
Titty-baby milk?"

Dustin's head snapped up, and he froze at the
sight of Eric and his best friend, Jimmy Ryker. Both
boys wore muscle shirts and ball caps with a baseball team logo embroidered on the front. Eric had a
cigarette stuck cockily between his lips.

"Screw off, Vanderhurst." Dustin moved to brush
past them, adrenaline pumping through his veins.

"Not so fast." Eric tossed the cigarette and
grabbed Dustin by the back of the shirt, pulling him
around to face him. Jimmy reached out and smacked
the plastic cup from his hand, laughing when it hit
the sidewalk and gushed open.

Dustin tried to shrug away, but Eric held tight and
Jimmy pushed up beside him, effectively cornering
him against the wall of a vacant storefront. "I heard
what you did to Eric," Jimmy snarled. His eyes were
nearly as dark as his short black hair. "Getting him
in deep shit with Somers."

"He did that himself," Dustin said, scowling. "Let
go of me before I break your fingers."

"O-oo, tough guy," Jimmy said. He laughed, tow-
ering over Dustin. "I'm real scared."

"You think you're tough, huh?" Eric said, leaning closer. "Well, I say you're a weenie."

"Who the hell cares what you say?" But Dustin felt so light-headed, he was afraid he might embarrass himself by hitting the ground.

"You're gonna care," Eric sneered, his face red with anger. "You and Somers got me in a shitload of trouble with my parents, too, Holbrook. Thanks to you, I'm doing crap-scoop duty at the local pound. I'd really love to kick your ass for that one. But me and Jimmy here, we've got a better idea."

"I doubt the two of you could fart a coherent thought if you used both your brains at the same time," Dustin scoffed.

Eric hit him. Hard, upside the head with the heel of his hand. Dustin saw stars and staggered, fighting to keep his balance, and at the same time wondering if he could shake it off and outrun Eric and Jimmy. He'd managed it in the past with a couple of his mother's boyfriends. But before he could get past the ringing in his ears, Jimmy grabbed him.

"Shut your smart mouth and listen." Jimmy darted a glance around to make sure no one was watching.

But it was after five o'clock, and most of the people who ran the small businesses in this section of town had gone home to dinner. The people at the wheel of the few cars that passed paid no attention to three boys on the sidewalk.

"You owe me," Eric said. "And if you think you're

so tough, then prove it, weenie. Prove you're not Somers' ass kisser."

Resentment overwhelmed Dustin. He liked Cody, but he sure as hell wouldn't be accused of brownnosing. "How?"

"Come with us," Eric said, "and we'll show you."

AT LEAST SHE'D AGREED to have dinner with him. At Fiesta Guadalajara. Their favorite Mexican restaurant, in nearby Glenwood Springs. The one where they'd celebrated their tenth wedding anniversary this past fall.

Maybe by the time they reached the restaurant he'd have her convinced that he was right about a few things. "Just let me…" He was about to run back inside the station to tell Jordan he wouldn't be joining him at the local sports bar when something caught Cody's eye. "I don't friggin' believe it!" He took off running.

"Cody! What are you doing?" Nikki called out after him.

Then she must have seen what he had—Dustin crouching beside Cody's squad car, letting the air out of the tires. He heard her sandals clicking against the sidewalk as she ran after him.

Cody resisted shouting at Dustin, hoping for the advantage of surprise, though he knew it was a slim chance, what with him and Nikki pounding across the pavement. Sure enough, Dustin heard them. He looked over his shoulder at Cody, wide-eyed. He didn't even try to run. Instead, he let out a groan and sagged against the squad car.

"What the hell are you doing?" Déjà vu gripped Cody as he stopped in front of Dustin. But just then, out of the corner of his eye, he caught movement; it wasn't Nikki. "Stay put," he said, sprinting after Eric Vanderhurst and another boy about his age who Cody didn't know. The two kids had been hiding behind Jordan's squad car.

Since he knew where Eric lived, he decided he'd be better off nabbing the other kid. Cody pumped his arms harder, running after the long-legged boy who moved almost as fast as Dustin.

He really did need to get back to the gym.

CODY TOOK DOWN Jimmy Ryker's name and address and sent him off with a stern reprimand and a promise to follow up with a visit to Jimmy's parents. He shook his head as he walked back toward the squad car, frustration making him irritable.

What had possessed Dustin to do something so stupid? Cody could've written Eric and his pal each a ticket for criminal mischief, but then he'd have to write Dustin one, too, and he really hated to do that. Instead, he intended to probe until he found out exactly what was going on.

As he approached Dustin, he noticed something that gave him a pretty good idea. The boy's cheek-

BRENDA MOTT   133

bone was bruised near his temple. Cody motioned for him to follow. "Come on. You and I need to talk." He glanced at Nikki. "Do you feel like waiting? I'm going to take Dustin home after we chat, and I'd like you to come with us."

Dustin groaned and opened his mouth as though to protest.

"Don't say a word." Cody pointed a finger at him. "You're the one who made a bad choice."

"Yeah, yeah. I've already had the refresher course on choices and my stupid journal."

"Yeah, well that refresher course is just starting," Cody said. "Let's go." He looked at Nikki.

"I'll wait in the car," she said.

Cody walked with Dustin to a small park three blocks from the police station and sank onto a wooden bench. A massive globe willow spread its branches above them, offering a canopy of cool shade in the setting summer sun. "I'll bet you can guess what I'm going to ask," Cody said, studying the expression on Dustin's face. Sullen. Resolved.

"Why." It wasn't a question.

"That's the one."

Dustin scowled and let his shoulders droop as he studied his hands, clasped in the lap of his baggy jeans. "I had to."

"Explain."

"What's to explain?" He narrowed his eyes at Cody. "You ought to realize why I had no choice."

"Dustin, there are always choices."

Abruptly, the boy met his gaze. "No, there are not." Each word was articulated, taking Cody by surprise.

"Okay. You're right. But I don't think this particular situation applies to that philosophy. So tell me what just happened back there in the parking lot."

"Eric and Jimmy were piss—ticked because I'd gotten Eric in trouble for what he tried to do to the kittens. They made me prove I wasn't kissing up to you."

Cody sighed. Bullying. How many times had it escalated into violence? School shootings, suicide…the old saying that names couldn't hurt just wasn't true. "So, letting the air out of my tires would prove different."

Dustin nodded. "They wanted me to slash them. But I told them we'd get into even deeper crap because knife marks left evidence—you know. CSI stuff."

"They had knives?"

"Yeah. I told them if we just let the air out, there wasn't any real damage, and no hard evidence. That since the tire stems were ridged, they wouldn't hold fingerprints."

"And they bought it."

"Yeah." He grimaced. "They're not exactly bright."

Cody almost laughed. "No, and you're not too smart either, letting them push you into something dumb.

But," he added, "I do have to hand it to you for your resourcefulness. And I understand peer pressure."

Dustin snorted. "They aren't my peers. I just didn't feel like getting my ass kicked."

Now Cody did chuckle. "You keep saying we. But you were the only one doing the tires."

"I know. Call me stupid. No, don't." Dustin held up his hand. "They were supposed to flatten one, too. Only once I started in on a tire, they ducked over behind the other cars. I guess they set me up."

"So why didn't you stop?"

"I figured I'd just let the air out of a couple of your tires real quick and be done with it. Be done with Eric and Jimmy."

"That's where you were mistaken, Dustin." Cody spoke gently but firmly. "You start doing things like that with people like Eric and Jimmy—or Chad and Ryan—and pretty soon you get in way over your head. Situations like that tend to escalate. Don't you think now's a good time to stop before that happens?"

Dustin slumped against the park bench. "Yeah, I guess."

"Well you'd better do more than guess," Cody said. "Because you know what you've committed today, screwing with my squad car again?"

"What?" Dustin eyed him suspiciously.

"POPO. Pissing off a police officer." He stared down the smirk on Dustin's face. "I'm serious, Dustin. We've been getting along pretty well, or so

I thought. But you keep messing with my squad car, well, I've got to draw the line. Understand?"

"Does this mean I'm in for more community service?" He made it sound like a life sentence.

"That's up to you. I can write you a ticket and we'll replay what you went through with the spray-painting. Or we can work something out between me, you, Frank and Sylvia."

"Like what?"

"Well, for starters, I'd say since you let the air out of the tires, you can put it back in."

"You're not going to call Joe's Garage to tow it or something?" Dustin's face scrunched in dismay.

"Nope. I've got an air compressor at the ranch." He tapped the bill of the boy's cap. "And you're all the help I need."

"What about Eric and Jimmy?"

"Oh, I'll be having a nice little talk with their parents. I thought about writing them tickets. But that would probably only make things harder on you, right?" He could imagine that the boys would want even more revenge against Dustin if that happened.

"They'll still be ticked off when you talk to their parents."

"Maybe so, but I can't ignore what happened, either."

Dustin shrugged. "So what else are you going to make me do besides airing up your tires?"

Cody stood, thinking about the trash he'd seen

lying on the river embankment. Trash that seemed to add further insult to Anna's death.

He smiled without humor. "I'm sure we can come up with something. Now come on. Let's take you home."

AT FRANK'S AND SYLVIA'S, Nikki got out of the car to say hello, then sat on the porch while Cody went inside to talk to the Thompsons. What Dustin had done was police business, not hers.

The Thompsons' dog, Jake, joined her on the porch and shoved his head into her lap, begging for attention. Nikki scratched his floppy ears, fighting the urge to look through the open kitchen window where she'd caught a glimpse of Cody as he sat at the table with Frank, Sylvia and Dustin. She could make out the sounds of Dustin's foster siblings, playing in the adjoining living room. The television blared with the SpongeBob SquarePants theme song, accompanied by Michelle's and Michael's laughter and Jessica's joyful shrieks.

"Quiet down in there," Frank called out.

His words sent a pang of envy through Nikki's heart. This is how it would be if she were a parent. Still, the thought of adopting Dustin did not sit well with her at all. That had to be what Cody had wanted to discuss with her over dinner, before they'd been interrupted by Dustin.

Nikki changed her mind about remaining a neutral party in the discussion inside and rose from the chair. She rapped lightly on the screen door, then stuck her head inside. "May I come in?"

"Of course," Sylvia called from the kitchen. "You didn't have to knock."

With a quick glance in Cody's direction, Nikki sat in the chair she'd pulled out. "I don't mean to interrupt," she said, seeing Cody's raised brows. "I wasn't going to come in, since what Dustin did is between you two and Cody. But I do need to talk to you both."

"What's going on?" Frank asked, his forehead creased.

Nikki lowered her voice to make sure none of the kids could hear her. "Is there someplace we can talk out of earshot?"

Sylvia nodded. "We were about to send the kids packing anyway, so we could talk to Cody." She went into the living room, her voice carrying back to Nikki.

"Dustin, take Michael and Michelle outside to play, would you please?"

He grumbled a protest, wanting to play video games.

"Now." Sylvia spoke more firmly, then returned a moment later with Jessica in her arms. From a cupboard set low near the floor, she retrieved two pots and pans with lids, and a wooden spoon. "Jessica can cook, can't you, baby girl?"

Again, a pang of longing shot through Nikki as she watched Sylvia arrange the dishes on an area rug centered in the spacious kitchen.

"Make Mama Sylvia something good to eat," Sylvia cooed. She gave Jessica an empty cereal box and some plastic, toy vegetables as well, and within seconds the little girl was absorbed in her play world.

Back at the table, Sylvia folded her hands beneath her chin, and gave Nikki her attention. "What's on your mind?"

Nikki took a deep breath and jumped right in. "I understand Cody came here and talked to you the other day about Dustin."

"Nikki—"

"Cody, please. Just let me say my piece and then I'll leave you to your police business." She hadn't meant for the words to sound curt, and she turned toward the Thompsons, softening her expression and her voice. "I'm sorry to be so blunt, but frankly, I'm pretty sure I know what Cody spoke to you about."

Frank's frown lines deepened. "He asked us about the two of you becoming Dustin's temporary guardians. Have you changed your mind?"

Nikki met Cody's gaze, and she wished she hadn't jumped the gun. *So that was what he'd wanted to talk to her about.* Telling herself it was a moot point, she hurried on. "Honestly, Cody and I hadn't gotten the chance to talk about that at all. What we'd originally discussed was the possibility of adopting Dustin."

"Why, that's wonderful!" Sylvia's face lit up, and Nikki could've kicked herself. *Crud! She wasn't handling this right at all.*

She hurried on. "No, that's not what I mean. We talked about it briefly, and meant to discuss things in further detail. But I'm going to be honest with you. I never wanted to be the instant mother of a preteen son." Her mind had been set on mothering a newborn. Her newborn. "I know that deep down Dustin is a good kid. But still, he has his problems." Ones she didn't care to deal with.

"Yes, he does," Sylvia said. "But we're working on those."

"Exactly." Nikki gestured to them. "Dustin needs parents as committed to him as you and Frank. Who can fully support him in working through his issues. He needs complete and total devotion, and I can't give him that."

Sylvia reached out and covered Nikki's hand with her own. "I know what you've been through, hon. We heard about the baby, and we're so very, very sorry."

"Thank you." Nikki's stomach churned painfully.

"Is your sister all right?" Frank asked. "I understand she moved to Tennessee."

"She did, and she's doing well."

"I'm glad to hear that."

"Me, too," Sylvia said. "And really, Nikki… Cody…Frank and I would never want you to take Dustin in, short-term or permanently, if you aren't one hundred percent committed to it."

"Of course not." Cody spoke in a civil tone, but he glared Nikki's way. "And if we decide we can make that commitment to him, we'll come over and talk to you then. In the meanwhile, we need to address what Dustin did to my tires."

Nikki rose from her chair, pasting a smile on her face. "I think I'll head back outside."

CODY BID GOODBYE to Frank and Sylvia and stepped out on the porch where Nikki sat with the Thompsons' hound. "Let's go," he said, barely able to contain his anger. After saying her farewells, she followed him to the car. He brushed past her and slid behind the wheel, ignoring her indignant huff.

"I'm perfectly capable of driving my own car," she said as he backed out of the driveway.

"Yeah? Well, obviously I have no idea what you're capable of. How could you blurt your plans to everyone else without telling me first?" He glanced at her. "Why the hell did you do that?"

"Do what? Tell Frank and Sylvia the truth?"

"I thought we were going to discuss this over dinner."

"I was willing to listen to what you had to say, Cody. But I already told you, adopting Dustin is not a good idea, and taking him in temporarily isn't any better."

"I was only going to suggest we meet with his social worker, and the Thompsons, and see what it would take for us to become his temporary guardians. But you're right, okay?"

Nikki crossed her arms and stared straight ahead. "What—so now you're going to freeze me out?"

"How do you expect me to react? You were trying to manipulate me into doing something I don't want to do."

"No, I was trying to work on setting things right between us."

She rolled her eyes and smacked him on the shoulder. "God, Cody, you can be so dense! Taking in a child is not the answer to our problems."

Cody ground his back teeth together. "Do you want to have supper with me or not?"

"I'm not hungry."

"Fine." His appetite was zapped to hell, too. He finished the drive in silence, his stomach churning with anger and frustration.

At the ranch, he parked the car and got out, pausing near his pickup truck. "I'm meeting Frank and Dustin back at the station with the air compressor."

"Good idea."

"I'll see you later."

He headed for the garage, and thought he heard her mumble something behind his back.

He couldn't be sure, but it sounded a lot like *jackass*.

CHAPTER NINE

NIKKI WOKE UP alone and grumpy. The argument she'd had with Cody last night left her feeling as though they'd taken a giant step backward, and as if that weren't enough to start her day off on a sour note, she remembered she had an appointment with her ob-gyn this morning for her annual pap. *Terrific*.

She showered, fed Max and checked to see that Cody had taken care of the horses, then headed for Glenwood Springs. Doctor Rosa Sanchez's office stood in a quiet section of town on Cooper Avenue, a pale green, framed building that had once been a residential dwelling. A giant blue spruce towered over the yard, a scattering of fragrant needles forming a bed at the tree's base where two gray squirrels chattered and foraged.

Doctor Sanchez had been Nikki's ob-gyn for the past ten years, and Nikki felt comfortable with her and trusted her completely. She'd been Nikki's rock through her miscarriages.

After a seemingly endless wait, she was admitted to the exam room. Doctor Sanchez's friendly smile and quiet way of speaking helped Nikki relax, and soon the dreaded examination was over.

"So, how are things going for you overall?" Doctor Sanchez asked, leaning back in her chair as Nikki sat up and scooped the backless cotton gown around her as best she could.

Nikki shrugged. "As well as could be expected under the circumstances, I guess."

"Mm-hm." The doctor flipped through the notes in Nikki's records folder. "How are you doing on refills for your birth control pills?"

Nikki hesitated. Unable to bear the thought of losing yet another baby, she'd been on the Pill ever since her last miscarriage. But she'd stopped taking them a couple of months ago when Cody had begun to sleep on the couch. "Actually, I don't need them at the moment."

"I see." Doctor Sanchez studied Nikki with her dark eyes. "So you and your husband are not having sex?"

"No," Nikki said. "We're...separated." The words seared her throat. "But we're trying to work things out."

"Nikki." Doctor Sanchez laid a hand on her shoulder. "I don't mean to intrude on your personal life, but I know the trauma you've been through. Why don't you let me give you a refill for your prescription, just in case, hm-m?"

"All right."

"Unless, of course, you've thought more about what we've discussed?"

"A tubal ligation?" The idea had been in the back of her mind for some time; before the surrogacy, before the crash. Before everything had gone to hell. Yet she stubbornly, illogically clung to the notion that if she went through with the procedure, it would be too final. It would confirm what she already knew was fact—that she couldn't have a baby of her own. She felt as if her womanhood were slipping away.

"It is something to consider, as I said before." Doctor Sanchez spoke softly. "Since you are high-risk—should you become pregnant again—perhaps a more permanent alternative to birth control would ease your mind."

Nikki gave a humorless smile. "I suppose that's true. But I'd like to think about it a little while longer."

"All right, then. I'll write you a prescription for the pills, and you can let me know what you decide." She scribbled some information onto a prescription pad and tore the sheet off for Nikki. "You take care of yourself."

"I will. Thank you, Doctor." Nikki tucked the piece of paper into her purse as Doctor Sanchez left the room, then got dressed.

Outside, she pulled from the parking lot, passing the pharmacy as she drove home.

She wouldn't need to fill the prescription right now. She still had the better part of a month's supply of pills sitting uselessly in her dresser drawer.

NIKKI LOADED the dishwasher, her thoughts scattered. Where had the past two weeks gone? As usual, summer seemed to fly by and with July coming to a close, she would soon have to make preparations for the start of the new school year, less than a month away. She looked forward to getting back to her kindergarten class, to having something constructive to focus upon daily. She normally enjoyed her summers off, but this one hadn't brought much pleasure.

With Cody pulling a lot of double shifts lately, undoubtedly working overtime looking for the hit-and-run driver, they had yet to make up after their last argument. Normally, they talked after they'd fought. But things hadn't been normal in so long, she wondered if she was expecting something that wasn't going to happen. They'd barely spoken to each other lately.

She closed the dishwasher and flipped the On switch. "I'm not going to let him avoid this," she said aloud. Max perked his ears, watching her from his place on the throw rug at the back door. "If your handler isn't going to get things out in the open once and for all, Max, then I will." *Lord, she was talking to a dog!* And the worst of it was, Max seemed to be listening intently.

Whining, the big German shepherd moved over to stand beside her, nudging her hand with his muzzle. Nikki petted his head, then moved to the cupboard and scanned the variety of a half dozen boxes of dog

biscuits and jerky treats. She selected barbecue fla-
vor, the kind Max seemed to like when Dustin fed
them to him.

"Here you go, boy." She held the bone-shaped
biscuit out. Max sniffed disdainfully at it, then
walked back over to curl up on the rug, his brown
eyes looking up at her as though she'd insulted his
dignity.

"He won't eat them for anyone but Dustin." Cody
spoke through the screen door, and Max immediately rose, tail wagging.

"Cody." Nikki laid the dog biscuit on the counter-
top. "I didn't hear you come up the drive."

"And neither did you, you worthless bum." He
stepped inside and bent to scratch behind Max's ears.
"Some police dog you are."

"I'm glad you stopped by," Nikki said. "I wanted
to talk to you."

"Me, too, but I'm on my way to the station." He
hesitated.

"So, what's up?"

"I'm sorry I got so mad at Frank and Sylvia's." His
eyes told her he was being sincere.

"Thank you, Cody. I also wanted to apologize—
for jumping to conclusions. Clear slate?"

"Clear slate…. The department's holding a fund-
raiser this Saturday, to benefit the women's shelter."

"I heard about it."

"Would you go with me?"

Nikki sighed. "Cody, we need to talk, not date."

He stared at her, eyes filled with determination. "You were right, you know—the other night. As soon as I sat down at the kitchen table with Frank and Sylvia, I realized Dustin's got a good home with them. And when I watched him interacting with the other kids, I knew we could never offer him a better home unless it was permanent." He took her hand. "That's why I was mad at you for blurting out what you had to say. But again, you were right. We have to start with us. Living in the bunkhouse has made me realize how empty my life is without you."

"Cody." Aware of the warmth and strength of his hand around hers, Nikki fought the urge to dive into his arms and tell him everything would be all right. She struggled to find the right words to express what she was feeling. "I'm really glad you feel that way. But going out on a date isn't going to solve anything."

"Why not?" He ran his hand up and down her arm, making her shiver.

She'd missed his touch. A very real, physical ache gripped her, and Nikki gently pulled away. "We're not in high school. This is serious. We need to go back into counseling with Regina. It's not doing me a hell of a lot of good to talk to her by myself."

"I'm still not real wild about that idea," Cody said, his blue eyes holding hers. "But I'll think about it, if you'll go to the fund-raiser with me."

"That's blackmail."

"Hey, whatever it takes."

"Blackmail. From a cop."

"Your word against mine."

Nikki fought a smile. How many times had she enjoyed bantering with Cody like this?

And remember where that silly bantering usually led?

"Come on, Nikki. It's just a fund-raising dinner, and it's for a good cause."

She sighed, already weakening. She'd always made a point to support women's and children's charities as much as possible. And she missed Cody so much. "Where's it being held?"

"The Elks Lodge."

"What time?"

"Seven-thirty." He gave her the sort of grin that had always left her unable to say no. "And you won't believe who'll be providing the entertainment for the evening. Jordan's got a cousin who has a friend who has an uncle who knows the brother of a guy who once played in a band with a guy who almost got hired to play for Reba McEntire."

Nikki laughed. "You expect me to follow that?"

"Bottom line, he's got connections. Guess who's going to play for the fund-raiser?"

She already knew, from the poster she'd noticed taped to the entrance of the grocery store, but Nikki played along. "Hmmm…let me see. Give me a hint."

"He's recently been the opening act for your favorite singer. The one you're in lust with."

There was only one man she was in lust, and in love, with. And he was standing beside her, melting her heart just as easily as he'd done when she was sixteen. "Toby Keith," she teased, knowing that wasn't the answer.

Cody chuckled. "No. The other one."

"Oh. Then it must be Josh Turner."

"Hey, I didn't know you had the hots for him, too." He lowered his voice to a growl. "How many guys are you lusting after?"

She laughed. *Only one.* "I saw the poster, Cody. It's Travis MacKenzie."

"You got it. So will you go?" The hopeful look in his eyes was enough to undo the last of her resolve.

"Yes," she said. "But only because it's for a good cause."

"It is." He moved closer and brushed a kiss against her lips. "It's for the only cause that matters to me, Nikki. I'll see you later." He slipped out the door, Max on his heels.

Leaving Nikki alone in the kitchen, her heart pounding like a runaway horse. Had she made a mistake in accepting his invitation? No. Either they moved forward, or they stepped back and let each other go.

THE ELKS LODGE was housed in a building left over from another era, the outer walls made of rough-hewn half logs. Multipaned windows fronted either side of the entrance, and the American flag waved proudly in the breeze from atop a flagpole near the front walk.

Inside, Nikki noticed rows of photos of the Ladies' Auxiliary and the Exalted Rulers on the walls of the entry. As she and Cody passed the main room on their way to the basement stairs, she caught a glimpse of a polished bar with an impressive rack of elk antlers hanging above it. A pool table stood centered in the room surrounded by rectangular tables and padded chairs. The fund raiser was to be held in the spacious basement.

Cody took her elbow as they headed down the stairs, and Nikki couldn't help but enjoy the familiarity of the gesture. They were seated by one of the Elks at a long table covered with a white linen cloth. Several people were already there. Some, Nikki knew. Others were strangers. Conversation buzzed around them, and she made an effort to focus on the event rather than on the intimacy of Cody's leg brushing against hers beneath the table. She began to think maybe she and Cody should have come here in separate cars.

"What're you thinking about?" Cody leaned close, his cologne overwhelming her. Bringing back memories.

"That it feels weird to be on a date with my husband."

He took her hand and brought it to his lips, pressing a kiss against her knuckles. "Precisely why we *should* be on a date." He kissed her again, before letting her hand go. "To start on a new track."

Nikki reminded herself of why she'd given in to him. Cody was a man of his word, and he wouldn't back out on his promise to reconsider counseling sessions with Regina. "At least we can say we gave it an honest try."

A delicious meal followed the keynote speaker, and by the time Travis MacKenzie took the stage, everyone was in an upbeat mood. The crowd cheered and whistled as his name was announced, and the ladies in the room whooped and eyed Travis in his tight jeans, and black-and-red western shirt. The man was sexy and good-looking, but he couldn't hold a candle to Cody.

Nikki sighed, the two glasses of wine she'd drank with dinner flowing warmly through her body. Out of the corner of her eye, she watched her husband sip from his glass of Coke. They'd always had a zero-tolerance rule to never drive even after one drink, even before the accident. *Crash,* Nikki reminded herself. Lord, what a fitting word.

"Would you like to dance?"

Nikki looked into Cody's eyes. It might be their last night to dance. "Sure," she said, taking his hand.

The upbeat song Travis MacKenzie played had just come to an end. Now the singer spoke into the microphone. "Many of you know my inspiration to cut a record came from my general love of country music. But there's one artist in particular I've always looked up to, and that's Vince Gill. I'd like to do one of his songs for you right now. Ladies, cuddle up to your honeys, because this one's for you."

Travis's sultry voice rang out over the strumming of his guitar. And Nikki's knees trembled as Cody swept her into his arms.

"I can't dance to this," she said.

"Sure you can." Cody's eyes implored her. "Please, Nikki. Let it be our song at least one more time."

Swallowing against the constricting of her throat, Nikki pushed aside her hesitation and let herself lean into him. Closing her eyes, she swayed against his warm body to the song they'd danced to at their wedding. "Look at Us." As Travis poured out the words about a man and woman who were meant to be together, whose love lasted forever, Nikki felt a pain in her heart like she hadn't known since Anna's death. Abruptly, she pulled away from Cody.

"I'm sorry," she whispered. "I really can't." She made her way unobtrusively back to the table where she got her purse before heading upstairs to the exit.

Cody was already there. He didn't say a word as they got into his pickup and headed back to the ranch. Country music played softly on the radio, one love song after another, until Nikki felt like screaming. She reached over and turned the music off. Minutes later, she climbed out of the truck as Cody let the Chevy idle in the driveway.

"Hang on a second," he said. He turned off the engine and came around to the passenger side. "Let me walk you to the door." He gave her a sad smile. "After all, it wouldn't be a proper date if I didn't."

Why argue? *Just get it over with.* She let Cody take her arm, telling herself she wouldn't let him get to her. Ignoring the fact that he already had.

"Did you have a good time?" Like a polite suitor, he paused on the doorstep with her.

"Yes, I did." She eyed him warily. "Are you going to keep your end of the deal?"

He nodded. "Yes. Set up an appointment with Regina and I'll go." His blue eyes studied hers. "I'm sorry the song upset you. Can I kiss you good night?"

Not a good idea. "I don't think…"

"Good." He moved close, slipping his arms around her, cutting off her protest. "Don't think." He brushed a kiss across her lips. "Don't think at all." His tongue found hers, and Nikki melted. A single tear slid from the corner of her eye as she realized how much she'd missed kissing him, holding him.

"Cody." She breathed his name, wrapping her arms around his neck, letting her mouth respond to his. She returned his kisses until what had started like the flicker of a small candle flame grew into a fiery furnace. She lost herself in the arms of the only man she'd ever loved.

With one hand, Cody fumbled for the doorknob only to find it locked. With a mumbled curse, he reached into his pocket for his keys, which were still in the Chevy's ignition.

"Here." Nikki handed him hers even as she recognized this was a good place to stop. A locked door. A symbol of the barrier between them. From inside, she heard Max's eager whine, but barely noticed the dog as he brushed past them when Cody opened the door.

Leaving the shepherd to his business, Cody elbowed the screen wide and pulled Nikki back into his embrace. His mouth found hers as they stepped inside. On their wedding day, Cody had scooped her into his arms to carry her over the threshold. This very threshold.

"Cody, we can't."

"We can." He stopped kissing her long enough to look into her eyes. Even in the dim light of the small kitchen lamp she'd left on, Nikki could see the intensity in his expression. "Nikki, please, just give into your heart. Please."

Not sure if it was really her heart speaking or her overpowering need for the physical kind of loving any healthy woman craved, she kissed him again. *Liar. You know you still love him.*

Eagerly, they peeled each other's clothes away and fell onto the couch like lovers in a forbidden tryst.

Lying across her body, Cody stroked the hair away from her temple with one hand. "I love you, Nikki. That's not going to change."

She fought back a sob as he held her, his eager caresses softened by the tenderness of two people intimately familiar with each other's bodies, each other's minds and souls. And when he entered her, Nikki moaned and writhed with pleasure, and the satisfaction of being with Cody again. She let the rhythm of their bodies wash away all the negative thoughts. All the questions.

Cody tucked his hands beneath her hips and raised her body to press more tightly against his. Nikki wrapped her legs around his waist and hungrily took him in completely. Kissed his mouth, his neck, his shoulder with the need that had consumed her for so long. And as they climaxed in near perfect synchronization, she realized something. She still hadn't taken her birth control pills, the prescription Doctor Sanchez had written for her over two weeks ago forgotten in the bottom of her purse.

How could she be so stupid?

"Oh my God, no!" She pushed Cody away, rolling from the edge of the couch onto the floor. Sobbing, her emotions and hormones overwhelming her.

"Nikki." Cody leaned on his elbows breathing hard, speaking her name half in question, half in protest.

"What have we done, what have we done?" She tucked her knees to her chest as hot tears streamed down her cheeks.

Awkwardly, he stroked the hair away from her neck, her face. She didn't have to see his expression to sense his puzzlement. "Nikki, it's all right. It's you and me, babe. Just enjoy what we've shared." He kissed her temple. "I know we got a little ahead of ourselves, but we're going to work through this somehow. And Regina—"

"No." She looked over her shoulder at him. "That's not what I mean. Cody, we just made love without protection. I haven't been taking my pills." She raked her hand through her hair. "God, what if we made a baby!"

For Nikki, a baby meant disaster. She couldn't go through another miscarriage. Couldn't stand the pain of one more loss. And neither could Cody, neither could their marriage.

Doctor Sanchez was right.

"I want to get my tubes tied." She blurted the words without thinking.

"What?" Cody looked as though she'd struck him with a baseball bat. He sat up and put his feet on the floor. "Nikki, slow down. I'm still processing the fact that you stopped taking the Pill…. Why did you do that?" He raked a hand through his hair and stared blankly at the wall. "Oh my God. I didn't know, or…"

Nikki stood and turned the light on, then reached for her dress where it lay pooled on the rug.

"Will you stop?" Cody stared at her as he put his jeans on.

He looked far too sexy, shirtless, his hair tousled. She turned her back and strode over to stare out the window. "I should've stopped all right. Before we got this far."

"Nikki, please don't make any hasty decisions."

"Hasty?" She spun around to face him. "You think I'm being hasty, when we just risked making a baby?"

"I just want you to think things through before you take such a serious step."

"I already have."

Cody shrugged into his shirt. "Why didn't you talk to me about it sooner?"

"I did."

He looked dumbfounded. "Yeah, I remember Doctor Sanchez brought it up a long time ago. But you wouldn't consider it. Why didn't you say something?"

"It's my body. Besides, we should've listened to Doctor Sanchez back then. It's just foolish to keep taking risks. Even the Pill isn't one hundred percent guaranteed."

"You're right." Cody reached out to touch her. Softly, his fingers grazed her cheek. "I feel like an ass." He let his hand fall to his side and gave a humorless laugh. "Every time you miscarried, it tore me up. Not just because we'd lost another child, but because of how deeply it hurt you."

"Maybe we should call it a night, huh?" She spoke quietly, looking down at her bare feet.

"Yeah." He cupped the back of her neck, massaging it with his fingers. "Are you going to be okay? Because I can sleep on the couch if you want."

"No." After what had happened on that couch, she wasn't sure she could ever sit on it again, much less crawl beneath the covers in their bed upstairs knowing Cody was down here sleeping. "That's probably not a good idea." Still, she appreciated his consideration. Why did this have to be so hard? If he were a jerk, she'd have no problem walking away.

"Maybe what happened tonight wasn't such a bad thing after all," Nikki said. "It reminded us of things we need to work on, sex not being one of them." She quirked her mouth. "Still want me to make an appointment with Regina?"

He nodded. "Yes." But he looked scared. "If we can't get past this, there's no hope is there?"

She knew *this* referred to their inability to have children. Could they ever find their way back to just him and her? To a happy life without children? Many couples did. But somehow Nikki knew that the door they'd opened on having children could never be closed. It would have to be all or nothing.

Suddenly, she felt drained, both physically and emotionally. "I don't know," she said.

"Just promise me something."

"What?"

"If you decide to get your tubes tied, I want to be there with you."

"I have decided."

"Okay." He held up his hands. "You're right. It's

your body, and it's the responsible thing to do. Or I could get a vasectomy."

Emotions roiled inside of her all over again. She'd thought about that, too, after she'd lost their second child. But, *God,* she'd wanted so badly to have Cody's baby.

And with that thought, another edged its way into her mind. Probing like a tongue in a sore tooth. *Cody can still have children. With someone else.*

If things didn't work out for them, if their marriage ended in divorce, it wouldn't be fair to expect him not to. But the thought hurt her so deeply, it left her literally light-headed.

Cody. With another woman.

Happy. Living his life as he'd always wanted, as the two of them had always dreamed of. With children of his own.

"No." She shook her head.

"Why not?" And then she saw by his face that he knew what she was thinking. "Nikki." He took hold of her. "Damn. Don't even go there. Our marriage is not over yet. And if I have my way, it never will be." He held her and she let him. "Please don't give up on us like that."

She squeezed her eyes shut and folded herself into his arms. She had to prepare for the worst, because it just might happen. There was a chance that she and Cody would find that not even counseling, or great sex, or all the best wishes, could change what was fact.

Their marriage had been altered by all that had happened, as had they themselves.

Could they live with those changes?

CHAPTER TEN

THREE DAYS had passed since he'd held Nikki in his arms, and still Cody couldn't get what she'd said out of his head. As he drove straight to Regina's office after his shift, that particular night stuck in his mind as though it had happened hours ago.

I want to get my tubes tied. That she thought she had to go through more physical pain, and had brushed aside his offer to get a vasectomy, upset him to no end. She'd been through enough. He'd wanted to stay with her, hoping that after a good night's sleep wrapped in his arms, Nikki would listen to reason. But instead, she'd booted him unceremoniously back to the bunkhouse. He'd decided not to push her; not to ruin what had happened between them. Maybe she would listen to Regina.

Cody parked his squad car behind Nikki's Saturn and made his way inside the building to Regina's office. Nikki sat in one of three chairs that formed what Cody supposed was intended to be an intimate triangle; a small, round glass table topped with a pitcher of ice water, and three clean glasses in the middle.

Instead, the setup made him feel as though he'd been called into the principal's office, which might explain why Nikki felt comfortable here. Yet he'd vowed to give this a try, and he meant to keep his word.

"Hello, Cody." Regina smiled pleasantly as he took his seat. "It's nice to see you again."

"Likewise."

Nikki looked at him nervously, while Regina poured them all water before leaning back in her chair. Her nut-brown hair fell in loose waves to her shoulders. With a reddish-orange scarf around her neck, she reminded him of a robin—ready to pounce on an unsuspecting worm.

And he felt like the worm.

"So, Cody, tell me why you decided to return to our sessions."

God, he hated this. He groped for an honest answer that would satisfy the woman. "I think Nikki and I can salvage our marriage, and I'd like to give it every possible shot."

"Good." Regina tapped her thigh with one hand. "Nikki, how do you feel about that?"

Nikki sat with her slender fingers folded in her lap. "I'm glad Cody's here." She took a deep breath. "But some other issues have come up, as you know, since our last session together."

"Meaning since the three of us talked as a group."

Nikki nodded, looking at Regina, not him. "I'm going to have a tubal ligation."

"That's obviously a pretty serious choice, Nikki. Have the two of you discussed it?"

"Yes," Nikki answered.

"And you're both in agreement?"

"I, uh, offered to get a vasectomy instead." Cody shifted uncomfortably in his chair. "I think Nikki's been through enough."

Regina smiled. "That's a generous gesture, Cody. But before you go through with a permanent form of birth control, I have to ask: Nikki, did your doctor ever talk to you about the possibility of a cervical cerclage?"

"Yes, she did," Nikki said. "After my third loss." It was a surgical procedure in which the cervix is tied shut with a suture early in the pregnancy in order to give it more support. "We also discussed the possibility of a tubal ligation."

"I see. Did she explain to you the success rate of cervical cerclage?"

Nikki glanced at her folded hands before answering. "It wasn't so much a question of the success, Regina, as it was the rate of failure—as much as twenty percent. I didn't, and still don't, feel I could handle losing yet another baby."

"That's understandable. I just want you to be certain you've examined all your options before you do anything drastic." She looked from Nikki to Cody. "Either of you."

"I agree," Cody said. "I think we should wait."

"I don't want to wait," Nikki said irritably. "As I told you the other night, Cody, it's my body."

"That's true," Regina said. "And while Cody needs to respect that, you also have an obligation to respect his opinion. His wants and needs as they pertain to this marriage. There are, of course, other means of having a family, such as adoption."

"We've discussed that, too." Cody couldn't help shooting a dark look Nikki's way.

"Good," Regina responded. "But I encourage you both to give your relationship more time before you take any action in that direction, or toward sterilization surgery. For the moment, you need to focus on the here and now." She crossed her legs, her gaze traveling between the two of them. "I truly believe the root of your problem is dealing with the loss of Anna. Have you come to an agreement about a joint, constructive outlet to help you release your feelings, your grief?"

More psychobabble. Cody bit his tongue...with effort, certain Nikki was going to bring up Dustin's name.

Instead, she glared at him. "I'm afraid not. Cody is still hell-bent on revenge. He's obsessed with searching for the hit-and-run driver."

He held his breath and counted to ten before releasing it. "I am not obsessed." He spoke the words slowly, enunciating each one. "I'm doing my job, Nikki." He glared back at her.

"I know you believe that," Nikki said, "but you've

gone beyond just doing your job. How many hours of overtime have you spent…how many hours of your own time…looking for the guy? Why can't you agree that we need to find a constructive way to move past our grief? You could consider joining MADD, you know."

"Time out," Regina said, making a ridiculous hand signal.

This isn't football, Cody thought, frowning. This wasn't a game, it was his life.

"Let's not attack one another here. Let's just concentrate on what we can do to get the two of you back on track."

"I think we've been over this ground before," Cody said, unable to restrain himself any longer. "Frankly, Regina, I came here today because I promised Nikki I would give counseling another shot. But I don't really see that it's getting us anywhere." He gestured with a lift of his hand. "It's obvious she sees things one way, I see them another."

"You both need to learn to compromise if you're going to make this marriage work." She leaned her elbow on the arm of the chair, index finger bracing her cheek. "What would the two of you say to an exercise in compromise?"

"What do you have in mind?" Nikki asked.

"I'd like you to go home and make a pros and cons list. Nikki, you look at things from Cody's perspective. Write down the reasons why, in your opinion, the things *he* thinks will help your marriage will or will not work. Cody, you do the same, from Nikki's perspective."

"How am I supposed to do that? I can't crawl inside her mind."

Regina chuckled. "Try. That's the whole point of this exercise. I want the two of you to make an effort to see things from the other's viewpoint. Maybe if you put it all down in black and white, you'll find a way to meet in the middle. You can share your results with one another right away, or you can wait and do that here at our next session. It's up to you. But either way, I'd like to discuss what you come up with. Agreed?"

Cody sighed. "All right."

"I'm certainly willing to give it a try," Nikki said.

"Good." Regina rose from her chair. "Don't forget the main issues at stake. Think hard about what it is that has come between the two of you over the past few months. And I'll see you back here next week, or sooner."

"Thank you," Nikki said.

"Yeah, thanks." Cody spoke grudgingly. He left the office, walking ahead of Nikki in order to hold her car door open for her.

"You're upset," she said, pausing before she slid into the driver's seat.

He leaned on the Saturn's door, his face close to Nikki's. Remembering how it had felt to make love to her. So right...so unbelievably good. Until they'd come down from their sexual high, back to cold, hard reality.

He shook his head. "I'm just not wild about this whole counseling thing. And making a pros and cons list?" He scoffed. "Come on. What is this, homework 101?"

To his surprise, his comment brought a smile to Nikki's face. A smile that sent a shock of warmth through him all the way to his extremities. *God,* he wanted to touch her.

She pointed her index finger at him. "If you don't do your homework, mister, you're going to have this teacher to deal with. We're paying Regina an hourly fee, so do it."

"Hey, I said I'd do it."

"Okay." She swung the car door shut, but rolled down the window. "How about if you work on your list over the next few days and I work on mine, then we compare notes on the weekend?"

"You don't want to wait and show them to Regina first?" Somehow, he worried that going this alone would only make things worse. He hated the thought of taking two steps back after the one forward they'd made the other night. Or at least, he'd felt as if making love was taking a step forward.

"We could. But I'd rather not wait. What do you say?"

"Sure." *Whatever.* He tapped the roof of her car in a send-off, then waved and headed for his squad car.

Pros and cons…homework.

No wonder Dustin hated writing in his journal.

NIKKI CAME HOME from Wal-Mart midmorning on Saturday with supplies for making classroom decorations, to find Dustin in the driveway waxing Cody's squad car. Nearby, Cody sat in a lawn chair beneath a cottonwood tree, dressed in jeans and a T-shirt. He wore sunglasses and sipped from a glass of what appeared to be iced lemonade. Max lay at his feet, snoring.

It was Dustin's third week of the two-month punishment assigned by Frank and Sylvia—washing the car twice a week, waxing it once. They'd also allowed Cody to choose a task, and Cody had made him pick up trash along the highway.

Nikki parked and climbed from the Saturn. "Hi, Dustin. How are you?"

"I'll be better when I'm done waxing this cruddy car," he grumbled, shooting Cody a glare out of the corner of his eye. "I'm glad to see *someone* is enjoying himself, drinking cold lemonade in the shade."

Nikki smothered a chuckle. "Would you like some lemonade, Dustin? That sounds pretty good to me, too. I'm pooped from shopping."

"I'd love some, but you'll have to ask the Gestapo over there if it's all right if I take a break."

"I heard that," Cody said.

This time, Nikki couldn't hold back her laughter.

"Come on." She gestured for Dustin to follow. "You can help me carry my stuff in from the car, then we'll get the lemonade."

"Cool." Dustin laid down the round, wax-covered sponge he held, and wiped the palms of his hands on his jeans.

Nikki opened the trunk, nearly backing into Cody when he stepped up behind her. "I'll take a couple for you," he offered.

"We've got it. Thanks, though." She closed the trunk lid with her elbow and followed Dustin up the walkway. She'd be glad to get the assignment Regina had given her and Cody over and done with. Maybe once they put everything in writing, he'd see what she already knew. That she was right about moving forward and leaving their dream of parenthood behind them.

Not that she was the kind of person who always had to be right. It was just that making love with Cody had made her realize how much her heart ached for him. Why couldn't he come around and see the situation in a sensible light? See that there was more to a marriage than parenthood and dwelling on the past.

After pouring lemonade into plastic cups, Nikki spent a few minutes with Dustin watching the kittens, laughing over their antics. They were now, by her veterinarian's estimation, nearly five weeks old and quite playful. Dustin had helped her name the four— Cheeto, Toulouse, Pepper and Tater Tot. Cheeto and

Pepper played a game of tag that culminated in a wrestling match, while Toulouse and Tater batted a catnip-filled mouse across the linoleum.

"They've sure grown," Dustin said.

"They have." Nikki paused. "Would you like to have one of them? I mean, if it's all right with Frank and Sylvia."

"I'd love to, but I'd feel kind of bad taking it away from the other three."

"That's okay. I wasn't really planning on keeping all of them anyway," Nikki said. She glanced at Cody, who pretended grave interest in trying to coax Max into eating a jerky treat.

Dustin's face clouded over. "You mean you're going to separate them?"

"Well, yeah," Nikki said. "I mean, providing I can find them good homes. I've decided to keep two and give the other two away."

"Why?" His face pinched with worry. "Can't you keep them all so they can stay together? You've got plenty of room here."

Nikki pursed her lips thoughtfully. "I suppose we do at that." Again, she looked toward Cody for his opinion. They hadn't had enough time lately to sort out their problems, much less talk about other things. "Cody?"

"Hmm?"

As if he hadn't been listening in on her and Dustin's every word.

"Did you want to let the kittens all stay here at the ranch?"

He shrugged. "Why not? We can always use good mousers."

Dustin looked expectantly at Nikki, and she turned her palms up in willing surrender. "I guess it's settled then. They stay."

"Cool." He nodded approvingly, then slowly sipped his lemonade.

"You can take that outside with you," Cody said pointedly.

Dustin shot him a glare. "I want to finish it in here."

"No, you want to stall." He pointed. "Out."

"Damn!"

"And watch your language."

Grumbling, Dustin stomped outside, lemonade in hand.

Cody tried once more to offer Max the jerky treat. The shepherd sniffed it, then turned and trotted after Dustin, pushing the screen door open with his nose. "Traitor," Cody muttered. "I'd swear he was a cat in another life."

"Could be." Nikki gathered up some of the shopping bags on the table. "Guess I'd better get busy, too. School will be starting before we know it, and kindergarten orientation is a week from Monday."

"Hold up a second."

She waited expectantly.

"About our pros and cons lists…did you get yours finished?"

"Uh-huh."

"Good. So did I. Do you want to go over them later this evening? Maybe grab a bite to eat first?"

Nikki tensed. It wasn't wise to fall into the same sort of trap as she had the last time they'd had dinner together, a trap she was equally responsible for. Even though her morning trip to the bathroom had indicated they hadn't made a baby. "I can do the list, Cody, but I don't know about supper."

"Okay." He quickly hid his disappointment. "One other thing. Would you consider spending a little time with Dustin today when he gets done with the car?"

She frowned. "Doing what?"

"I don't know. I thought maybe you might take him riding or something. He seems to like the horses."

"Riding?" She gave a half laugh. "Has he ever been on a horse? Or better yet, would he even want to get on one?"

"Why don't you ask him?"

She gave him a stern look. "I know what you're trying to do, and it won't work."

"Regina suggested it."

Nikki put one hand on her hip. "How do you figure that?"

"You're supposed to look at things from my viewpoint."

"On paper."

"Please, Nikki?" He removed his sunglasses, his expression serious. "Give him a chance. That's all I ask."

"I thought this subject was closed."

"I can't help it," Cody said. "I can't turn my back on that boy."

And neither could she.

"Just get to know him a little better," Cody went on.

"We've been feeding the kittens together all this time."

"Yeah, I know. But all you ever talk about are the kittens, as far as I've heard. Maybe you could talk to him about other things."

"Like how much he wants parents?" She shook her head. "Cody, get real. I'm not going to set that boy up for more heartache."

"Fine. Talk about the weather. Talk about his schoolwork. See if you can get him to put some effort into bringing his grades back up again. Frank and Sylvia don't seem to be getting anywhere with him, from what they've told me." His eyes pleaded with her. "Just this once? The kid needs all the positive influence he can get."

"No fair," she said. "Now you're appealing to my sensible side."

He grinned. "Then you'll do it?"

"I'll ask him to go riding. But if he says no, don't push it."

"YOU WANT ME to wear boots?" Dustin looked at her as if she'd lost her mind.

"For safety's sake, yes," Nikki said as Dustin followed her reluctantly into the house. "Running shoes are dangerous to ride in because you can get hung up in the stirrup if your foot slips all the way through it. A boot heel generally prevents that."

"Man, I ain't a cowboy," he grumbled.

Nikki fought her irritation. "And I'm not trying to make you be one. But if you want to go horseback riding, you have to wear boots." She paused in the middle of the living room. "Of course, you don't *have* to go if you've changed your mind."

"Naw, I'll go."

She could tell by the eager look in his eyes that Dustin was more anxious to go on a trail ride than he let on. Poor kid probably hadn't had a lot of luxuries in his life, and these days, owning a horse was definitely just that. "I'd bet Eric Vanderhurst can't ride a horse to save his sorry butt," she said.

"Yeah?" Dustin's ears practically perked.

She nodded. "I passed him on the road one day while I was riding Cheyenne, and he stepped way off to the side like he was scared to death of her."

"Really." Dustin smirked. "I wouldn't mind being good at something that creep is afraid to try. He thinks he's so hot."

"Then you'll wear the boots?"

"I don't think a pair of Cody's will fit me."

"I have an old pair you can borrow."

He looked down at her hot-pink Ropers. "No way."

Nikki laughed. "Don't worry. They're plain brown. If they don't quite fit, we can dig up an extra pair of tube socks for you, too. Hang on and I'll get them."

In her room, she retrieved her Tony Lamas from the closet. The boots smelled pleasantly of worn leather and sawdust from the barn, and Nikki cradled them to her chest for a moment, remembering the day she and Cody had been cleaning stalls together and ended up in the hayloft making a baby....

She carried the boots to the living room. Dustin made a face as he slid out of his runners and put on the Tony Lamas. "Man, these look stupid!"

Nikki covered her mouth with one hand to smother a chuckle. "They do look a little funny with your baggy jeans. Hang on." She went back to her closet and pulled out a pair of Levi's she'd worn when she'd lost so much weight right after Anna's death. She couldn't begin to fit into them now. She returned to where Dustin waited. "Try these on." She tossed the pants at him. "If they're a little big, it shouldn't bother you. Just cinch them up with that belt of yours."

He shook his head. "Man, the things a guy has to do."

But she could tell he wasn't as unhappy as he pretended to be, looking forward to their ride. A short time later, the two of them walked to the pasture, and Nikki chose the horse for him that was the most docile.

"What's his name?" Dustin asked as she saddled the sorrel gelding.

"Cowboy."

Dustin clutched his chest with a groan. "It's not enough that you're making me wear these lame clothes? I have to ride a horse named Cowboy?"

Nikki gave him her stern teacher look. "Like I said, you don't have to go if you don't want to."

"I'm already here." He held his arms wide in exaggerated surrender. "What the heck."

"How about we take a short lesson in the arena before we set out on the trail? I'll show you the basics."

"All right."

She saddled Topaz—her buckskin mare—and they led the two horses to the arena, Dustin holding gingerly to the end of Cowboy's reins. "He's not going to bite you," Nikki said. "Besides, dude stables take people who don't know how to ride out on the trail all the time."

"I never said I didn't know how to ride."

"You've ridden before?" Nikki arched her brow, surprised.

"Once. Frank and Sylvia took us to a riding stable a few months ago for Michelle's birthday."

"Well, then you should do fine." She showed him the proper way to mount and, after adjusting the stirrups to fit his legs, how to correctly position his legs and feet. She gave instructions on the right way to hold the reins, how to stop, turn, and back up. When he seemed pretty comfortable, the two of them left the arena and headed up the bridle path.

"Cody told me he goes riding whenever he's got something on his mind. He said it helps him relax and think."

"That's right." Nikki guided Topaz around a fist-sized rock in her path, suddenly realizing that Dustin had been quiet since they'd left the arena. "Are you okay, Dustin?" She wondered if he was more scared of the horses than he cared to admit. "Is something troubling you?"

"Not really." He lifted one shoulder. "Well, sort of."

"Is it the horses? We can turn back."

"No, it's not that." He fell silent again.

"I'm a good listener."

He hesitated, as though weighing his words. "Some people came to meet me the other day. A lady and her husband. They set up an appointment with my social worker and everything."

Nikki's heart picked up speed. Was Dustin finally going to get a home?

"And?"

"And nothing. They decided they didn't want me." He stared stonily at the trail. "Same sh—stuff, different day."

Nikki's heart twisted inside her chest. "This has happened to you before?"

"Oh, yeah." He made it sound like it was no big thing, nothing more than a trip to the local mall. "People come and talk and 'oooh and aah' over me like I'm some damned puppy at the pound or something." His voice thickened and he cleared his throat. "But then they decide I'm not perfect or that I'm older than what they want, and they move on to the next kid."

Nikki's heart dropped all the way to the bottom of her stomach. "Nobody's perfect, Dustin. I'm sure the right home for you will come along."

He shook his head.

"Well, you've still got Frank and Sylvia. They're cool people, right?"

"Yeah. But it's not the same as being adopted. You never know what's coming day to day."

She studied him. "Are you sure nothing else is bothering you?"

He blinked, then scowled to hide the tears in his eyes. "Jessica got adopted. She went home with her new family yesterday, and I miss the little bugger more than I ever thought I would."

Nikki recalled the way Dustin had been concerned that the kittens would be separated from one another. "Well, that's good news," she said. "Even though I'm sorry the two of you can't be together anymore."

"Yeah. Jessica will be happy."

Dustin needs a permanent home with parents of his own.... We could give him a home. Cody's words.

"And I'm glad for her," he continued. "It's just hard watching the kids you live with come and go."

"I imagine so." For the first time, Nikki really thought about how difficult that would be, how hard on a child. She was so used to moving on from one kindergarten class to the next, loving each year's group of children as much as the previous one, that she'd been more or less seeing things from Frank's and Sylvia's perspective. Not Dustin's.

"And Michael and Michelle's parents get to take them back pretty soon."

"Oh?" She wasn't aware of the two kids' specific situation or that they were biological brother and sister.

"Yeah. Their mom and dad went through something sort of like my mother, with alcohol. Only they cleaned up their act. My mom never did."

"Where is she—your mother?"

He shrugged. "I don't know. I haven't seen her in a few years."

"Well, believe it or not, I can sort of relate to what you're going through," Nikki said.

"How?" He glanced skeptically at her.

"My mom has never been much of a mother, either. She left my sister and I with my granny a lot when we were kids, and she moved Amanda and me around so often, it was hard to make friends. We attended about a bazillion different schools, until we started high school."

"Really?"

"Really." She nodded. "We'd had enough of it by then, and we made her promise to stay put so we could finish through our senior year in the same place. But as soon as we graduated and went to college, she took off for Texas. She's moved so many times I can hardly keep track of all the places she's been, and she never bothers to visit." She'd come to Anna's funeral, but hadn't stayed, leaving Nikki and Amanda to lean on each other—as usual.

"Where does she live now?"

"Alaska."

"Well, at least she's not a drunk or a druggie."

"True."

"What about Cody?"

"He's not a drunk or a druggie, either."

Dustin laughed, and for a moment she could see the happy child beneath his tough exterior. "No, I mean, are his parents cool?"

"Yeah, they are." She gestured toward the land surrounding them. "At one time, Cody and his family raised cattle on this ranch. It used to be over five thousand acres, plus they had permits to graze on the surrounding BLM land."

"Damn! I mean, dang. That's huge."

"Uh-huh. It's down to five hundred now. When cattle prices started to tank, Cody's folks got out of ranching. They sold off most of the land and turned the rest over to Cody."

"Where are they?"

"Living in Las Vegas. Cody's dad is a retired sheriff as well as a former cattle rancher."

"Lucky you," he said dryly. "Cops in every branch
of the family."

Nikki couldn't help but chuckle. "Hey, that can
come in handy." Then she sobered. "Dustin, don't
ever give up hope. I'm sure the right family will find
you before you know it."

"Yeah, whatever." He flicked a huge horsefly off
of Cowboy's neck. "Hey, can this old nag go any
faster?"

"Are you insulting my horse? He may be mellow,
but he's definitely not a nag."

"Prove it." Before she could object, Dustin slack-
ened the reins and bumped Cowboy's sides with his
heels. Startled, the gelding leapt into a rapid trot,
nearly unseating the boy, then broke into a lope.

"Dustin, be careful!"

But the kid clung to the saddle horn with one hand
and managed to right himself. He flopped around like
a sack of potatoes before finding his center of balance again. "Yee-haw!" he shouted.

Nikki shook her head. The kid could drive her nuts
at times, but he touched her heart in spite of her reser-
vations. She nudged Topaz into a lope and when they
caught up with Dustin, made sure he kept Cowboy at
a reasonable pace as they continued down the trail.

She did her best to put what he'd told her out of
her mind. Still, her thoughts continued to dwell on

the fact that she could indeed relate to Dustin. She knew how it felt to be abandoned. But at least she'd had Amanda and Granny Satterfield.

Nikki looked over at the boy who really had no family at all, and felt tears sting the back of her eyes.

Stop it! He's not your problem.

And she had no intention of changing her mind.

CHAPTER ELEVEN

SKATEBOARD TUCKED under one arm, Dustin walked along the sidewalk toward the skate park. He couldn't shake the bad mood he'd been in ever since he found out his foster siblings were leaving. He'd had a pretty good time with Nikki this afternoon and had enjoyed the horseback ride, though his legs and butt were sore. Maybe he could work out the kinks—among other things—on his board.

Frank and Sylvia would get more kids in—some girl was supposed to be arriving on Monday. But he'd been with the other three for a while now, and it was hard to start over.

Dustin rounded a corner near the convenience store and immediately ducked behind the Dumpster. Eric and Jimmy were just leaving the store. Eric had his gym bag slung over one shoulder, but the two were acting weird. Not talking, not cutting up the way they normally did. He'd barely had the chance to wonder why when a store clerk ran out the door after them.

"Hey! You guys, stop!"

Immediately, both boys took off running. Curious, Dustin left his hiding place and circled around the back of the building, out of sight of the store clerk and the few people who'd been in the parking lot. He knew the neighborhood like the back of his hand and was able to duck up an alley and head down a side street within seconds. He scanned the area, looking for possible places where Eric and Jimmy might've gone. Moments later, he caught sight of them as they slowed to a jog down another alley. Dustin barely had time to duck behind a pile of old tires.

He followed at a discreet distance, making sure to keep out of view by walking behind hedges and trees as he made his way up the alley in their wake. Twice, Eric and Jimmy cast nervous glances over their shoulders; they nearly saw him once. Heart racing, he hid behind a tree until he was sure they hadn't spotted him, then continued following them. They ducked around the corner and ended up at the same empty storefront where they'd hassled him the other day. *What the hell were they up to?*

Dustin cut through a vacant lot and came around the opposite side of the building, sneaking behind a brick wall that bordered a staircase that led down to a basement entrance. From the depths of the stairwell, he heard them. Laughing, talking in low voices.

"Dawg, that was too cool!" Jimmy's voice carried on the quiet air.

"You know it." Eric snickered. "Cheers, dude."

Dustin heard the clunk of aluminum cans striking one another, and crawled on his hands and knees around the brick wall for a look. Carefully, he peered into the stairwell.

The two boys sat with their backs to him on the bottom step, Eric's gym bag open at their feet. Each held a tall can of beer—which Eric had obviously jacked from the convenience store.

Losers. He didn't regret for an instant throwing eggs at their houses after they'd set him up with the cop car.

Cautiously, he backed into a squatting position, sidled around the wall, then took off for the skate park. Maybe he ought to tell Cody what he'd seen. Being a snitch wasn't cool, but in this case it would be fun. He smiled to himself, picturing Jimmy and Eric in real trouble.

Shitheads.

Then again, giving up Eric and Jimmy might bring more trouble down on his head. He'd stood up to them before, but he wasn't in any hurry to have his ass kicked.

As he crossed the street that led to the skate park, Dustin caught movement out of the corner of his eye. For one heart-stopping moment, he thought Eric and Jimmy had followed him. He snapped his head around in time to see Ryan come up behind him just a few yards away and bolt across the street without so much as a glance in his direction.

"Hey!" Dustin hollered. "What's up, dude?" But Ryan ignored him and before Dustin could go after him, a big black-and-tan Doberman raced out into the street on Ryan's heels. Right into the path of an oncoming car.

Old Man Parker's dog.

"Thor!" Dustin shouted, finding the dog's name out of the blue. At the same time, he tossed his skateboard onto the grass near the sidewalk, then vaulted away from the curb. He couldn't let the dog get hit.

But he knew he couldn't reach him in time, either. The events unfolded as if in slow motion. The car drew closer, the driver attempting to slow with a squeal of brakes. Thor hesitated, looking back as Dustin called his name. What the hell was it Dustin had heard the admiral say? Some sort of military thing….

"Thor, fall out!" Dustin shouted, hoping that was right.

The dog spun around and took a step toward him.

The driver of the car blared the horn.

And suddenly Dustin wasn't so sure he'd done the right thing after all.

Thor's spiked collar glinted in the sunlight, and his white teeth showed above his lolling tongue as he began to run again.

Only this time, the Dobie was coming straight at Dustin.

CODY PAUSED on the front porch. The thought of knocking on his own door still struck him as ludicrous.

But then Regina had said he and Nikki needed to respect one another's feelings and opinions. So he raised
his fist and gave the screen a rap. Max ran to the door,
barking, then wagged his tail when he saw Cody.

"Come in," Nikki called. She stood with her arms
folded against her waist, looking as nervous as he felt.

He sat on the couch, remembering what had happened the last time the two of them were together in
this room. If he'd gotten Nikki pregnant, he would
never forgive himself.

"Would you like something to drink?" she asked.

"Sure."

She went to the kitchen and returned carrying two
cans of pop. "Want yours over ice?"

"No, this is fine, thanks." He opened the can and
took a sip, not really thirsty, but grateful to give his
hands something to do.

She picked up a piece of notepaper from where it
lay on the end table, then sat down in a chair near the
couch. "Do you have your list?"

"Yep." He dug it out of his pocket. "But before we
get started I was wondering…is everything okay with
you? After the other night, I mean?"

Her face flushed. "I'm all right."

"What about…" He groped for the right words.

"The fact that I wasn't on the Pill?" She crossed
one leg over the other, drawing his gaze to her calves.
"We got lucky."

He tore his roaming eyes away, forcing himself

not to think about how sexy her legs looked. Relieved she wasn't pregnant, he also felt a familiar tinge of sadness.

"So, how do you want to do this?" she asked. "Should we take turns reading our entire list to each other, or one thought at a time?"

He shrugged. "You're the teacher. You decide."

Nikki quirked her mouth. "You're the cop. We could go by Cody's Law and string things along."

"Or Nikki's Rule," he said. "And just get it over with." His smile softened the words.

"Okay, let's be serious. Maybe it would be easier to compare one thing at a time. That way we each get equal opportunity to speak."

Cody shifted on the couch, feeling like he was at some damned job interview. *Wanted: Husband. Worn-out cowboys need not apply.* "Fine. You go first."

"All right." She smoothed the paper against her knee and read aloud. "Cody's way of coping with the crash—tracking down the drunk driver. Pro…" Her voice cracked, and she paused to clear her throat. "Anna's killer may end up in jail, paying for what he did. Con—Cody's feelings of anger and his need for vengeance only grow stronger and may eat him up inside." She looked at him. "Your turn."

Feeling ridiculous, he read from his notes. "Nikki copes with Anna's death by trying to change herself. She seeks comfort in food, dresses in loud, bright colors. Pro—these things might make her feel better for a while, or maybe even long-term. Con—she's denying her deeper feelings."

Nikki glared at him. "I am not."

"Yes, you are." He wagged a finger at her. "No arguing, remember? We promised Regina to keep open minds."

"Fine." She continued reading. "Cody's answer to our marital problems—adopting a child, specifically Dustin Holbrook, in order to form a family and reestablish the bond we once shared. Pro—Cody feels this will help solve our marital differences. Con—"

"Hey," he interrupted her. "I already admitted that wasn't the best idea right now."

"You're not supposed to interrupt," she said. "Con—" she gave him a stern, teacher-like stare "—Dustin could get hurt by such a hasty decision." She raised an eyebrow and waited for him to go next.

"Nikki thinks her kindergarten class will be enough to fulfill her mothering needs. That it will satisfy and offset her natural instincts to raise children. Pro—her job is important, she's a great teacher and she enjoys her work. Con—she's hiding from her true feelings of wanting to have a child of her own."

"I'm not hiding from anything!"

He fixed her with the toughest interrogation-method-look he could muster. "I think you are."

"Well, it doesn't matter what you think." She rattled the notepaper with a flick of her wrist. "We're supposed to be doing these lists from the other's perspective."

"Yes, but we're allowed to give our own reasons why we feel these things will or won't work."

"But you're not supposed to accuse me of...stuff."

"You can't even say it out loud," he scoffed. "Yet it's okay for you to write down that my 'need for vengeance' is eating me up inside?"

"Sure, if you're going to sit there and say that I'm 'hiding from my true feelings.'" She gave him a triumphant smirk. "There, I said it. Satisfied?"

He raked one hand through his hair. "This isn't getting us anywhere. Maybe we'd better wait and show our lists to Regina."

Nikki made an obvious effort to control her irritation. "Okay." She laid hers on the end table. "We have an appointment with her again on Tuesday."

"Good." He knew he should get up and leave. But he hated to end their short evening on such a sour note. He took a sip of his cola. "So, how was your ride with Dustin this afternoon?"

"It went pretty well." But her voice carried an odd note.

"Did something happen?"

"He opened up to me quite a bit."

"And?"

"You're right, Cody. He really does want a home. But—" quickly, she held up one finger "—I'm not saying I want to adopt him."

His premature excitement faltered. "What exactly did he tell you?"

"That Jessica was adopted by a nice couple and went home with her new family yesterday, and that Michelle and Michael are being returned to their parents."

"Wow." Cody sat back against the cushions, stunned. "Poor kid. He must feel like the proverbial redheaded stepchild."

"More like an unwanted puppy at the pound. That's the way he worded it."

It wrenched Cody's heart. "There's got to be something we can do. What if we double up on our counseling sessions with Regina? Is there any way you could reconsider adoption?"

"No, I won't." She looked at him as though he were dense. Maybe he was. "That's not fair," Nikki went on. "Not to us, and certainly not to him." She gestured with the flat of her hand. "You can't put a time line on solving our problems. You can't just speed up our counseling and hope that works. And— hello—Dustin's *not* a puppy!"

"I know *that*." He sighed. "I want to fix it all, but every time I try things turn out all wrong."

"Exactly. You can't do it on your own, Cody. And neither can I." A look of comprehension dawned in her expression. "I get it now. That's why Regina had us make up our pros and cons list, to show us that we can't solve things one way or the other as individuals. She's trying to get us to experience compromise."

He shrugged, extracting the claws of the yellow kitten from his jeans. "The list was a dumb idea."

Nikki frowned. "Don't be so negative. At least it got us talking."

"I guess Regina—" The ringing phone interrupted him. Before he could move to answer it, Nikki rose and picked it up, and again he was reminded that he was no longer living in this house with her.

"Hello? Yes, he's here, Jordan." She held the phone out, and Cody took it, standing.

"Jordan, what's up?"

"Hey, Cody. Can you meet me at Admiral Parker's? There's been a fender bender, and it involves those punks Dustin hangs with."

"I'm on my way." He hung up the phone.

"What is it?" Nikki looked worried.

"I'm not sure, but Jordan mentioned Chad and Ryan. Let's just hope Dustin isn't involved. I'll let you know when I find out."

With a sinking feeling in the pit of his stomach, Cody headed for the door.

CODY ARRIVED at Parker's house to find a group gathered on the sidewalk between curb and lawn. Directly in front of the house, two cars sat in the middle of the street, one having rear-ended the other. Nearby, Jordan's Dodge Dakota was parked along with Henderson's and Schmidt's squad cars. Jana was one of the people standing on the sidewalk and, to Cody's surprise, so was Dustin.

"What's going on?" Cody addressed Jordan after parking his squad car behind his partner's truck.

"Parker had some trouble with those punks again. I'll let him explain."

Cody hurried forward and greeted Henderson and Schmidt. Schmidt was busy scribbling down a report as he spoke to a man—presumably the driver of one of the cars—while Parker told his story to anyone and everyone who would listen. He seemed to be enjoying the attention.

"I'm telling you, Thor was nearly killed!" Parker said. He turned toward Henderson. "I want those boys arrested and put in jail." He patted the shoulder of the Doberman at his side on a leash. Then, still scowling, Parker looked at Dustin.

For a moment Cody thought he was about to accuse the boy. Parker pointed. "This young man here is the only reason Thor is alive. If he hadn't happened by, there's no telling how things might've turned out."

"Okay, try to calm down, sir," Henderson said, pen poised over his clipboard. "Just tell me what happened."

"I was in the bathtub when I heard Thor barking. As if someone was at the fence teasing him again. Officer Somers and his partner took the call the other day—you remember?" This last he directed at Cody.

Cody nodded. "I do."

"By the time I got my pants on and went outside, those punks had let Thor out of the yard. Near as I could see from leaning my head out the bathroom window, one of them had been up on the garage roof, and the other climbed that tree over there." He turned and pointed at the massive cottonwood that stood between his fence and the garage. "The kid on the roof baited Thor by teasing him, while the other one leaned down over the gate, hanging from the tree branch, and used a stick to lift the latch and push the gate open. I shouted, and the boy on the roof leaped down and took off through the alley.

"I rushed outside and saw the other one sprint across the street and down to the corner. Thor went after him, and that's how my dog was almost killed." He patted the Dobie again. "He nearly got hit by that car." Parker gestured toward the silver Toyota that had been rear-ended. "And one down by the corner, too."

"He jumped right out in front of me." The owner of the Toyota, a young woman with blond hair spoke up. "I slammed on my brakes as hard as I could. I didn't realize there was anyone behind me."

Cody could hear Henderson, still lecturing the driver of the second car about keeping a proper distance from the vehicle ahead of him.

"Why would those kids want to goad Thor into chasing them?" Cody asked. "That doesn't make any sense."

"I don't believe that was the way it was sup-posed to work out," Parker said. "I think they'd planned to hide up on the roof and in the tree and open the gate so Thor would run away. Maybe to get back at me for calling the police out here the other day. Maybe hoping I wouldn't have a guard dog around anymore, so they could cause more mis-chief, like painting graffiti on my garage. Who knows with kids these days?" His voice turned to a growl. "All I can tell you is they hadn't counted on me. I don't think they thought anyone was home, because I've got my car and my Suburban parked in the garage."

"So, no one knows where the boys went?" Cody asked.

"I only saw the one who dashed across the street in front of my car just before the dog did," the blonde said. "I darned near hit the kid, too." She pressed both hands to her heart. "My God! I'm still shaking."

"You said he ran toward the corner?" Hender-son asked.

She nodded. "That way." The woman pointed across the street at an angle.

"How do you fit into the picture, Dustin?" Cody asked.

"It was Ryan who cut across the street," Dustin said, pointing toward the corner as well. "I had just crossed Oak Avenue, heading toward the skate park, when I saw him. Thor was chasing him, and there were cars coming at him." He shrugged. "I called him and grabbed hold of his collar so he wouldn't get hit."

"And he would have for sure," Parker boomed, then repeated, "I want those two punks arrested."

But Cody's mind was still back at the part where Dustin had grabbed hold of the dog. A dog he himself wouldn't want to tangle with. "You grabbed Thor by the collar?"

"Uh-huh. It was the only way to keep him from darting into the street again."

"Did he try to bite you?" Cody couldn't hide his astonishment.

Dustin shook his head. "No. I didn't have much time to think about that, I guess. I just yelled at him to fall out." He cast a glance Parker's way. "I've heard you say that to him before, when you were walking him on a leash down by the park."

"That's fall *in*," Parker said with a nervous chuckle.

Dustin shrugged. "Anyway, Thor came to me, so I just snagged his collar."

Awkwardly, the admiral patted Dustin's shoulder. "That's all right. You did good, son. You did real good."

"Thanks." Dustin shifted self-consciously, obviously not used to so much attention.

Or at least, not so much *positive* attention.

"Where's your skateboard?" Cody asked.

"Oh, crap. I dropped it on the grass by the street. I forgot all about it."

"You'd better go get it," Cody said in a mild tone. "I'm sure Frank and Sylvia wouldn't appreciate you losing a skateboard they paid good money for." But secretly, he was proud of Dustin.

"Now don't be giving the boy a lecture," Parker said. "He's a hero, if you ask me." He gave Dustin's shoulder a squeeze. "You come by anytime, son. I'll have cold soda pop and peanut butter cookies waiting." He lowered his voice. "Thor's all I've got, you know."

Dustin nodded, meeting the old man's gaze. "That's cool." He glanced at Cody again. "Guess I better head back for my skateboard." He hesitated.

"Something wrong?" Cody asked.

"Naw." Dustin shook his head. "I'll see ya later." He turned and jogged away.

Cody tried to focus politely as Admiral Parker continued to ramble about Thor and how much the dog meant to him. The old man was finally interrupted as the tow truck from Joe's Garage pulled in. Lester, wearing his usual sleeveless shirt and ball cap, got out and conversed briefly with Schmidt and the owners of the two cars before hitching up the Toyota. A second tow truck showed up for the other car, and the neighbors began to drift back to their houses. Parker, still fussing over Thor, took the dog inside. Henderson and Schmidt had driven away as well, and Jordan bade Cody goodbye before climbing into his truck.

"Hey, Cody." Jana walked up beside him. "How's it going?"

"Not bad. Guess our quota of excitement for the day is over."

"Guess so." She chuckled. "That's what I love about small-town life." Then she pressed her lips together, studying him. "So, how was the fund-raiser for the women's shelter? I missed it—had to do inventory at the bookstore."

"It was great. I think the Elks Lodge raised quite a bit of money for the cause." He grinned. "I know Nikki and I gave till it hurt."

"I'm glad to hear it," Jana said. The look she gave him said her question had really been about how things had gone between him and Nikki. But she was too good a friend, and too polite, to pry more. "So, that was Dustin, huh?"

Cody nodded. "Yep. He can be ornery at times, but deep down he's a pretty good kid."

"I can see that." She tilted her head respectfully. "I don't think I would've been brave enough to grab Parker's Doberman by the collar."

"Dustin has a way with animals."

"So I've heard. How are the kittens?"

"Good. The little curtain climbers." Cody smiled, remembering the one that had climbed his pant leg while he and Nikki were hashing over their lists.

Jana laughed softly. "Curtain climbers they are…. Nikki told me she really got a lot out of the MADD meeting last month."

"Yeah." He didn't want to admit that they hadn't actually talked about it.

"The group is always looking for informed speakers, you know." Jana's tone carried a heavy hint.

"I'll keep that in mind." But he couldn't picture himself getting up in front of a group, speaking as an officer of the law about drunk drivers, when on a personal level he was having more than a little trouble coming to terms with the subject. And the person who had made him a victim, putting him on the other side of the fence.

Neither could he bring himself to do what Nikki had—share his grief over Anna's death with a group of relative strangers. "Listen, Jana, I've got to run. It was nice seeing you."

"Sure. Take care, Cody." She lifted her hand in a wave. "Tell Nikki I said hi."

"Will do."

He got into his car and drove homeward, wondering exactly how to handle it if he and Nikki picked up where they had left off.

CHAPTER TWELVE

NIKKI WAS in the middle of cooking supper when she heard Cody's car pull into the driveway and stop in front of the house. She really hadn't expected him back this soon, if at all, since the call he'd gotten from Jordan had sounded serious.

Worried about Dustin, she turned the burner down on her skillet of chicken and went to the door. Maybe if she stepped out onto the porch, she could discourage Cody from coming inside. She wanted to be sure Dustin was okay, but she'd meant what she'd told Cody earlier about not having supper together. Her heart couldn't take any more of the swing back and forth of emotions she'd been through lately.

"Is everything all right?" Nikki asked, standing at the top of the steps.

Cody had gotten out of his squad car, and a ripple of sexual awareness shot through Nikki at the sight of him. He was in his cowboy clothes, not his uniform, since he'd officially been off duty when the call from Jordan had come in. But he'd driven the squad car rather than his pickup, since technically an officer was never off duty.

Cowboy, cop…

Nikki quelled her fantasies with effort and stepped back to give him room as Cody climbed the steps— to give herself room. She wanted to wrap her arms around his neck and devour his sexy mouth.

"Everything's fine," Cody said. "Just a minor fender bender, like Jordan said."

"So how were Dustin's buddies involved?" She bit her lip. He might be a brat, but she didn't want anything bad to happen to him. He'd had enough of that in his life. "Is Dustin okay?"

"Yeah." Cody proceeded to tell her about how Chad and Ryan had let Thor out of Parker's yard, and how Dustin had rescued the Doberman. "I've got to give the boy credit—he sure acted unselfishly."

"And bravely," Nikki said. Pride welled, and she told herself it was the teacher in her, always happy to hear that a student had done something out of the ordinary.

"I'm sorry we were interrupted earlier," Cody said, leaning against the porch rail with his hands in his pockets. He inhaled deeply, closing his eyes. "Man, something smells good. Is that fried chicken?"

Nikki squirmed, fully aware of the tempting aroma wafting through the screen door. "Yes, it is. I, uh, thought I'd make up a big batch so I'd have some leftovers to eat cold."

"Did you make potato salad, too?"

He knew her too well. "Yes." She chewed her bottom lip, doing her best to ignore his blatant hints.

"Man, I'm hungry. Are you sure you don't want to have supper together and talk?" There it was again: that grin that was impossible to resist. "I mean, not that I'm trying to just invite myself to eat your chicken. I would've gladly taken you out."

"There's plenty," she said finally, gesturing toward the door. "Why don't you come in. I've already fed the horses and Max."

They made small talk while she finished cooking the meal. Cody set the table, and the familiar pattern of the routine made Nikki ache. She missed him more every day.

A short while later, Nikki sat across from Cody, a platter of golden-brown fried chicken and a bowl of potato salad on the table between them. She'd also thrown together some baked beans and a tray of biscuits once she knew Cody would be joining her for the meal. For dessert, she'd pulled a chocolate boxed cake out of the freezer.

Nikki took a sip from her glass of milk before speaking. "So, getting back to our lists, do you agree with me that that's what Regina was showing us?"

He chewed a bite of chicken, nodding. "But what she wants us to do about it, I don't know."

Nikki poked her fork into the potato salad on her

plate. "*Would* you consider going to a MADD meeting with me? There's one coming up on Wednesday."

Cody's expression hardened. "I don't think so, Nikki. I'm sorry, but I can't share my personal feelings about Anna's death with a roomful of people."

"Caitlin Kramer's mother was there when I went last month."

"Who?" He frowned, then his expression cleared. "Of course. Caitlin." His mouth quirked. "I'm sorry, it's not that I'd forgotten her. It's just…"

"Me, too. I told Evelyn—her mother—that I'd meant to follow up on Caitlin's condition."

"How *is* she doing?"

"Not real well, from what I gathered. Apparently she's been through a tough regimen of ongoing physical therapy. But at least she wasn't killed."

"That's what I mean," Cody said. "Every person at those meetings has a burden of their own, some worse than others, all horrible in their eyes. But I can't help feeling ours is right up there at the top of the list. You almost lost your sister. We lost our little girl…."

She took his hand. "We need to find some middle ground. I thought MADD might be it." She paused. "If you don't feel comfortable in coming to a meeting as a victim, how about if you give a talk to the group as an officer?"

He shook his head. "Jana already suggested it."

"See, even Jana thinks it's a good idea. She

cares about you. She wouldn't suggest you do something if she didn't feel it was beneficial for both of us."

"I can't, Nikki. Please try to understand."

But she didn't. "Okay. Then how about this. A lot of the people in the MADD group have put up memorial markers at the crash sites where their loved ones were killed. Could you do that with me? Put up a marker for Anna?"

He laid his fork down and stared at her. "You know how much time I've spent combing that stretch of highway, looking for evidence? But when I took Dustin out there to pick up trash…" He shook his head. "Bottom line is, I can barely stand driving past there anymore, much less put a—a—wreath—" he waved his hand in the air "—at the spot to remind me of what happened. As if I need a reminder!"

"But that's exactly the point," Nikki said. "To *remind* other people. To send out a message, that drinking and driving kills."

He scowled. "I'm sorry, it seems morbid to me."

"How can you even say that? It's no different than marking a grave."

"Precisely. And that spot on the highway is *not* Anna's grave." His hand trembled. "Our baby is buried in the cemetery, with a marble angel to mark her place of rest. She's in God's hands now. I don't want to put some cross or flower arrangement or whatever up on the side of the road for everyone to gawk at."

Nikki felt like crying. Out of frustration, out of anger. Out of hurt. "Fine. I'll do it myself."

"I don't want you to do it at all." He pushed his chair back from the table. "Damn it, maybe we'd better stop this conversation right here before we both say things we'll regret."

"You're going to leave then. Just like that." He hadn't even finished his supper.

"I'll stay if we talk about something else."

Change the subject, as if pretending everything was all right would make it go away. Nikki stuffed a chunk of biscuit into her mouth to keep from snapping at him. The silence lay between them like a wet blanket. She chewed and swallowed. "Will you at least agree to talk about this with Regina next week?"

He gave her an exasperated look. "I'll agree to discuss the list of pros and cons and take it from there. Will that work?"

"Do I have a choice?"

"Yes. We can forget the whole thing." He held up his hand. "Sorry. That was uncalled for. I'm tense."

"I guess we both are." All the fight drained out of Nikki.

They ate in silence. "You know what?" Cody finally said. "I can't stop thinking about what you told me Dustin said. About missing the other kids and all that."

"Now it's my turn. I think Dustin is another subject we need to wait to discuss with Regina." Actually, as far as Nikki was concerned, the subject was closed.

As though reading her thoughts, he said, "I know you're not interested in adoption. But that doesn't mean we can't talk about him at all, does it?"

"What did you have in mind?"

"Something seemed a little off today, in the way he was behaving after he brought Parker's dog back."

"Oh? How so?"

"I don't know. I couldn't put my finger on it, and maybe it was only my imagination. But he had something on his mind."

"It was probably exactly what you said. Missing Jessica, knowing Michelle and Michael are leaving, too."

"I suppose." He fell silent until the end of the meal, then began loading the dishes without her asking.

"You don't have to do that," Nikki protested.

"Yes, I do. You cooked."

Tired of arguing, she let it go. "All right." She sliced a second piece of cake and slid it onto her plate. But she'd only finished half of it before the sharpness of her pants cutting into her waist made her stop. She laughed dryly. "I told myself I wasn't going to do this anymore, and look at me." She gestured at her plate, then stood and dumped the rest of the piece of cake into the trash. "I really need to start working out."

"Me, too." He chuckled, and the sound washed over her, warming her inside.

Cody had a great laugh. A sexy laugh.

"As a matter of fact," he said, "the day I chased Dustin when he spray-painted my squad car, I told myself I'd start working out at the gym more often." He paused. "What would you say to working out together? It's something neutral we could do with each other, and it would motivate us to stick with the program."

Focus on the word neutral. It wasn't as if they planned on doing something personal, like going dancing. *Or making love.* "Okay. Do you want to join a health club? The gym in Glenwood offers memberships."

"That would be good. And we could also ride the horses more often." He held up his hand. "We don't necessarily have to ride together if you don't want to. We can take turns going with Dustin, or ride alone. Whatever."

She knew what he was thinking. When they'd ridden together, their outings often turned romantic. Countless times, they'd packed a picnic in their saddle bags and ended up beneath the shade of a tree at the far corner of the ranch, sometimes sipping a glass of wine while the horses grazed nearby. Once, they'd made love beneath a full moon.

Nikki struggled to rein in the memory. "Yeah. Riding is good."

"Speaking of which," Cody said. "Tom Lockhart's mustang roundup is coming up next Saturday. Were you planning on going?"

Another thing they'd done together.

"I don't know," Nikki said evasively. "I'll have to see what's going on."

The Lockhart roundup was an annual event in Deer Creek. A widower and longtime resident of the town, Tom ran a mustang sanctuary on his six-thousand-acre ranch. Horse Haven was home to over two hundred wild horses deemed unadoptable for one reason or another. Horses that had fallen through the cracks of the Bureau of Land Management's adopt-a-horse program, because they were too ugly, too old or too wild.

Tom had taken the animals in a few at a time, and all yearling colts were gelded to prevent exacerbation of the ongoing problem the BLM faced—too many wild horses, with not enough land to support them and not enough adoptive homes available.

Every year at the end of summer, Tom and his ranch hands rounded up a group of about thirty horses and herded them from Horse Haven to the county fairgrounds, where they were placed in sturdy pipe-rail pens. The roundup itself drew a crowd to Deer Creek from all the surrounding communities. People lined the streets, getting a kick out of watching the old-time wild horse roundup. Main Street and the surrounding side streets were marked off, as if it were a parade route, with all motor traffic banned while the horses came through the little town.

After watching the horses and cowboys go by, the crowd gathered at the fairgrounds where Tom and other volunteers spoke of the plight of the mustangs. They educated the public on the care and needs of the wild horses, both in captivity and out on government-owned rangeland. Tom talked about how Horse Haven had come into being, and invited everyone back to the holding pens to look the horses over. Each year, many of his so-called "unadoptable" horses found new homes, enabling Tom to then take in other mustangs from the BLM and continue the process.

"I thought the roundup might be something Dustin would enjoy, too," Cody said.

Nikki ignored the hint. Cody let the subject drop, and finished loading the dishwasher. Once he was done, he wiped the table down, then looked around the kitchen. Was he stalling?

Taking matters into her own hands, Nikki moved to kiss Cody's cheek. "Good night," she said. "Thanks for doing the dishes."

He lifted his hand to touch the place where she'd kissed him. "You're welcome. Let me know when you want to go set up our memberships at the health club. Or when you've gotten yours set up—whatever. I can do mine." Awkwardly, he backed toward the door. "Good night."

Nikki stood alone in the kitchen for a long while before turning off the light and heading upstairs to bed.

ON MONDAY, she went to the school to begin readying her classroom for students. She couldn't wait for the school year to start. It would make her feel productive again.

The familiar scents of the school hallway washed over her as she entered the building. Lingering odors of kids' running shoes and sweaters, sack lunches and pencil lead. She greeted the office staff, also preparing for the opening in two weeks, then retrieved the key to her classroom from her mailbox before making her way to her room. She unlocked the door and entered, breathing in the wonderful smell of chalk and erasers, paint and glue. Smiling, Nikki placed her shopping bags of supplies on her desk. Clean now, it would soon be cluttered.

On the bulletin board, she hung cutouts she'd made of a floppy-eared dog, a doghouse and a collection of bones with each child's name—taken from her class roster—written on them with colorful magic markers. From construction paper, she'd also formed letters to spell out *Bowwow Welcome.*

She stocked the shelves with supplies provided by the school: paper, books, extra scissors and crayons, along with colored wooden letters to assist in teaching the alphabet and plastic magnetic numbers. The morning passed quickly, and by the time Nikki left for home shortly past noon, she was satisfied that her room was almost completely in order. She had a few little things to do yet, but they could wait until later in the week. She would have eighteen students this year, a good number and one that allowed for added individual attention.

Reaching the parking lot, Nikki spotted Dustin riding his skateboard across the blacktop. He did a complicated trick against a cement handicap ramp, then seeing her, picked up the board and headed her way.

"Hi, Nikki."

"Dustin, what are you doing?" She wagged her finger at him. "You're not supposed to ride your skateboard on school property."

His shoulders slumped. "But that's such a cool ramp.... What are you doing here?"

"Getting my classroom in order. Are you ready for the new school year?"

"I guess." But his tone let her know he'd prefer summer stayed around a good while longer.

"So, are you coming out to the ranch later to wash Cody's car?" she teased.

"Naw, not today." His brow furrowed. "I'm supposed to stay home the rest of the afternoon. We've got a new girl coming to live with us. She'll be here at two-thirty."

"Really?" Nikki brightened. "Are you excited about getting a new sister?"

"She's not my sister," Dustin said. "I don't think of the other kids that way anymore, because they never stay."

His solemn words made Nikki regret speaking without thinking. "I'm sorry. I just meant, are you excited to meet her—the new girl?"

"Not really. She's *thirteen*." His tone said it all. He

fully expected the new arrival to be a major pain in his neck.

"Does she have a name?"

"Brittany."

"No last name?"

"Spears," he said with a sarcastic snort. "I'm not kidding. Maybe she can sing."

Nikki laughed, placing her hand on his shoulder. "You're too much, Dustin. Well, if you make it out to the ranch later this week, we can go for another horseback ride if you want."

"As long as you don't make me wear pink boots."

"I won't." She laughed again. Then she sobered. "Dustin, can I ask you a question?"

"I guess."

"Was something on your mind the other day? Cody told me what happened with Admiral Parker's dog, and he said it seemed as though you had something you wanted to get off your chest."

Dustin's expression shifted so abruptly, she knew Cody had been right. "It was nothing," he said, with a casual lift of his shoulders.

"Are you sure?"

"Uh, *yeah*." The defensive sarcasm was back, and Nikki fought her frustration.

At that moment, Cody's squad car turned up the street alongside the school. Spotting them, he swung into the parking lot.

"Speak of the devil," Dustin said.

Cody leaned out the window. "Hey, Dustin. Hi, Nikki."

"Hi," Nikki replied. Dustin merely nodded a greeting.

"Dustin, have you got a minute?"

"Why?" he asked warily. "I have to be home before two or my butt's in trouble."

"No problem. I can give you a ride."

"Terrific." He rolled his eyes. "Just what I want the neighbors to see. Me coming home in a cop car."

Nikki couldn't help laughing. "Beats walking, huh?"

"I can ride my board." But he went around the front of the squad car to the passenger door.

"'Bye, Dustin." Nikki waved at him, said goodbye to Cody, then walked to her own car.

As she climbed behind the wheel, she watched Cody pull out of the parking lot and wondered what he wanted to talk to Dustin about. She hoped nothing was wrong.

And she hoped that whatever Cody was planning to talk to him about wasn't too personal, either. Come to think of it, she shouldn't have offered to take Dustin horseback riding. Here she was, not wanting Cody to get more attached to the boy, and she'd opened herself up.

Too late, her inner voice whispered. *Cody's already way too attached.*

And like it or not, Nikki was beginning to suspect she was, too.

"So, WHAT'S up?" Dustin asked, making an obvious effort to keep his tone of voice casual.

"I was about to ask you the same thing." Cody studied him out of the corner of his eye as he pulled the squad car over to the curb on a quiet street and shut off the engine. "You wouldn't happen to know anything about Eric Vanderhurst and Jimmy Ryker shoplifting some beer from the convenience store the other day, would you? The same day, and around the same time, you saved Thor?"

"Why would I?"

Dustin was a lousy liar, but for the moment, Cody let it ride. "I don't know. I'm just asking, that's all."

"How should I know what they do? I don't hang with those jerks. "

"I realize that. But the convenience store is only a couple of blocks away from where you said you found Thor. And the store clerk who ran out into the parking lot after Eric and Jimmy said they took off running toward the west end of town. That would've put them in the same vicinity as you. I thought it was a bit coincidental."

Dustin sighed. "Okay, I'm going to tell you some-thing, but not because I'm a snitch, all right? Only because I want you to know that I had nothing to do with what happened. Eric and Jimmy didn't even know I saw them." He went on to explain how he'd seen the two boys drinking the stolen beer. "I didn't feel like sticking around, so I headed for the skate park. A couple of blocks later, I saw Ryan run across the street, and that's when I grabbed Thor and headed for Admiral Parker's."

"And that's all you saw? That's all you know about it?"

"That's it. I swear." Dustin narrowed his eyes. "I wonder if Vanderhurst's parents know that he drinks?"

And with that simple statement, alarm bells went off in Cody's mind. Eric was a little more than a year older than Dustin, close to thirteen. And kids who lived in the country often learned to drive at an early age, especially on farms. Not that the Vanderhursts were farmers exactly. Did Eric already know how to drive and, if so, would he dare take his parents' SUV at night without their knowledge?

The crash that had killed Anna had coincided with the middle school's Valentine's Day dance, and the one for the high school as well. Kids were out partying that night, and Cody had already taken into consideration the possibility of an underage drinker behind the wheel. It might explain why the driver had fled the scene.

Eric was tall for his age.

And Cody had noticed that the boy's parents often left him alone at night. Could he be the one?

Cody tried to focus on Dustin. But in the back of his mind, he vowed to check out Eric Vanderhurst, just in case. It wouldn't hurt. He simply couldn't leave a stone unturned.

"I need to ask you about something else, too," he said. "Did you have anything to do with throwing eggs at Jimmy Ryker's garage?"

Dustin squirmed. "I don't know what you're talking about."

"Dustin." Cody pinned him with a serious look. "I want a straight answer."

"Maybe." He set his mouth in a stubborn line.

"That's not straight." Cody stared him down. "I'm waiting."

The boy crossed his arms defensively. "He had it coming. He's just a chickenshit like Vanderhurst."

Cody sighed. "Dustin, you can't go around doing stuff like that." He shook his head, at a loss. "What is it going to take to get through to you? Do you *want* to go to juvie?"

"I don't care."

"I don't believe you."

Dustin fell silent, scowling. Cody debated giving the kid a ticket. He'd given him enough chances and he shouldn't let his personal feelings interfere with his duty as an officer of the law.

But he had made so much progress with the boy. He hated to give him over to a system that was overworked. A system that often only made things worse for a foster child.

"So, are you going to come wash my car soon?" he asked.

Dustin narrowed his eyes. "You're not arresting me?"

"Not today."

It took the boy a minute to answer. "Nikki already asked me if I was."

"She did?"

"Said we could go horseback riding." Dustin paused. "Would you come with us?"

"Riding?"

"Ye-ah." He dragged the word out into two syllables.

Cody pictured the three of them riding together. Like it or not, his personal feelings were interfering in the way he handled the boy. He wasn't ready to give up the idea of adopting Dustin. Maybe the therapy sessions with Regina would help convince Nikki—or dissuade him. Although he'd rather pay a visit to the dentist than talk about his marital problems.

"I might just do that," he said. "Providing, of course, that you do a passable job of washing and waxing my squad car."

"Hey, you can already see your reflection in the paint. In the tires, even. What more do you want?"

"I want to have the cleanest, shiniest car in the whole patrol unit," Cody said. "I want to be the envy of every single officer in the county."

Dustin rolled his eyes. "The things a guy has to put up with for making one teeny little mistake."

"Teeny?" Cody started the engine and put the car in gear.

"Not just teeny." Dustin held up his thumb and index finger to indicate a minute amount of space. "I'd say more like eensy-weensy. You know, like the spider in the nursery rhyme."

"That's itsy-bitsy."

Dustin chortled. "Did you just say *itsy-bitsy?*" He threw his head back and roared with laughter. "A tough cop, who says *itsy-bitsy?*"

Cody felt his face warm. "Tell anyone," he threatened, "and you'll be washing and waxing this car until you're an old man."

"Oh, now we're making threats, are we?"

"That's no threat." Cody gave him a wink. "It's a promise."

CHAPTER THIRTEEN

"HEY, CODY, hold up a minute."

Cody paused in the process of lifting a bag of sweet feed from the Co-Op loading dock into the bed of his pickup, and looked up to see a grizzled old cowboy headed his way.

"Hey, Tom. How's it going?" Cody got the bag in the truck and nodded a thank-you to the young boy who had given him a hand with the grain.

"Fair to middlin'." Tom Lockhart tipped the brim of his hat back off his forehead. In his mid-sixties—his skin tanned and wrinkled from a lifetime of ranching—he could still outride most men half his age. "I was wondering if you had some free time this weekend? I know it's short notice, but one of my wranglers busted his leg the other day breaking a filly, and he won't be able to ride in the mustang roundup. Would you be interested in filling in for him?"

"I'd be honored." Cody smiled.

"Good. I wasn't sure if you'd be on duty monitoring the barricades and traffic and all that."

"Naw, we've got plenty of officers and sheriff's

deputies who volunteer for that," Cody said. "I'm off this Saturday, so my time is all yours." He clapped Tom on the back. "You know I admire what you do with those horses."

"I appreciate that." Tom squinted in the sunlight. "You're a good hand, same as your dad always was. I wouldn't trust just anyone with my mustangs, you know."

"Thanks," Cody said. "What time do you want me at Horse Haven?"

"Eight o'clock. We'll get everything in order so we can have the herd downtown by nine."

"Sounds good. I'll see you in the morning." Cody closed the tailgate on his truck and drove off, thoughts ticking.

He and Nikki had met with Regina two days ago, and their session had gone pretty well. Regina had been pleased to hear they'd discussed their lists of pros and cons, and that they had come to the conclusion—as Nikki had said—that each of them alone could not solve their problems. They needed to find a compromise that would satisfy them both. Regina had also applauded their plan to join the health club and work out together. She felt the exercise would not only benefit their relationship, but would help them feel better physically and mentally, putting them in a happier frame of mind to work out their differences.

The right mind-set is important in order to reach the correct resolution.

In the past, Regina's psychobabble had often put Cody off. But this time he thought she had a point. Sound mind, sound body and all that.

With that in mind, he pulled into the driveway of the ranch house and backed the truck up to the open barn door. Nikki stood in the stable aisle, grooming a bay mare that had been her Christmas gift to Cody three years ago. "Hey there," Cody shot her a grin. "What are you doing brushing my horse?"

"Well, for once it isn't because you procrastinated," Nikki said, returning his smile. "I went for a ride earlier, and when I got back I noticed that Dancer and Cowboy had rolled in the mud over by the pond. I thought I'd groom them, too, after I'd brushed Cheyenne down."

Cody chuckled. "They'll probably just do it again."

"I imagine." But she kept brushing Dancer's dark, red-brown coat, carefully picking dried mud from strands of the mare's ebony mane. "It doesn't matter. Grooming the horses relaxes me."

"Me, too," he said.

"Maybe it's something else we can do together." Nikki gave him a look and he backed off. Was she thinking about other things they'd done together in the barn? He certainly was.

"So," he said. "Did you decide if you're going to the mustang roundup?"

"I'm still thinking about it."

"I saw Tom at the Co-Op. He asked me to be one of his wranglers."

"Really?" Nikki paused with a currycomb poised in one hand. "That sounds like fun."

He hesitated, anxious not to rush things. Still, he couldn't help feeling as though time were slipping through his fingers. "If you do go, would you mind asking Dustin along? I think he'd enjoy it."

"Don't you think Frank and Sylvia will take him if he wants to go?"

"I suppose, unless Sylvia has to work or some thing." He shrugged. "He can walk downtown to watch, for that matter, but not to the fairgrounds. I just thought it might be more fun for him to go with you."

Nikki's arched brow let him know she saw right through his weak excuses. "Cody, I don't mind tak-ing Dustin if he needs a ride. But don't force the issue, okay?" Briskly, she went back to work on Dan-cer's coat. "If Frank and Sylvia plan to take him, let's leave it at that."

With effort, he held back a sigh. "Fine."

"Besides, I think I know why you really want him to go with me."

"Is that right?"

"Yes." She gazed at him over Dancer's back. "You want to show off for him, don't you? You want him to look at you the way a boy looks at his father, and be proud."

His jaw dropped, and Cody let the sack of feed

he'd shouldered slide onto the floor to rest at his feet. He stared at Nikki. "Where in hell did you come up with that?"

She shrugged. "I know how your mind works." But her words were softened by the look in her eyes. "And maybe I can relate a little to what you're feeling."

"I think you've been hanging around Regina too much." He shook his head. "You're starting to sound just like her."

Nikki ran the currycomb over Dancer's shoulder, a hurt look on her face. Instantly, Cody regretted his words.

"Maybe," she said. "But I felt some of that same pride the other day, too, when I showed Dustin how to ride. I'd always hoped to teach our children everything I know about horses."

"That's because you're a teacher."

"Yeah, I suppose so." Nikki pressed her lips together.

Damn! He hadn't meant it to come out sounding that way. Cody walked over and, taking Nikki's free hand, clasped it in both of his. "And it's also because of the mother in you," he said. "You'd make a fantastic mom." He pressed a kiss to the palm of her hand, then folded it closed as though sealing the kiss inside. "I'd better get the rest of that feed unloaded."

SATURDAY MORNING dawned pleasantly cool, the sun peeking above the mountains like a watchful eye. Cody drove to Tom Lockhart's and had Raven un-

loaded from the horse trailer and saddled by the time
Tom and his wranglers were ready to move the herd
of horses toward town. Wearing his black hat, brown
leather chaps and spurs for dramatic effect, Cody
rode point—at the rear corner of the herd—feeling
as though he'd traveled back in time a hundred years.
A few spectators had parked their cars off on the
shoulder of the road near the end of Tom's driveway,
and they cheered the cowboys on as Cody and the
other riders whistled and called to the mustangs,
driving them down the road.

Up ahead of the spectators, the road stretched into
the distance, quiet and empty, the sagebrush on either side creating a tempting place for the horses to
wander. It took concentrated effort from the half
dozen riders to keep the herd in line, along with the
help of Tom's two Australian shepherds. While the
mustangs weren't actually *wild,* having lived at the
sanctuary for some time, they weren't extremely
tame either. Tom fed them and handled them enough
to be able to take care of their needs but other than
that, he left them to run on the vast acreage, like a
free-roaming band.

As Raven trotted along, the gelding's ears swiveled
back, picking up a sound behind them. The rumble of
an engine. Cody glanced over his shoulder and saw
that one of the people who had been parked along the
edge of the dirt road had decided to try and drive
through the herd, rather than take the long way around.

Idiot.

The guy—a young man in a jacked-up four-by-four pickup, with an enormous black dog in the back—leaned out the open window to wave as he rumbled past Cody. "Howdy, partner."

Cody glowered at him. "You can't drive through the herd," he said. "You'll spook the horses."

Whatever the man was about to say was drowned out by the sound of the dog's excited bark. The animal raced across the pickup bed and leaned over the opposite side to take a snap at one of the mustangs. The chestnut gelding snorted and swiveled on his haunches, bumping into the red dun mare at his heels.

The driver shouted at the dog, leaning through the open sliding window between the pickup's cab and bed, and swung his fist at the animal. At the same time, he let the truck continue to roll forward, deeper into the herd. Realizing he was still moving, the guy slammed on his brakes, sending a spray of gravel into the air. A rock pinged off the hip of the red dun, and the pair of horses bolted.

Cody cursed and took off after them, hoping the rest of the herd wouldn't follow. The two horses had dodged behind the pickup and Cody's own horse, and now ran hell-for-leather across the sagebrush, manes and tails flying in the wind. Cody let Raven race after them, guiding him across the rocky terrain through the sagebrush. The gelding stretched his neck out, ears flattened, moving like a shadow skimming above the ground. In spite of the seriousness of the situation, the horse's speed exhilarated Cody. The wind, stinging his eyes, tugging at his hat brim, made him feel carefree.

The mustangs streaked toward the distant hills, sure-footed, slightly ahead of Raven. But though he carried the weight of saddle and rider, the black gelding could run, and as the mustangs topped a rise and started down the other side, he caught up with them. "Here! Hey!" Cody shouted, then whistled. He hoped the mustangs would remember Tom's whistle when he called to feed them. Hoped they might even be two of the many horses that had done the roundup before, and have some familiarity with being driven by men on horseback.

Down a ravine they went, toward an old barn in the sagebrush and rock-strewn hillside. The time-worn and weathered wood blended into the scenery like a painting from the Old West. The pair of mustangs made quite a picture as they sped toward the barn. Cody spotted a corral beside the building. A few of the rails were broken and falling down, but the majority seemed to be firmly in place. As he drew closer, he saw a feed trough running along one side of the corral, and the mustangs had come to a halt there, noses down, snuffling the trough for something to eat.

"Whoa." Cody spoke soothingly to the horses as he pulled Raven to a stop, blocking the corral's open gate. The red dun raised her head and blew loudly through her nostrils, neck arched as she studied something behind Cody. He turned in the saddle and saw Tom approaching at a gallop on his gray gelding, his Australian shepherds in tow.

"They okay?" the old cowboy asked, pulling back on the reins as he eased the gray up beside Raven.

"Yeah." Cody chuckled. "But they sure gave me a run for my money." He leaned over and patted Raven's damp neck. "Gave you a run, huh boy?"

Tom shook his head. "Danged fool kid in that pickup. I looked up just as his dog took a dive at the chestnut, and saw you take off after the horses."

"I'd hoped to cut them off a little sooner, but at least they cornered themselves."

"I'd forgotten that Dan Godfrey's old barn sits back here," Tom said. "He hasn't used it in years."

"Looks like it's seen better days," Cody said, turning Raven away from the corral to ride toward the barn's double doors. One of them sagged on its hinges, and some of the wallboards gaped in places. Sunlight backdropped the building, catching dust whirling in the beams of light, and Cody caught a glimpse of something shiny in the barn's dusty interior. Curious, he nudged Raven forward and leaned in the saddle to peer through a crack in the doors.

His heart began to race.

"Tom, you said Dan hasn't used the barn in quite a while?"

"That's right. He used to run cows, but not anymore. His uncle worked for me years ago when I was in the cattle business. Dan's got family strung from here to Ferguson." Tom waved one hand. "Matter of fact, his cousin Lester moved in with him right around the holidays. Works for Joe's Garage. Drives the tow truck?"

Cody clenched his jaw. "Yeah. I know who he is." He swung down from the saddle and looped Raven's reins around a corral post.

"Something wrong?" Tom asked.

"I don't know yet." Cody lifted the weathered latch on the barn's double doors, not surprised that they weren't locked. The ranchers in the area didn't bother to lock their houses most of the time, much less an old abandoned barn. There would be no reason to, unless there was something of value inside...or something to hide. Cody told himself he was probably wrong. Probably jumping to yet another dead-end conclusion. He swung the barn doors open.

Inside, the building was cool, but not as cool as the chill that ran down Cody's neck as he moved around the vehicle parked in the middle of the dirt floor. A dark green Jeep Cherokee. With a bent bumper, and a smashed passenger-side front fender.

Walking around to the front of the vehicle, Cody memorized the plate number—*John-Lincoln-David-7-3-8*. An emotion somewhere between excitement and disgust hit his stomach. He rushed back outside.

"Tom, can you stay here and watch this building for me? I've got to get to a phone."

"You're welcome to use the phone at my place, but why do you want me to stay here and watch an old barn?"

Cody swung up onto Raven's back. "I think I just found our hit-and-run driver's SUV."

Tom didn't need to ask which hit-and-run. "Lord have mercy," he muttered.

"You're okay here with the horses? I hate to run off and leave you short a hand, but—"

"Go!" Tom waved him away. "If I can't handle a couple of mustangs by myself, I'd better hang up my spurs. The dogs will hold 'em till you get back."

Already, the Aussies stood watch at the open corral entrance, poised to herd the two mustangs into whatever direction their master indicated.

"Thanks, buddy." Cody gave Raven his head and raced back across the sagebrush toward Tom's ranch.

NIKKI STOOD at the edge of the crowd on Main Street, Jana beside her. Spotting Frank and Sylvia nearby with Dustin and Brittany, she waved the boy over.

"Where's Cody?" Dustin asked, as the cowboys guided the herd along.

"He must be riding drag," Nikki said. Her eyes scanned the colorful sea of horses and the half-dozen cowboy hats bobbing along. But she couldn't see Cody anywhere, and by the time the herd had passed by and made their way out of town toward the fair-grounds, she realized he wasn't in the group. And neither was Tom.

"That's odd." Nikki stood, arms akimbo, scanning the area, looking back the way the horses had come. "Tom Lockhart wasn't with the herd, either."

Dustin smirked. "Maybe Raven bucked Cody off, and Tom had to take him to the hospital."

"Let's hope not," Nikki said lightly. But she was worried. She'd seen Cody drive away this morning with the truck and horse trailer, Raven stowed inside. She couldn't imagine any reason why he would change his mind about riding with the herd at the last minute. And even if he had, where was Tom?

"Maybe he got called in on duty," Jana suggested.

"No. Everyone knew he was riding today, and the shifts were covered." Nikki frowned. "What on earth could have happened?"

"I wouldn't worry," Jana said. "If it were anything serious, he'd get in touch with you. You've got your cell phone, don't you?"

"Back in the car." Nikki's stomach churned. "I guess we can head for the fairgrounds and I'll call him on the way."

"Can I ride with you?" Dustin asked.

Nikki nodded. "Sure, if it's all right with Frank and Sylvia."

"I'll go ask." He vaulted away and returned moments later. "It's fine. They'll meet us there."

"Okay, then, let's go." She smiled at Dustin as he walked with her and Jana to the car. But she couldn't stop worrying about Cody.

See, you do still love him.

Of course she still loved him. And their session with Regina had gone well the other day. Cody had agreed to look for new ways to work through his grief. And Nikki had promised to work harder on seeing things from Cody's perspective as an officer of the law.

Regina had reminded her that it was his duty to track down the hit-and-run driver, and that it had become all the more important because this was personal. That it wasn't so much a need for vengeance as it was a need for closure, for law and order to take their proper steps.

But what if Anna's killer was never found?

What then?

IN THE CLUTTERED kitchen of Tom's ranch, Cody spotted a battered telephone directory, thumbed it open and grabbed the handset of the old-fashioned wall phone. He dialed Dan Godfrey's number. *Be home.*

"Hello?"

"Dan. Hey, it's Cody Somers. There's a Jeep Cherokee parked in your barn." He described it. "Do you know who it belongs to?"

"No." Dan sounded genuinely surprised. "What are you doing on my place?"

"I was chasing a couple of horses. Listen, I'm

going to need you to come out to the barn. We're going to have to hook and tow that Cherokee, and I want it official that I have your consent to do that."

"I'll be there." Dan hung up.

Cody dialed the county dispatcher and identified himself. "I'm off duty." He gave his badge number. "I need you to run a vehicle registration for me." He rattled off the plate number of the SUV, then stood, waiting for what seemed an eternity before the dispatcher's voice came back over the line.

"Your plate—John-Lincoln-David-7 3-8—comes back clear on a green 1997 Jeep Cherokee. Registered owner is a Lester Dwayne Godfrey, D-O-B 10-15-69, address 2417 County Road 311, Ferguson, Colorado. Do you need the driving record?"

"Yes."

"Godfrey is revoked. D-L address is the same as registration."

Cody's hands began to shake. "For what?"

"Stand by."

He waited. "Three DUIs in seven years. The last was 9-21-01."

Cody squeezed the phone until his knuckles were white. He gave the location of Dan Godfrey's barn to the dispatcher. "Send a deputy out. I think I've found their hit-and-run vehicle."

TIME PASSED in a blur. Tom stayed behind, reassuring Cody he would take Raven back to the ranch, leaving Cody free to go to town with the sheriff's deputies.

Cody indicated the Jeep Cherokee. "You know this guy?" he asked Deputy Stillwell.

"Lester Godfrey? Matter of fact, I do. But I wasn't aware he was living in this area. Me and my partner had a run-in with him a few years back. He carjacked a little girl over in Ferguson while he was drunk." Stillwell held Cody's gaze, his eyes full of compassion. "Let's go pick him up right now and have a chat with him," he said.

"Oh, you're damned right I'm going to have a chat with him." Cody clenched his fists at his sides.

"We're gonna take care of this," Stillwell said. "But you need to be rational, buddy. We want this done right. Okay?"

Cody took a breath. "Yeah, okay." He slid into the passenger seat of the deputy's patrol car, and they headed for the garage where Lester worked. "Tell me one thing," Cody said. "If this asshole's a repeat offender, and his license is revoked, how the hell did he get a job driving a tow truck?"

"I imagine employers don't always check references and driving records, especially if they have a hard time keeping somebody on the job." Stillwell shook his head. "It sucks."

"Yeah." Cody clenched his teeth, furious. He couldn't change the system, but he could work his end of it to the best of his ability. Putting the bad guys back behind bars gave him a rush of satisfaction like no other.

Stillwell parked in front of Joe's Garage and got out. Cody walked ahead of him to the bay where Lester stood bent over an engine, a wrench in his hand. He turned, and the expression in his eyes said it all when he looked at Cody.

"Officer Somers." He pasted on a smile. "What can I do for you?"

Cody wanted to knock the smile off his face. With effort, he contained himself. "Lester, we found your Jeep Cherokee in your cousin's barn. It's got some damage on it. Can you tell us how that happened?"

"Well," Lester stalled, wiping his hands on a greasy rag, "I lent it to Dan and he hit a deer."

"Cut the shit, Lester," Cody snapped. "Why did you hide it, then? Why didn't you bring it in here to the garage and fix it?"

Stillwell said nothing. He only stared at Lester.

Lester avoided their gazes, his eyes flitting nervously to the door. "I think I need an attorney."

Cody reached over and grabbed the handcuffs from Stillwell's belt. Slapping the cuffs on Lester, he took pleasure in tightening the steel around the man's wrists. "You have the right to remain silent...." He rattled off the Miranda. "You're going to jail for hit-and-run, Lester." He leaned in closer. "And I wish to God I could hang you for murder. You son of a bitch."

CHAPTER FOURTEEN

NIKKI GOT Cody's voice mail and left him a message.

"Maybe he did get called to the station," Jana suggested. "Why don't you swing by?"

"Yeah, I will." But Cody's squad car wasn't in the parking lot when they drove past, and neither was his truck. "That's odd," Nikki said.

"He's probably at the fairgrounds," Dustin said.

"I suppose Raven could've thrown a shoe or something." Nikki shrugged. "That's the only thing I can think of that would stop Cody from riding today." But it still didn't explain where Tom was.

The parking lot at the fairgrounds was crowded, and Nikki barely managed to find a space. All around the lot, vendors had set up souvenir and food booths. The holding pens for the mustangs were just outside the arena. Nikki walked with Dustin and Jana to the grandstand and found a place to sit and watch the activities.

"When will the horses get here?" Dustin asked.

"Soon," Nikki said.

"You're not anxious, are you?" Jana asked with a

smile. She gave Dustin a nudge with her elbow. "I thought you didn't like cowboy stuff."

"I never said that. I only said I'm *not* a cowboy."

"Oh, I see." Jana pressed her lips together and nodded.

"Hey, I like horses," Dustin said. Then he grinned. "Anybody hungry? Those caramel apples at the snack booth sure looked good, and I'm buying."

"Is that right?" Nikki stared at him, surprised by his generosity. "Well, in that case, I'd love one. How about I spring for soft drinks?"

"Cool."

She reached for her fanny pack, only to realize all she'd grabbed was her cell phone. "Crud. I left my fanny pack in the car. Do you want to get it on your way out, Dustin? There's a twenty in there you can use to buy pop."

"You mean you trust me not to skip town?"

"You wouldn't get very far on twenty bucks," Nikki said. She waved him away. "Go on, you rotten kid."

Dustin sprinted down the bleacher steps.

"He might be ornery, but he's a cutie," Jana said. "I can see why Cody's so attached to him."

"Yeah," Nikki mused. "I hate to admit it, but I'm starting to get attached, too." She noticed the look Jana gave her. "Don't go there." Nikki wagged her finger. "That still doesn't mean I want to adopt him. I'm a teacher, not a mom."

"Hey, I didn't say anything." Jana held up her hands in surrender, then pointed. "Isn't that Tom?"

"Where?" Nikki turned to look, scanning the area. Several men in cowboy hats were clustered around the holding pen near the announcer's booth where Tom would speak. "Yes, it is. But I don't see Cody." Worry churned her stomach.

"That is sort of odd," Jana said. "I thought for sure he'd show up by now. Maybe you should go talk to Tom."

But no sooner were the words out of her mouth when Tom climbed the stairs to the announcer's booth. "Okay, folks, looks like the horses will be here shortly. In the meantime, I invite you to come to the information booth to chat. I'll be there answering questions and passing out brochures..." His speech went on.

"Guess I'll have to catch him down at the booth," Nikki said.

"I'll wait here for Dustin," Jana replied.

"Thanks. I'll be right back."

DUSTIN OPENED the driver's door of Nikki's Saturn and leaned inside. He spotted the fanny pack where it had slid onto the floor near the gearshift. As he reached for it, he noticed a sheet of paper tucked into the car's console between the passenger seats. His name jumped out at him from the rows of neatly formed handwriting on the paper's surface. Curious, he reached over and picked it up.

"Pros and cons?" he mumbled, frowning. He sank sideways onto the edge of the seat, legs sticking out the open door, and smoothed the paper out on his lap.

Cody's answer to our marital problems...adopting a child, specifically Dustin Holbrook...

What the hell?

He read on. *Pro—Cody feels this will help solve our marital differences. Con—Dustin could get hurt by such a hasty decision.*

Stunned, Dustin stared at the sheet of paper, then read it again. Nikki and Cody had thought about adopting him? His heart raced. Then the words sank in. Nikki thought it was a bad idea. And Cody only wanted to save their marriage.

He hadn't even realized they were fighting. They acted so nice around him. When he'd helped fix up the bunkhouse, Cody had told him they were going to use it as a guest cabin. Come to think of it, Cody never seemed to really be in the house all that much. He was mostly either outside or at the bunkhouse. Was he living there? Were he and Nikki getting a divorce?

Dustin pushed the sheet of paper back between the seats where he'd found it and retrieved Nikki's fanny pack. How could she and Cody lie to him like that? And Cody wanted to use him. Everyone always stabbed him in the back.

The caramel apples no longer held their appeal, but Dustin stopped by the snack booth anyway. Minutes later, he carried a cardboard tray with three drinks in the holders, the apples tucked into a slot in the middle. He felt numb.

No one cared about anyone but themselves.

He was better off alone.

DEPUTY STILLWELL dropped Cody off at Tom's ranch after they'd taken Lester in for questioning. Cody had wanted to stick around the police station, but he wanted to tell Nikki what had happened more. By now she must be wondering where he was. He'd asked Tom not to say anything. Cody wanted to tell her the news himself.

Tom had brought Raven back to the ranch, unsaddled him and put the tack in Cody's pickup. The horse now waited in a round pen, and Cody loaded the gelding into the horse trailer, then reached for his cell phone. No signal. *Damn!* He drove toward town, keeping an eye on the phone until he reached a spot in the road where the mountains opened up enough to allow him to get through. He pulled over and dialed.

"Cody?" Nikki answered, her voice on edge. "Where on earth are you?"

"I'm on my way from Tom's place. Are you at the fairgrounds?"

"Yes. Is something wrong?"

"No. Just sit tight, and I'll be there in a few minutes." He wanted to tell her he loved her. "Meet me in the parking lot, okay?" He didn't want a crowd of people around when he told her Lester had been arrested. They'd find a quiet spot to talk.

"Okay." She sounded perplexed as they disconnected.

The drive to the fairgrounds seemed endless. Cody pulled into the parking lot but had to search for somewhere to put his truck and trailer. He'd already spotted Nikki nearby, leaning against her Saturn. Leaving his rig, he hurried toward her as she walked his way.

"I was worried about you," she said. "Why weren't you with the other riders?" She glanced toward the horse trailer. "Did something happen to Raven?"

"No. Listen." He took her by the shoulders, wanting to kiss her, hold her. He swept her into his arms and buried his face in her hair. "We caught him."

"What?" She pulled back and looked at him, her eyes studying his face. "The hit-and-run driver? Are you serious?"

He nodded, then explained what had happened.

"My God." Nikki gripped his arms, shock clearly visible in her face. "Lester Godfrey. I—I can't believe that."

"Neither can I."

"You're sure it was him?"

"He lawyered up as soon as I started asking questions, so I don't see any other explanation. I doubt he's covering for someone else." Cody shrugged. "His Jeep Cherokee fits the description, and Lester had no reason to hide it if there was some other explanation."

"Oh my God," Nikki repeated. She pressed her fingers against her lips, and a tear squeezed from the corner of her eye. "I didn't think you'd ever find him," she whispered.

Cody pulled her closer. "You knew I wouldn't rest until I did."

"Yes." She nodded. "And that was what frightened me so much. What would have happened if you never found him?"

"Well, I did. And it's over now." He rubbed his thumbs against her arms, caressing her soft skin. "I have to go back to the station. I want to be there when Lester is charged. But I had to tell you before you heard it someplace else."

She nodded. "I imagine word will get around fast. I need to call Amanda."

"Can you swap cars with me?" he asked. "That way you can take Raven home. Unless you were planning to stay for the festivities."

"I'll have to see what Jana wants to do, but I'm definitely going home." She fished her keys out of her pocket and handed them to him.

"I'll meet you at the ranch as soon as I can," Cody said. "We need to talk."

"Yes. Of course."

He leaned down and kissed her. She felt good in his arms.

Lester's arrest would surely take them another step toward closure.

By the time Nikki returned to the grandstand, Frank, Sylvia and Brittany were sitting next to Dustin and Jana.

"Everything okay?" Jana asked.

"Yes, but I'm afraid I'm going to have to leave." She smiled at the Thompsons. "It was good seeing you, and nice meeting you, Brittany. Dustin, I imagine we'll see you out at the ranch tomorrow?"

"Yeah, whatever," he said, his attention on the holding pen where the mustangs were being herded inside.

Nikki frowned, surprised by his abrupt change of mood. She offered to drop Jana at home, which her friend took her up on.

"Where's your car?" Jana asked as they crossed the parking lot.

"Cody took it. I've got to run his horse home for him."

"You want to tell me what's going on?"

Nikki met her gaze. "Cody caught the hit-and-run driver. He arrested him."

"You're kidding." Jana stopped dead in her tracks, eyes wide. She laid her hand on Nikki's arm. "Who is it? Can you say?"

"Lester Godfrey, the mechanic down at Joe's Garage."

"Oh my God!" Jana clutched one hand to her heart. "I just saw him the other day, over at Admiral

Parker's." Her mouth gaped as she resumed walking. "I can't believe it!"

"I know." Nikki shook her head. "I don't know who I expected the driver to be. Some monster or something."

"Wow. Goes to show you never really know your neighbors, do you?"

"Lester hasn't really lived in Deer Creek long enough to get to know him. Cody said he was from Ferguson."

"Did he tell you all the details?"

"Just about the arrest. He'll know more after they question Lester."

They reached the truck and Jana climbed inside. Nikki walked back to check on Raven before sliding behind the wheel. She dropped Jana off at her house, then went home to wait for Cody. She tried phoning Amanda, but got her answering machine. She left a message for her to call, then hung up. The time dragged endlessly by, and she was pacing the floor by the time Cody pulled into the driveway.

She met him on the porch. "How'd it go?"

Cody sank onto the steps, looking tired yet elated. "Better than we'd hoped. Lester confessed to everything. Said it had been eating him up, especially once he started working at the garage and actually met me." He shook his head, his expression bitter. "I can't believe it was him. I've done business with Lester. Hell, I considered him a friend of sorts."

Nikki's stomach churned painfully. She didn't want to have to relive the night of the crash. But she needed to know exactly what had happened. "Tell me everything," she said.

Cody took her hand and pulled her close. "Lester is a repeat offender," he said. "He's had several DUIs."

Nikki sucked in her breath. It was in keeping with the statistics she'd learned through MADD. "I guess that shouldn't surprise me."

"The last time he was arrested it was for carjacking and kidnapping."

"Kidnapping?"

"Yeah, but there was no intent, so it didn't stick. He got drunk and took a truck from a convenience store. There was a nine-year-old girl in the passenger seat, but Lester wanted the truck, not the kid. Anyway, he plea-bargained down and got what amounted to a little jail time. More like a slap on the wrist. But his wife had had enough of him, and she kicked him out of the house."

"He's married?"

"Was," Cody said. "With four kids."

"Sweet heaven." Nikki closed her eyes.

"He left Ferguson to move in with his cousin—Dan Godfrey—when his wife kicked him out." Cody looked faraway. "He was drinking his sorrows away that night at the sports bar. After a twelve-pack at home. He was so damned drunk, he didn't even realize he'd hit Amanda or Caitlin." Cody's voice cracked and he fisted his hand. "He thought he'd hit a deer and a parked car. He went home and passed out on the couch, and when he came to the next day he heard on the news about the crash, and he knew. The son of a bitch knew he'd killed our baby. Knew he'd hurt two innocent women, and instead of facing what he'd done, he hid his SUV in Dan's barn like the coward that he is."

Nikki began to cry. "How could he?" she asked. "How could anyone do such a thing?"

"It happens every day." Cody hugged her protectively against him, rubbing his hand up and down her arm.

His embrace felt warm and strong, and Nikki wanted to lose herself in it. "Why didn't Dan Godfrey turn him in?" she asked. "Can't he get in trouble for that?"

"He didn't know," Cody said. "He was in New Mexico at the time of the wreck, and when he got back and asked Lester where his SUV was, Lester said his ex-wife took it." Cody cursed again and shook his head. "He's been driving Dan's car on a revoked license. I see this crap all the time, yet it never ceases to amaze me." He swallowed. "I'd like to string Lester up with my own two hands."

"We need to fight for stronger laws," Nikki said, slipping her arms around Cody's waist. She leaned her head against his shoulder. "That's one of the things I admire most about MADD." She sniffed and wiped her cheek with the flat of one hand. "Cody, I'm so sorry. I knew it was your job, but I just couldn't…" She leaned back against the steps. "When Anna died, I didn't want to fight anyone. I only wanted to crawl into a dark hole and stay there."

"I know," Cody said. "I felt like that, too, for a while. But I was too furious to let it go—that some bastard could come along and destroy everything for all of us, just like that." He snapped his fingers. "And then be able to drive away and disappear."

"They say the drunks hardly ever get injured," Nikki said. "They hurt people—kill people—and nine times out of ten, walk away from the crash with nothing more than a few scratches. It isn't fair."

"No, it isn't. What's even worse is that he could drive away with no remorse. With no damned knowledge of what he'd even done." He clenched his jaw. "I can't fathom that, and I can't tolerate it."

Nikki squeezed his hand. "I only wish you would've opened up to me instead of shutting me out."

"I'm sorry." He kissed the top of her head. "I couldn't deal with my feelings, much less know how to deal with yours." His eyes grew moist. "Anna was our last chance for a child of our own. That ate me up inside."

"I understand," Nikki said. She laughed without humor. "You were right. I changed my hair and my clothes thinking it would make me feel better. Like someone new. And when you stopped sleeping in our bed, I started munching and I couldn't seem to stop." She patted her thigh. "Now look at me."

"Oh, I am," Cody said, turning to face her. "And I like what I see." He ran his hand along her hip. "Your curves are sexy." He closed his mouth over hers, and her eyelids fluttered shut.

She kissed him, savoring the sweet warmth of his lips, his tongue. Then she pulled away. "I feel more vindicated than I imagined I would, with you finding Lester. We've still got to find a way past everything else." She looked him in the eye. "I'm not ready to adopt a child, and I might never be. Can you live with that?" Dustin's welfare couldn't be her business. She couldn't try to replace one child with another.

"I guess I'll have to," Cody said.

"No." Nikki stood. "That's not what I asked. Not will you live with it, but *can* you live with it? Willingly, happily? Can you face knowing you'll never be a father, that you'll never have a son or daughter to play ball with or take horseback riding?"

Under different circumstances, maybe she would've been willing to consider adopting him. But until she sorted herself out, Nikki could never bring herself to be a mother to anyone.

He took his time in answering her question, sitting with his fingers laced, elbows resting on his knees. "I love you," he finally said. "And I want you back, whatever that takes. I want things to be the way they used to be."

"I don't think that's possible," Nikki said. How could she explain? "I don't feel like my old self, Cody. I look in the mirror, and I see a stranger. And it has nothing to do with my clothes or my hair." Her lip trembled, and she reached down and took his hand, tugging him to his feet. "Please help me. Please help me find myself again."

He wrapped his arms around her. "I don't know exactly what you want me to do," he said, "but I'm here for you." He held her, then brushed the hair away from her forehead. "I have to be honest with you, though. I can't turn my back on Dustin, Nikki. He's come to mean too much to me for me to do that."

Suddenly Nikki felt cold, in spite of the summer sun. "Are you giving me an ultimatum? Either I accept Dustin or our marriage is over?"

"I didn't say that." He frowned. "Nikki, I want us to be together. But I can't move back in with you if I'm not completely honest about everything I'm feeling."

"Who said anything about you moving back in?" she asked, her heart breaking. Lord, she wanted nothing more than for him to do just that. "Why can't I be enough?" she asked. "Why can't we be enough?" She smacked her palm against her forehead. "Listen to me—I sound like a selfish brat." She bit her lip. "I care about Dustin, too. But I can't be his mother."

"So now you're giving me the ultimatum."

"No." Damn it, she didn't want to do that! "I don't know what I'm doing." All the energy drained out of her. "Look, we've had quite a day. We've got a lot to think about. I wasn't able to get hold of Amanda earlier. She could be at work, but I didn't want to call her there. I need to try her again at home." She was too impatient to wait for Amanda to return her call.

Cody nodded. "Okay. We'll call it a day." His eyes looked so sad, a part of her screamed to give in to him. To tell him she'd be the mother Dustin needed. But she couldn't. Grief still lay like a hard lump in the pit of her stomach. And new doubts swirled in the back of her mind.

Maybe there'd been a reason why she couldn't have a baby. Maybe she wasn't meant to be a mother because she wouldn't be any better at it than her mother.

Confused, Nikki moved to the front door. "I'll see you later, Cody." She paused with her hand on the screen. "The MADD chapter is having a special event next weekend. We're going to meet at town hall and walk down to the park to tie ribbons on the trees along the street. One to represent each of the people who've been killed in Colorado in the past year by drunk drivers. If you'd like to go with me, let me know." But she could tell by the look in his eyes that he wouldn't.

It all came back full circle. He'd cope in his way, and she'd cope in hers.

They couldn't find a middle ground. Nikki felt alone and empty as she went inside the house and headed for the phone.

CHAPTER FIFTEEN

NIKKI SAT in her classroom, the ticking of the wall clock abnormally loud in the silence. *One more week,* she told herself. One week, and her kindergarten kids would be here. And in the meantime, today was kindergarten orientation. The kids would be coming in for a few hours for a mock school day, to get them accustomed to the classroom atmosphere. Nikki had a fun agenda planned, including an art project making farm animals out of construction paper and story time. She loved reading out loud to the children. Watching their faces as she lent drama to the story using exaggerated voices and silly noises gave her such pleasure, especially if she could coax a few giggles.

"Excuse me." A woman's voice came from the open doorway, and Nikki looked up into a pair of friendly brown eyes. "Are you Mrs. Somers?"

"Yes." Nikki rose from her desk. "Welcome." She extended her hand.

The woman took it. "I'm Melinda Woods, and this is Katy." Melinda ushered a dark-haired little girl into the room, who stood shyly beside her mother, her face half buried in her mother's slacks. "We're new in town, and when we came to register for school today, they told us about the orientation."

"Ah." Nikki smiled and leaned forward. "Well I'm glad you could make it, Katy. It's nice to meet you." She held out her hand and the little girl shyly clasped it. "Oh, a firm handshake," Nikki said, giving the girl's small hand a gentle pump. "I like that." She looked at Melinda Woods. "Where are you from?"

"Los Angeles. My husband was recently transferred, which worked out well since we wanted to get Katy out of the city." She shrugged. "I was raised in a small town myself, and I'd like her to have that experience. Less crime and all that."

Not always. But Nikki managed to smile. "Deer Creek is a great place to raise kids." She looked down at Katy again. "I think you'll like it here, Katy. You'll make lots of nice friends."

"I'm getting a puppy," Katy announced, coming out of her shell with a crooked smile that immediately won Nikki's heart. The little girl had dimples and freckles and a missing tooth.

"A puppy? Wow!"

While Nikki chatted with Katy and Melinda Woods, other children and parents began to file into the classroom. And as each of them dropped their child off, Nikki witnessed the emotional goodbyes she'd seen so many times, yet which had never hit her as hard as they did now. Mothers with tears in their eyes, and a couple of fathers as well, letting their babies take that first step on their journey toward independence. They were putting their children in the hands of total strangers. That had to be tough.

At the end of the day, Nikki closed her door, then sat at her desk and looked around the empty room. Scraps of construction paper lay scattered across the rug. Books and educational toys were stacked haphazardly on their shelves. She loved the disorder, the clutter, the happy atmosphere. The children's presence seemed to linger in the room.

Sudden emotion overwhelmed her, and Nikki laid her head on the desk. The surface felt cool against her forehead, and she blinked her eyes. *You can't cry in here, for pity's sake!* But she couldn't stop. She never would have the opportunity to experience what the mothers today had. She'd been trying all along to convince herself that her students were all she needed. But they weren't. She wanted to raise a child. To watch that child's first steps, hear her first words, and be the one crying when she went off to school. She wanted to watch her child grow and change and learn.

Being a teacher wasn't nearly enough. She wanted to be a mother.

CODY RODE DANCER across the hillside past the bunkhouse. He'd done little else but think of Nikki. And Dustin. Something wasn't right with the kid, but try as he might, Cody couldn't get him to talk about what was bothering him.

Hoofbeats behind him drew Cody's attention. He turned in the saddle and saw Nikki riding up on Topaz. He started to smile, thrilled that she'd decided to join him on his ride, but then he saw that her face was pinched with worry. He pulled Dancer to a halt. "What's wrong?"

"It's Dustin. He's run away."

"What?"

"Sylvia just called, frantic. She went to wake him up and he wasn't in his bed. He'd left a note on his pillow."

"What did it say?"

"To not worry about him. That he'd decided to hit the road."

Cody mumbled an expletive. "That's it?"

"Yep. Sylvia's already called the police, but she wanted me to tell you, too. She's hoping since the two of you are pretty close…"

"I'm on it." He turned Dancer around and headed at a gallop back toward the barn.

Nikki caught up. "You go," she said, swinging out of the saddle to take Cody's reins. "I'll take care of Dancer."

"Thanks." He rushed toward his squad car, digging his keys out of his pocket.

"Call me if you hear anything!" Nikki shouted after him.

"I will." Cody got in the car and, lights flashing, headed toward town. He'd stop by the station and see who had taken the call, then go over to Frank's and Sylvia's. But blocks from the station, he slowed his car. There was Dustin, wearing a backpack, trudging down the sidewalk—with Admiral Parker and Thor. Pulling over, Cody flicked off his lights and got out of the car.

"Officer Somers." Parker greeted him with a wave. "Good to see you again."

"Likewise."

Thor met him with a growl.

"At ease," Parker commanded.

Cody stared Dustin down. "You want to tell me what's going on?"

Dustin's face reddened. "Guess you heard."

"That's right." He folded his arms, resisting the urge to plant his feet. These days, Dustin brought out the father in him more than the cop.

"Don't be too hard on the boy," Parker said. "He's already told me what happened, and we've had a good, long talk, haven't we, son?"

Dustin's posture remained stiff, his attitude surly. "Yeah."

"Great," Cody said. "Maybe you'd care to en-lighten me?" He motioned with his hand for Dustin to follow him.

The boy shrugged, his posture indicating he didn't give a damn. With a mumbled "See you later" to

Parker, he followed Cody to the squad car. Cody radioed dispatch to let them know he'd found Dustin, safe, and that he'd be taking him home. Then he faced the boy, waiting.

"What do you want to know?" Dustin said, staring Cody down.

"All of it. Start from the beginning."

The kid was silent, and Cody wondered if he was going to refuse to answer. "I saw Nikki's list," he finally said.

"Her list?" It took a minute for the words to register. "Her pros and cons list?"

Dustin nodded. "She had it in the car the day we went to the fairgrounds."

Cody briefly closed his eyes and let his head fall back against the seat. "I see. So, you obviously saw what she'd written, about me wanting to adopt you."

"Yeah."

"And that was such a horrible idea you ran away?"

Dustin looked away. "I'm just tired, you know?" He took a deep breath. "People put on acts and they lie, and I'm never going to find a home, so why bother?"

"Whoa, whoa, wait a minute. Back up." The thought that this bright, fun-loving, eleven-year-old boy could already be weary of life hit Cody like a sucker punch. "What lies are we talking about here? Nobody lied to you."

"Yes, you did. You and Nikki are obviously getting a divorce."

"No, we're not." Cody shook his head. "We never told you that."

"That's right. You never even told me you two were fighting. You just acted like a happy family. But you were having marriage problems."

Cody pressed his lips together. "I don't know what to say. Yes, Nikki and I have had some problems ever since our baby died."

"She told me about the baby."

"She did?"

"Uh-huh."

"Well, then I guess maybe you can understand that our lives haven't been the same since that happened. I mean, imagine what it would be like if something happened to someone you care about. It messes you up." He gestured toward his temple. "Makes your head feel like it's not on straight. But we're not getting a divorce." At least, he hoped they weren't. Nikki's talk of ultimatums the other day worried him. "And we didn't see any reason to involve you in our troubles."

"Because I'm a kid."

"Well, yeah. Kids ought to be happy and have fun."

"Get real." Dustin looked at him as though he'd come from another planet. "What century are you living in? I thought cops knew about the stuff that goes on out there."

He did. And that was the problem. He wanted things in his own life, his own world, to be different.

To not be like what he saw at work, what he read in the papers and heard on the news. He wanted to be happy, with Nikki and with Dustin. He wanted this boy to be happy and enjoy life.

"Where did you plan on going?"

"I don't know. Denver or someplace. I thought I'd hitch a ride and see what happened."

"Oh, now there's a great idea with all the nuts running around in the world. Assuming you'd gotten there safely, what did you plan to do next?"

Again, the boy lifted a shoulder. "I'd hook up with some homies or something."

Cody shook his head. "Dustin, if you think you've gotten in a little hot water hanging out with Chad and Ryan, just stop and think a minute about the things you see on the news. The things you hear at school." He paused. "Do you really believe living on the streets of Denver, hooking up with a gang, is a good plan?"

Dustin wrinkled his nose. "There are worse ideas."

"Are Frank and Sylvia really so terrible?"

"No."

"Okay. Then be grateful you've got a nice home with people who care about you." Cody's own words left a heavy weight in the pit of his stomach.

Dustin threw his cap on the seat. "Does this mean I'm going to get more community service?" He met Cody's gaze. "I suppose I'll have to muck your barn, wax your car, shine your shoes…"

Like the proverbial lightbulb going on, Cody understood. Dustin *wanted* more chores. He wanted to spend time at the ranch.

But Nikki's words rang in his mind. *I can't be his mother.* Maybe not, but surely she could be his friend.

He smiled. "I guess that will be up to Frank and Sylvia. But honestly, I can always use the help."

Dustin rolled his eyes. "I suppose I'll have to wear boots and gloves." When they'd found out it was a safety issue, Frank and Sylvia had bought him a pair of cowboy boots of his own to ride in. "The next thing you know, I'll be wearing a cowboy hat."

"Hey. Cowboy hats are cool." Cody tipped the brim of his own black Resistol. "So, are you ready to go home?"

"I suppose."

Cody pulled away from the curb, waving to Admiral Parker. The old man gave a sharp salute as he walked Thor back and forth along the sidewalk, putting the dog through his paces. "By the way, how did you end up running into the admiral?"

Dustin cast a glance back over his shoulder at Parker. "He's pretty sharp for an old guy. He saw me when I was walking to the convenience store. I was going to spend the last of my money on beef jerky and stuff for the trip. He asked me why I had my backpack, and ended up figuring out that I was running away. He can trick you with questions," he added. "He ought to be a cop."

Cody laughed. "I'll take that as a compliment. So, what did Parker say to you?"

"Pretty much what you did. That my idea was dumb." Dustin narrowed his eyes. "You know, he's not such a bad guy. He's just grumpy because of what happened with his daughter."

"Oh?"

"Yeah. He said he got a divorce when she was four years old. He told me fathers didn't have rights back then, and her mother took her and moved away. He hardly ever got to see her, and she hasn't come to visit him in years. That's why he doesn't like having kids around. He told me it reminds him of what he's missed."

"I see," Cody said quietly. Why was it that people who didn't have kids longed for them, and those who had them often took them for granted?

"I told you everyone gets divorced."

"Not everyone."

"Then you and Nikki really aren't?"

"Not if I can help it." Cody pulled up in the Thompsons' driveway. "Ready to face the firing squad?" He grinned at Dustin.

"If I must." He got out of the car, then paused. "Hey, Cody. Thanks."

Cody smiled. "You're welcome."

NIKKI UNSADDLED Dancer and Topaz and turned them out in the pasture before returning to the house to wait anxiously by the phone. Still, it startled her when it rang. "Hello?"

"I found him. He's safe." Cody's words brought a rush of relief.

"Thank God. Where was he? What happened?"

"I'll tell you when I get home. I'll be there in a few minutes." He hung up.

Nikki stared at the phone. It wasn't like Cody to be so abrupt. He arrived a short while later and didn't bother to knock. He didn't mince words, either.

"How could you leave your list of pros and cons where Dustin would see it?"

Her mind went blank for a moment. "What? I didn't..." Then she realized what must have happened. She'd left the list in her car, and she'd sent Dustin to retrieve her fanny pack. "Oh, Lord." Nikki squeezed her eyes shut and pressed her fingertips against her forehead. "He saw the list?"

"Yep."

"That's why he was acting so strangely." She stared at Cody, racked by guilt, knowing how her blunt statements about adopting Dustin must have looked from a child's viewpoint. "Is that what made him run away?"

"Let's just say it didn't help." Cody slumped onto the couch. "Do you know what that boy told me—a kid who's only eleven years old?" He didn't wait for her to answer. "He told me that he's tired. Tired of people lying to him. He's sick of everyone putting on acts, and he believes no one wants him, that no one will ever want him, and that you and I are getting a divorce and lied by omission."

Nikki sank onto the ottoman, stunned. "Oh, no," she whispered. "Cody, I feel so awful. Did you tell him why we'd written the lists?"

"I tried to explain. I'm not sure he really understood." His eyes darkened. "I know you told me you can't be his mother. But he sure could use all the friends he can get right now."

"I care," Nikki said. She scowled at him.

"Then I hope you'll let him know that."

"I'm not that coldhearted," she said. "Of course I'll talk to him."

"Good." He stood. "I've got to go."

"I'm sure Frank and Sylvia need some time with him today, but I'll see if Dustin can come over tomorrow afternoon."

Cody paused in the doorway. "I appreciate it." Then he walked out without a backward glance.

Nikki stood in the living room for a long while, feeling as if she'd kicked a puppy. She hurried to the phone and dialed the Thompsons' number.

NIKKI DROVE to the town hall the next morning for the MADD ribbon tribute. Today was Cody's day off, but after the heated words they'd exchanged yesterday, she knew he wouldn't change his mind and show up. The guilt she carried for having put Dustin through something so traumatic still weighed heavily on her, and she hadn't slept well the previous night.

When she'd called Sylvia, Nikki had asked if she could pick up Dustin this afternoon after the ribbon tribute, so she could talk to him. Instead, Sylvia had offered to bring him out to the ranch herself, since she had a hectic schedule today and wasn't sure what time they might or might not be home. Nikki had spent hours last night thinking about what she wanted to say to him. She couldn't blow this. The poor kid had been hurt far too much in his young life, and knowing she'd inadvertently added to that pain had left her literally sick to her stomach.

She now turned her attention to the event at hand. Savannah Webster spoke to the group in the meeting room before the march to the park got under way.

"I'm glad to see so many of you here today," she said. "We need to do everything we can to make the public more aware of the problem of alcohol-impaired driving. I'm hoping that with this ribbon ceremony, we can give people a vivid picture of exactly how many loved ones were lost this past year. I'd like to make the ribbon tribute an annual event." Everyone murmured agreement. "And I pray that the day might come when there are no ribbons on those trees."

Everyone in the room burst into applause, then gathered their belongings and headed outside. A lot of people had made placards to carry. Like Savannah,

Nikki was pleased to see the large turnout, spotting many new faces in the crowd. Some of the townspeople had come to take part in the event purely out of curiosity, but that was good. Curiosity sparked interest and would hopefully draw more members to join MADD's cause.

Still, she wished Cody were there. Nikki walked down the street with the group, carrying a placard of her own. They headed for the park, and she smiled as Jana appeared on the sidewalk and dropped into step with them. "Hi, stranger. You made it."

"I didn't think I was going to be able to, until the last minute."

"Shorthanded at the bookstore?"

"Aren't I always?" Jana grinned. "I'm not about to complain about extra customers, but one of these days I'm going to have something that resembles a social life."

"That's exactly what you need," Nikki said. "A good-looking man to brighten your days. And maybe your nights." She winked.

"Speaking of which," Jana said. She nodded toward a nearby intersection, and Nikki looked over and saw Cody's truck pulling around the corner.

Her heart picked up speed. "Can you take this?" she asked Jana, indicating the placard.

"You bet." Jana gave her a smile and took the sign.

Nikki stepped away from the crowd and stood on the sidewalk, waiting. Cody parked the Chevy and got out. He wore his best hat—a white Stetson—and a black western shirt and jeans.

"Hi."

"You're here."

"Yeah. I, uh, decided it was something good to do. In memory of Anna, and for everyone else who's ever been a victim of someone like Lester Godfrey."

Nikki felt a tightness in her throat. "Thank you," she said.

"I'm sorry I was so hard on you last night."

"You had every reason to be. I'm sorry I hurt Dustin."

"I'm sure he realizes that." Cody reached out and took her hand. "I want us to do things together again, starting now. And I want to be with you, no matter what that takes." He folded her fingers over the crook of his elbow. "Can we talk about it later?"

She blinked back moisture in her eyes, then smiled. "You'd better believe it." She laid her head against his shoulder, before hurrying with him to catch up with the group.

Everyone gathered around the row of aspen trees that lined the edge of the park. Savannah spoke to the crowd again, and then each person stepped forward and tied their ribbon on a branch of one of the trees. Many of the people were crying, and Nikki felt her heart twist painfully. She reached up to tie her red ribbon and, as she did, Cody laid his hand on her arm.

"Wait," he said. He took hold of one end of the ribbon. Together, they tied it on the tree, then Nikki stepped back and stared. The leaves whispered in the breeze, making a musical sound unique to the quaking aspen.

"Hello there." The soft voice behind her drew her attention. She turned to see Evelyn Kramer.

"Evelyn. Hello." Nikki smiled. "I didn't even spot you in the crowd."

Evelyn smiled back. "We did have quite a nice turnout, didn't we?"

Nikki introduced Cody to the woman.

"I'm very sorry about what happened to your daughter," Cody said. "I hope her recovery gets easier."

"Thank you," Evelyn said. "As a matter of fact, that's why I came over here to talk to you. I heard about the arrest of the hit-and-run driver. I wanted to thank you for what you did, Officer Somers. From what I've gathered, you were relentless in your pursuit of the investigation, and I can't tell you how much that means to me…to Caitlin and our entire family."

"I'm just glad to see that scumbag behind bars."

"Yes," Evelyn said. "But it's a crime Lester Godfrey can't be charged with murdering your baby. I'm so sorry for your loss."

"You and me both, ma'am."

"Well, I won't keep you," Evelyn said. "Please take care of yourselves."

"You do the same," Cody replied.

"Please tell Caitlin she's in our prayers," Nikki said. "I'll come by and see her sometime."

"Thank you."

Nikki walked with Cody and the others back toward the town hall. They stopped when they reached his pickup. "Your car is parked over by the station?"

She nodded. "Want to meet me back at the ranch?"

"No. I want you to come with me."

She frowned. "But then we'll just have to come back later for my car."

"That's all right. We're not going far." He indicated the pickup and, puzzled, Nikki moved toward it.

As Cody opened the door for her, her gaze fell on the bench seat. With a gasp, she brought both hands up to cover her mouth.

In the middle of the seat lay a memorial wreath, made of pink and white silk rosebuds woven around a white cross. On the cross were the words *Never forget.*

Nikki let out a sob and whirled around. "Oh, Cody."

He folded her into his arms and kissed the top of her head. "You were right," he said lovingly, "and I'm sorry I ever thought otherwise. I want people to remember Anna. Maybe it will keep someone else from losing their child."

Nikki wrapped her arms around his neck and held on tight. "I love you," she whispered. She slid onto the seat, carefully lifting the wreath onto her lap.

Cody drove from town down the two-lane highway to the crash site. Nikki's heart picked up a pace.

She hadn't been to this spot in months. She'd come here only once, after the wreck, and had become sick to her stomach.

Cody pulled onto the shoulder—in the same spot where Amanda had parked that night when she'd meant to help Caitlin. Nikki began to tremble inside. She closed her eyes and took a deep breath.

"Are you all right?" Cody asked. "I can do this if you'd rather not."

"No way," she said. She reached over and squeezed his hand, then got out of the pickup.

From his toolbox in the pickup bed, Cody got a hammer. The base of the white cross had a point on it that would stick into the ground. He walked to the edge of the road and stood for a moment, looking down into the ravine. Nikki stood next to him, picturing Amanda's Chevy Blazer lying at the bottom of it. Crushed. Amanda trapped inside, already losing the baby even before the EMTs could arrive.

Nikki shook her head. Amanda was happy—with Ian. Nikki envisioned Amanda's stomach, rounded with child once more. And this time, everything would be okay. She was going to be an aunt, and the thought thrilled her.

"We got something in the mail today," Nikki said. Cody looked at her, puzzled. She slipped her arm around his waist, holding onto the wreath with her free hand. "Amanda sent us a wedding invitation. She and Ian have set a date near the end of September."

Cody smiled. "I'm happy for them. Really." He held her beside him, and they said nothing for a long while. "I want to move back into the house, Nikki," he said. He brushed a gentle kiss across her lips. "I can't live without you. It's killing me."

Nikki embraced him, holding the wreath behind him. It was almost a symbol. They were putting Anna's death behind them, finally. Moving on. Letting go of her little girl didn't come without sorrow. But she would always know that her baby was in God's hands…a little angel.

"I can't live without you, either," she said. "I don't want to. Maybe we can't go back to the way things used to be. But we can move forward." Gently, she extracted herself from his arms. "Come on. Let's get this done—for Anna."

He nodded. Taking the hammer, he drove the cross into the ground between the ravine and the dirt-and-gravel shoulder of the road. Putting it in clear view of passersby, where wildflowers bloomed. Nikki touched the silk rosebuds. "Let's go visit her grave," she said.

Cody nodded.

Holding hands, they walked back to the truck.

CHAPTER SIXTEEN

"ARE YOU SURE you don't want me to wait here with you until Nikki or Cody gets home?" Sylvia looked at her watch. "We're way too early." They'd dropped off Brittany and a couple of friends at the movie theatre, then grabbed a burger at a fast-food restaurant.

"Naw." Dustin shook his head. "I know what I'm supposed to do. I don't need somebody watching over my shoulder."

"All right." Sylvia gave him a smile. "I'm proud of you, you know."

He felt his face warm. "What for? It's just a bunch of dirty horse stalls. Anyone can shovel manure."

She laughed. "Yes, and anyone can dish it out, too." Her gaze skimmed his newly cut hair and Levi's. "You look nice, Dustin."

"Whatever." He straightened his cap. He actually liked the way it fit with his hair short. He got out of the van and shut the door behind him. "See ya."

Sylvia waved and pulled away. Max was in the driveway, wagging his tail and rubbing up against Dustin's legs. "Hey, boy." He rumpled the dog's fur.

"How ya doin', buddy? Look what I've got." He pulled a treat from his pocket and fed it to the shepherd, then headed for the barn.

Whistling, he opened the barn door. The horses were already out in the pasture, which made his job easier. But still, he was a little disappointed. He liked working with them, and Nikki had shown him how to catch and feed them in the evenings and lock them up for the night. They were fed again each morning, then turned out for the day.

Dustin stood on a metal tack box to reach the radio Cody kept hanging on the wall. He flipped the on switch, then cringed as country music blared through the speakers. Shaking his head, he moved the selector dial until he picked up a station he liked, then hopped down and made his way to the storeroom.

The pleasant odor of wood shavings mingled with that of the horses—a scent he'd come to appreciate—as Dustin pushed the wheelbarrow to the first stall and set to work with the rake and shovel. Cheeto and Toulouse played nearby, wrestling and climbing on a few hay bales that lined the aisle. Dustin scooped the used bedding from the stall into the wheelbarrow. The radio blared with the sound of N.E.R.D, and he moved to the beat, swinging the shovel.

Laughter from the doorway made him jump, and he whirled around to face Eric.

"Man, I thought I'd seen lame before." Eric snickered. "Look at you, weenie." He shut the door in Max's face, then stood there, puffing on a cigarette, acting tough.

"What the hell are you doing in here?" Dustin asked.

Eric didn't answer. Instead, he eyeballed Dustin's clothes. "Are those shit-kicking boots you're wearing there, hick?"

Dustin glowered. "Screw you, Vanderhurst. I'm no hick."

"Could've fooled me." Eric blew a plume of smoke into the air.

"Get out."

"Make me." Eric snickered. "I see you're still brownnosing Somers. Waxing his car. Shoveling his horseshit. What's he going to have you doing next? Wiping his ass?"

Fury shot through him, and Dustin gripped the shovel's handle, barely resisting the urge to smack Eric upside the head with it.

"I said get lost. You're the reason I'm waxing his damned squad car."

Eric snorted. "Only because you screwed up. Why didn't you run?"

"What good would that have done? He caught you, didn't he?" He smiled, proud of Cody. "You're a loser, Vanderhurst." Turning his back on Eric, Dustin slid the shovel into a pile of manure. With a smirk, he pivoted around and flung the manure in Eric's face.

Eric cursed and stumbled backward. "Oh, you're gonna pay for that, you little shit." He lunged at Dustin, and Dustin dived sideways and vaulted from the stall.

From outside the barn, Max barked. Dustin wished Vanderhurst hadn't slammed the door shut. Max could've bitten the jerk. But he knew the dog was trained only to attack on command, or when his handler was threatened. *Crap*. He'd figured maybe he could beat Eric to the door and take off running, but he'd have to stop to open it...

"You told Somers about me and Jimmy jacking that beer, didn't you?" Eric accused.

"No." But he wondered if the other boy could see it in his eyes, that he had known about the beer.

"Liar. The cops came to my house. Jimmy's, too, and now we have to go to court." Eric shoved him, and Dustin stumbled backward.

He doubled up his fists and moved to swing at Vanderhurst. But Eric dodged the blow, and punched him in the eye, then tripped him. Arms flailing, Dustin fell. His head struck the corner of the metal tack box he'd stood on earlier, and his vision swam.

Then slipped away into nothing.

NIKKI PULLED INTO the ranch. After visiting Anna's grave, Cody had dropped her off at the town hall parking lot to get her car, with the intention of following her home. But as she'd pulled out from the parking lot, Nikki passed Tom Lockhart in his battered pickup and, in her rearview mirror, she saw that he'd slowed down and stopped in the middle of the street, leaning out his window to talk to Cody.

She hadn't bothered to wait. Dustin should be arriving any time, and she was anxious to talk to him. She'd found such peace and closure in putting up Anna's wreath with Cody. She had to make things right with Dustin.

Nikki parked in front of the garage, and as she got out of the car, heard Max barking in the distance. Toulouse and Cheeto streaked past her as though the hounds of hell were on their tails and vanished in the shrubbery. What in the world? Frowning, Nikki hurried toward the barn. Eric Vanderhurst stood not far from the building, pinned against the fence. Max was in front of him, holding him in place, the hair on the back of the dog's neck raised, his teeth bared.

"Max! *Nein!*" Nikki called. *"Hier!"* But the shepherd ignored her.

"Mrs. Somers!" Eric looked petrified.

Nikki walked over and took Max by the collar, tugging with all her might in an effort to pull him away from the boy. "What's going on here?" She glared at Eric.

He gestured toward the barn. "It's Dustin. He's in the barn." His voice cracked and, to her surprise, he looked remorseful. "He fell and hit his head. There's blood everywhere. My God, I think he's dead!"

"What?" Nikki's blood turned to ice.

Smoke curled from the barn's open door. And she could hear the crackle of fire. "Dustin!"

She let go of Max's collar and ran.

CODY SMELLED SMOKE as soon as he pulled into the driveway. He frowned. This didn't smell like burning weeds or trash. When he looked toward the barn, his heart leapt. It was on fire.

"Shit!" Cody grabbed his cell phone and dialed 911, then threw the phone on the truck seat and raced toward the building. He reached the doorway and his heart nearly stopped at the sight of Nikki, inches from the blaze, trying to drag Dustin from the barn. "I've got him. Get out!" Cody lifted the boy into his arms and, coughing through the thick cloud of smoke, rushed outside in Nikki's wake.

They stopped a safe distance away, and Cody laid Dustin gently on the grass. The boy's eyes were closed, and he wasn't moving. The blood matting his hair had smeared Cody's shirt and arms as well as Nikki's blouse. "Dustin, can you hear me?" Gently, Cody smacked the kid's cheeks with his fingers. Max circled them, whining and barking.

"Oh my God!" Nikki knelt beside Dustin. Tears streaked her soot-smudged cheeks. "Is he dead?"

Cody checked for a pulse. "He's breathing. What the hell happened?"

"I don't know, I don't know." She cradled the boy

in her arms. "Dustin? Honey, wake up." Cody saw that she'd torn off the bottom half of her blouse, and now held it to the wound at the back of Dustin's head. "I sent Eric to call 911," she said. "But I don't know how fast they can get here."

"Eric?" Cody frowned. "What was he doing here?"

"I have no idea. I came home and found him in the driveway, hysterical. Dustin was lying in the barn aisle, out cold." She looked at him, eyes wide with fright. "There was blood everywhere, the hay bales on fire. I couldn't pick him up. Oh God!"

"Calm down," Cody said, laying a hand on her arm. "Head wounds always bleed a lot. It's probably not as bad as it looks." Gently, he moved the scrap of material to examine Dustin's head and found a nasty gash there. "Dustin. Can you hear me?"

Slowly, the boy's eyelids fluttered open and he groaned, touching his head.

"Lie still," Nikki soothed. "Help's on the way."

Dustin squinted up at them, dazed. "What's going on? Did I fall off my horse?" He began to cough and tried to sit up.

"You're gonna be okay, partner," Cody said. "Just stay put." *Damn it, how far away was the ambulance?* Cody debated putting the boy in his truck and driving him to the emergency room himself, but he knew that wasn't the best choice. He needed to keep Dustin alert and talking. He checked his pupils for dilation.

It seemed an eternity before they heard the sirens, drawing rapidly closer. The white-and-orange ambulance pulled in first and parked beside them. Reluctantly, Nikki relinquished Dustin's care to the EMTs. The fire truck zoomed past them and stopped in front of the barn.

"I better call Frank and Sylvia," Cody said. He reached out to touch Nikki. "Are you all right?"

She nodded, but she didn't look okay. Her face was pale beneath the streaks of dirt and soot, and with her torn and bloody blouse, she looked like an accident victim herself. She waved the paramedics away when they tried to look her over. Cody left just long enough to call the Thompsons. Then he returned to stand beside Nikki and watch the firemen go to work dousing the flames. Dustin had been loaded into the ambulance.

Cody put his arm around Nikki and pulled her against him. "You did a brave thing," he said, "going into that burning barn."

"I had no choice," Nikki said, her voice hoarse. She looked up at him, and her eyes watered. "I love him," she said. "I didn't even realize it until I saw him lying there on the floor like that." She pressed her fingers to her lips, and Cody turned and pulled her into his embrace.

"Sh-h," he soothed. "He's going to be okay."

"I want to go to the hospital with him."

"That's fine. We'll follow the ambulance." Cody

cast one final look over his shoulder at the barn. The building would be saved, but the damage was extensive. He didn't care. All that mattered was that Dustin and Nikki were safe. He would deal with Eric later. Obviously, the fire hadn't started by itself.

At that moment, Jordan pulled up in his Dodge. "Everyone okay?" he asked.

"Dustin's hurt," Cody said. "Can you oversee things here for me? Nikki and I need to go to the E.R."

"You bet." Jordan shook his head. "Man, what a mess. The horses okay?"

Cody hadn't even thought of them. He looked at Nikki.

"They are," she said. "I'm pretty sure they're back on the pasture by the pond."

"Good thing." Jordan waved them away. "Go on. I'll stay here till you get back."

"Thanks," Cody said. He helped Nikki into his truck and drove toward town. They had to wait for a long time in the emergency room before they were able to see Dustin. Frank was there with him.

"Sylvia got called in to work," he said. "She's going to have a fit when she hears what happened."

Cody walked up beside the gurney where Dustin lay propped in a reclining position. "How're you doing, partner?"

The boy managed a grin. "Good thing I only hit my head."

Nikki smiled at him, her relief obvious. She

bent over to examine his wound. "Stitches, huh? How many?"

"Eight," Dustin said proudly. "The guys at school will think I'm the bomb."

Frank chuckled. "You're a bomb, all right, kiddo. You about made me go off when Cody called."

The boy looked around him at the circle of faces. "You were all *that* worried?"

"Ye-ah," Nikki said, drawing the word out the way Dustin always did. "What happened anyway?"

"Eric was smoking, and I guess I made him drop his cigarette when I threw the manure at him," he finished. "It must've lit up the hay or something." His expression was one of genuine remorse. "I'm really sorry. I messed up again."

Nikki touched his arm. "Don't worry about it. We're just glad you're okay."

"Heck, it would take more than a knock on the head to keep me down," Dustin boasted, then groaned as he moved too quickly. He put one hand to his temple. "Ouch."

Cody gave Dustin's shoulder a squeeze. "You're going to owe me chores until you're a hundred years old to pay for that barn, you know."

"Yeah, so what's new?" He grinned.

The doctor came into the room and explained the extent of Dustin's injuries to Frank, and Cody wished he could be the one acting as Dustin's guardian. But it was Frank who nodded and listened, and took the sheet of outpatient care from Doctor Lee after signing the required forms.

Dustin swung his legs over the edge of the gurney and cautiously tested his balance. The kid was tough, and Cody was proud of him for standing up to Eric yet again. Just the thought of Vanderhurst made his temper rise. What would it take to get through to the boy?

And why didn't he feel the need to mentor Eric back onto the road of good behavior, the way he had Dustin?

Because Dustin had Cody's heart.

THE FOLLOWING DAY, Nikki carefully prepared a special dinner. Cody was on duty, but she'd gone up to the bunkhouse earlier and left a note on his door. And a little present inside. One she knew he'd be unable to resist.

He'd be home by four—plenty of time for what she had in mind before the supper she'd prepared.

She opened the oven door and checked on the roast that simmered inside, nestled in a bed of baby carrots and new potatoes. The smell of parsley, basil and onion rose on the steam as she lifted the lid of the roasting pan. It looked good and smelled even better. She and Cody would have to work out extra hard this week at the health club they'd joined last Wednesday. Or maybe they'd get enough exercise in bed this afternoon.

Nikki moved around the house, closing both doors, pulling all the curtains. She'd turned on the swamp cooler, and the temperature in the house soon dropped to a comfortable level. She'd parked her car in the garage so he would think she wasn't home. She wanted him to find the note and the gift first.

She took a shower, then put on the sexy black lingerie she'd purchased and sprayed her neck, wrists and cleavage with her new perfume. Then she lit the candles she'd placed on the dresser, peeled back the satin sheets and lay on top of them to wait.

CODY DROVE homeward, debating whether to stop at the house and talk to Nikki, or go up to the bunkhouse first for a shower. When he saw that her car was not parked in its usual spot, his anticipation turned to disappointment. Then alarm. The fact that the door was shut made sense, since the swamp cooler was running. But why were all of the curtains pulled? Nikki generally didn't close them until it got dark.

Cody got out of his squad car and moved toward the door, his hand on his gun. Where was Max? Something wasn't right. He unsnapped his holster and cautiously turned the doorknob. It wasn't locked. He pushed the door open and stepped inside, moving as he'd been trained to do. Checking each doorway before entering the next room.

A mouth-watering aroma wafted from the kitchen as he made his way down the hall to the bedroom. It wasn't like Nikki to leave something cooking on the stove and leave. Had there been a home invasion? Someone attracted by the sight of a burned building, thinking he could ransack the place? Had he hurt Nikki—or worse—?

No. Cody refused to accept the possibility of yet another tragedy.

In one smooth movement, he rounded the corner of the bedroom, and Nikki let out a startled yelp, clutching her hand to her throat. "Good grief, you scared the life out of me!" She scowled at him as he stood there, his hand still on his gun, unable to tear his gaze away from her.

She sat sprawled in the middle of a swirl of ivory-colored satin sheets that were obviously new. And heart-shaped pillows. She wore something black and slinky, and barely there. A gold chain hung between the luscious cleavage of her full breasts, a heart dangling from the end of it. He'd given her the diamond pendant for their ninth anniversary.

Her look of surprise turned to one of desire as she looked him up and down. "My, my, officer. Have you come to arrest me?"

He chuckled and moved toward the bed. "I don't know. What did you have in mind?" He slipped off his duty belt and let it fall to the floor.

"I had in mind to seduce you," she said. Then she

glared at him. "But you weren't supposed to barge in here like that. Didn't you see the note I left you? And your present?"

"What note and present?"

"At the bunkhouse."

"I didn't go to the bunkhouse." He slid onto the bed and skimmed one finger along her bare thigh. "When I saw the curtains drawn, I thought something was wrong."

"I closed them for privacy. In case we decided to wander about the house naked." Nikki leaned back on one elbow and gave him a sultry stare. "So, you came in here to rescue me, huh?"

"Yep." He pursed his lips. "Or I could arrest you. Whichever you'd like."

She laughed, then started to purr. "Oo-oo, you're so big and strong." She tugged at the buttons on his shirt. "But you're wearing *waayy* too many clothes."

"I can fix that," he said. He helped her undo the buttons, then shrugged out of his shirt. His clothes soon lay in a pile on the floor. He took Nikki into his arms. "Mmm, you smell good." Her hair felt like silk beneath his fingers as he laced his hand through it to cup her neck, bringing his mouth down to meet hers.

They kissed and touched like lovers exploring each other's bodies for the first time. Cody traced Nikki's earlobe with the tip of his tongue, nibbling, tasting her. "I don't know what secret some woman named Victoria has," he whispered. "But you're not hiding anything from me." He tugged at the wisp of silky material that covered her nipples, and the one over the vee at her thighs.

"I have no secrets from you," she said, running her tongue along the curve of his neck. She reached down to stroke him into near mania. "But I did have that present I mentioned."

"It'll have to wait." He continued to explore and nibble.

"But you need it."

He nuzzled her throat. "All I need is you."

"No, really, Cody." She sat up. She bowed her lips in a cute way that he found irresistible. "It was a box of condoms. And not just any condoms." She ran her index finger down his chest. "It was a box of Japanese condoms." She dipped her hand lower. "Did you know that Japanese manufacturers have a reputation for making the world's most sensuous condoms?"

"No." He moaned and grasped her wrist, stilling her hand. "But I'd love to explore that idea one of these days when I'm not in such dire straits." He rolled over and reached for his pants, removing his wallet. "Lucky for us, I came prepared."

She graced him with a saucy pout. "What made you think this was going to happen?"

"I wasn't sure it would," he said, readying himself for her. "But I did have hope." He lay beside her once more and picked up where he'd left off, kissing and caressing her with light, tantalizing touches.

She pulled him on top of her. "Why don't you show me exactly what you hoped for."

She slid her arms around his neck, and he lost himself in making love to her.

NIKKI DOZED comfortably in Cody's arms, and awoke to the sound of someone pounding on the door.

"Hello? Is anybody home?"

It took her fuzzy mind a moment to clear. *Dustin. At the door.*

Nikki scrambled to find her clothes. Cody lay on his stomach, his arms shoved beneath the pillow, breathing the deep, heavy sleep of a man fulfilled.

"Cody," Nikki said, poking him with one finger. She shook his shoulder. "Cody, wake up."

"Hm-mm," he mumbled. Sloth-like, he blinked, then sat up abruptly. "What's the matter?"

"Dustin is at the door," she said, whispering, even though there was no way the boy could hear her.

"He is?" Cody grinned. "How about that. Our first taste of what it's like to be interrupted by a kid. Well, sort of interrupted." He slid from the bed and began to throw on his clothes.

And the sudden humorous reality of the situation hit her. "I want that." She blurted out the words without thinking.

Cody stopped in the midst of buttoning his shirt and stared at her. "What?"

"I want to be interrupted by our kid," she said, pulling on a pair of shorts. "*That* kid."

"What?" he repeated. Dumbstruck, he stood there, staring at her. "You're serious."

"Yes. I was going to tell you tonight. That's why I'd planned this big evening, with the lingerie and the dinner…" She clapped her hand over her mouth. "Oh my God, dinner! Our roast." Frantically, she looked at the clock, then bolted for the doorway. "It's going to be ruined."

Cody caught her by the arm, chuckling. "You're in your bra," he said. He laughed harder, then couldn't stop.

Nikki laughed with him.

"You take care of whatever is about to burn up in the oven," Cody said finally, "and I'll go outside and keep Dustin busy until you're presentable." He paused long enough to kiss her. "I love you."

"I love you, too. Now go!"

A short time later, the roast rescued by an added cup of broth, Nikki put on her blouse, combed her hair, and slipped out the door, feeling ridiculously embarrassed. To her relief, Cody and Dustin were nowhere in sight. Good. She'd have time to think up some plausible reason for why she'd been in the house with the curtains drawn, ignoring Dustin's knock.

She found him at the burned-out barn with Cody

and Max. "Hi," she said. "What are you doing out and about one day after you had your head split open?"

"There you are," Cody said. "I told Dustin you were finishing up dinner preparations."

Dustin gave her a look that was much older than his years. "Yeah, he said you had the curtains pulled and the house all closed up to keep the heat out, what with the oven on and all."

"Yes," Nikki said. "That's right. I guess we didn't hear you over the noise of the swamp cooler."

The kid gave her a saucy grin. "Sure. Whatever." Then he grew serious, turning once more to look at the barn. "I had Frank bring me out so I could see if you guys needed help cleaning up this mess. I feel really bad about what happened to your barn."

"Don't worry about it," Cody said. "It was insured."

"We'll rebuild it," Nikki said. She walked up and laid her hands on Dustin's shoulders, peering at his cap. "Doesn't that hurt to wear your hat with those stitches and all? How's your head anyway?"

"It's fine." He pulled the cap off to reveal the neat row of blue, nylon stitches. "It's a pretty good gash, huh?" He grinned proudly.

Nikki shook her head. "I'll never understand men."

His grin widened. "Hear that?" he asked Cody. "She called us men."

"That she did." Cody stood with his hands in his pockets. "Which is fitting, considering she'll have two men around the house from now on."

"Two?" Dustin looked puzzled. "What do you mean?"

"Yeah, two. You, me." He gestured between them, then pursed his lips. "Oh, that's right. We didn't tell you yet. Or should I say, we didn't ask you yet."

Dustin looked suspiciously at him. "Ask me what?" His gaze darted from Cody to Nikki and back again.

"If you'd consider staying here on a regular basis."

He stared at them. Then he gave a dry, half laugh. "You mean to be your hired hand?"

"Nope." Cody rocked back on his heels. "To be a permanent member of our family."

Nikki slipped her arm around Dustin's shoulders. "Dustin, would you consider living with us? Would you let us be your mom and dad?"

His face blanched, and for a minute she thought maybe his head wound had made him dizzy. "You're not sh—screwing with me, are you?" He stared at them. "You're serious?"

"Yes," Cody said. "We're very serious, Dustin."

"But I thought…" Dustin looked at Nikki. "I saw that list you made." His mouth set in a firm line, he took a step sideways. But she didn't let go of him.

"That's another thing I wanted to do—talk to you about that list." She cupped his chin. "I'd meant to talk to you yesterday, but then the barn caught on fire, and I found you there on the floor…. You scared me to death when I saw you like that, you know." She gestured. "All that blood and the fire. I thought I was going to pass out on the spot."

"I'm sorry, Nikki." He still looked distressed.

"No," she said. "I'm the one who's sorry. I had no intention of you ever seeing that pros and cons list. And I didn't mean what I wrote on it. That Cody was looking to solve our problems by adopting you."

"Then, that's not what you're doing?" He stared at her, still wary.

"No way," she said.

"We've become attached to you," Cody said. "Though Lord knows why." He grinned and hooked Dustin's neck in the crook of his elbow. "You've grown on us, kid. And we want you to be our son."

"But I thought you were getting a divorce."

Cody gave him a mock frown. "I told you we weren't."

"I didn't believe you."

"Well, believe it."

"That's right," Nikki said. She reached over and hugged both of them. "It took seeing you in that fire to wake me up, Dustin. I was hiding from my feelings, ever since Anna died. Have you ever done that?"

"Yeah," he said.

She nodded. "Then you can relate. You know, life's too short to waste. And it's also too short not to let people know how you feel about them. I love Cody very much, and I never, ever plan to leave him. And I love you, too, Dustin. I want to be your mom."

He looked back at her, blushing. Then his eyes welled with tears. He wiped at them. "Crap, there's still smoke in the air. It's burning my eyes."

"Yeah, mine, too," Cody said, knuckling his own eye. "We've got a lot to talk about, the three of us. Why don't we go in the house and eat something? We'll call Frank and Sylvia and see if they can join us."

"Okay," Dustin said. Max trotted over and sat at his feet, tongue lolling. "It's a good thing I'm staying," Dustin said. He reached down to pat Max on the head. "Nobody else in this family seems to be able to keep this poor dog in biscuits."

Nikki laughed. "Now that has been a problem." She reached out and took Cody by the hand, and Dustin, too.

The three of them walked together toward the house.

CHAPTER SEVENTEEN

Four months later...

MORNING BROUGHT the first white Christmas Deer Creek had seen in six years. Nikki awoke to the smells of hot coffee and frying bacon. She looked over at the clock. 5 a.m. She must be dreaming. With a groan, she nuzzled into her pillow again and dozed.

"Mom?" The stage whisper came from beside her bed.

"Mm-ph."

"Mom, I made breakfast for you guys, and it's snowing! Come on, get up. We've got presents to open."

Nikki opened one eye and peered at Dustin. He stood there in a pair of striped pajamas, Max beside him. The dog wore a red Christmas bow around his neck and a Santa hat. Nikki chuckled, coming fully awake. She poked Cody in the ribs. "Wake up. You've got to see your dog. Oh, that's funny." She grinned at Dustin and sat up, wearing the cotton nightgown she'd long ago traded for her silky lingerie. But she didn't mind. Having a child of her own, who sometimes barged in unannounced, was worth the trade.

Cody sat up, peered at Max through slitted eyes and flopped back onto the pillows. "Please tell me this is a visit from the ghost of Christmases never to happen," he said. He raised his head off the pillow to stare at the dog. "My police dog. Wearing a Santa hat. *And a bow?*" He gave Dustin a mock glare. "You've ruined him."

"I don't think so. Come on, get up."

"Is that coffee I smell?" Cody yawned.

"I told you I can cook."

"My man." He rumpled Dustin's hair, then slid from bed, wearing only pajama bottoms. "Brr-rr." He shivered. "It's cold in here."

"It snowed! Can we go for a ride later?"

"It depends on how good your coffee is." Cody slipped on a sweatshirt and slippers.

Nikki put on her robe, and a short time later, they carried plates of slightly scorched scrambled eggs, bacon and toast into the living room and sat cross-legged on the floor, eating while they passed the gifts around.

"You go first," Nikki said to Dustin. Her heart swelled with happiness. It was still hard to believe they were a family. She'd been planning to have a tubal ligation while off from school on Christmas break. But as she watched Dustin tear into his gift, she was glad she'd changed her mind.

It wasn't that she cared anymore if she and Cody had a baby of their own. They had Dustin, and he was their son in every way. She might have missed his first steps and a few other things. But she'd also avoided diapers and potty training and waking up in the middle of the night. It wasn't all bad.

Still, she hesitated in taking the final step of getting a tubal ligation. Regina was right. Sterilization surgery was a serious and permanent decision, and she didn't want to make a hurried choice. She had time to make up her mind. Meanwhile, she had a wonderful husband, who loved her with all his heart, and a great son.

"Oh my God!" Dustin flung the lid of a hat box aside and extracted the black Resistol she and Cody had picked out together. "You've got to be kidding me."

"What, you don't like it?" Cody's face fell. "I thought that since you've been wearing your boots and jeans a lot more lately, and since you like riding in the snow, you might want a cowboy hat. They're pretty good for protecting your head in all kinds of weather."

Dustin quirked one corner of his mouth, considering. "I don't know. Maybe." He put the hat on, then rose and walked over to look in the mirror above the fireplace. "Hey, I look kind of cool."

Cody laughed. "You do. Sort of like a younger version of Kenny Chesney."

"Who's Kenny Chesney?" Dustin asked.

"A really cool country singer," Cody said, "who once took a joyride on a policeman's horse."

"Really?" Dustin grinned. "Hey, any guy who would take a cop's horse is okay in my book."

Cody made a grab for Dustin's ankle, pretending to trip him. "You're not planning on stealing my horse, are you?"

"No." Laughing, Dustin hopped on one foot until he wriggled away from Cody's grasp. "Why would I?"

Nikki nodded at another box under the tree. "Why don't you open that one next?"

"All right." Dustin sat cross-legged on the floor once more and, still wearing the cowboy hat, ripped open the package. His face brightened when he lifted out the brand new, German silver-inlaid bridle. "Sweet. Thanks." Then he looked deeper into the box. "What's this?" He picked up a sheet of paper.

"Cowboy's registration papers," Nikki said. "And a signed bill of sale."

Dustin's eyes widened. "It's got my name on it."

"Sure it does," Cody said. "If you're going to ride him, you might as well own him."

"I don't know," Dustin said slowly. "A cowboy hat *and* a horse named Cowboy. I'm not sure I can handle all that at once."

"Yes, you can," Nikki said, laughing. She reached out and draped an arm across his shoulders, then leaned over to include Cody in a three-way hug. "You can deal with anything you put your mind to. We all can. We're family."

"Hey, what time are Grandma and Grandpa Somers going to get here?"

"Their plane is due in at noon, providing this snow doesn't delay their flight." Cody stood and looked out the window. "Wow, it sure looks beautiful."

Nikki came to stand beside him, wrapping her arms around his waist. She looked out at the peacefully quiet morning. The moon still glowed in the sky, and the entire area was covered in a blanket of pure, untouched snow.

"It sure does," she said. She leaned into Cody's shoulder. "Am I allowed to be this happy?"

"You're not only allowed," he said. "You're entitled." He kissed the top of her head. "Let's renew our wedding vows."

"What?" She drew back and looked at him.

"Start the New Year out with a bang."

"Cool!" Dustin thrust between them to look out at the snow, too. "Can I be the best man?"

"You'd better know it. Providing your mom says yes."

"Yes," Nikki said, giving Cody a shove. He pulled her close and kissed her.

"Yuck," Dustin said. "I tell you, I'm never getting married."

Cody chuckled. "That's what I used to say. You'll change your mind, son."

"No way. Hey, quit all that mushy junk and come open your presents."

They sat down again, and Nikki held her gift in her lap while she waited for Cody to open the one Dustin had given him.

She could wait to open hers. Because she already had the best Christmas gift she could ever ask for.

A family of her own.

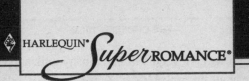

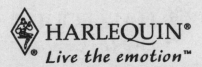

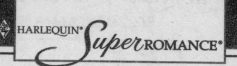

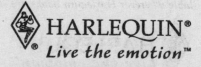

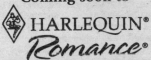
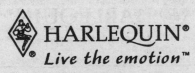

Curl up and have a

Heart *to* Heart

with

Harlequin Romance®

Just like having a heart-to-heart
with your best friend, these stories
will take you from laughter to tears
and back again. So heartwarming
and emotional you'll want to
have some tissues handy!

Next month Harlequin is thrilled to bring you
Natasha Oakley's first book for Harlequin Romance:

For Our Children's Sake (#3838),
on sale March 2005

Then watch out for....

A Family For Keeps (#3843),
by Lucy Gordon, on sale May 2005

Available wherever Harlequin books are sold.

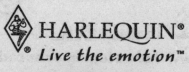

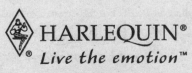

HARLEQUIN *Super*ROMANCE®

WELCOME TO *Crystal Creek*

If this is your first visit to the friendly ranching town located in the Texas Hill Country, get ready to meet some unforgettable people. If you've been here before, you'll recognize old friends...and make some new ones.

WILD HORSES
by Bethany Campbell
(Harlequin Superromance #1261)
On sale in March 2005
Wild horses might be the only things that could drag Mickey Nightingale into another disastrous relationship—especially one with Adam Duran. He has a secret that threatens the ranch of Carolyn Trent, a woman who happens to be Mickey's boss and the only mother she's ever really had.

MEET ME IN TEXAS
by Sandy Steen
(Harlequin Superromance #1271)
On sale in April 2005
When Del Rickman leaves the FBI, he can think of no better place to start his new life than Crystal Creek. Years ago he worked a kidnapping case here and never forgot the town or the people. He's surprised to learn that his new career has put him in opposition with his neighbors!

Available wherever Harlequin Superromance books are sold.

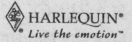

HARLEQUIN®
® *Live the emotion*™